Finding
Zach

Rowan Speedwell

Dreamspinner Press

Published by
Dreamspinner Press
4760 Preston Road
Suite 244-149
Frisco, TX 75034
http://www.dreamspinnerpress.com/

Finding Zach

Cover Art by Catt Ford

ISBN: 978-1-61581-446-6

Printed in the United States of America
First Edition
May, 2010

eBook edition available
eBook ISBN: 978-1-61581-447-3

For my mother,

who always believes in me—
even if I won't let her read what I write.

Chapter One

"THE hostages are secure, Captain. All present and accounted for. Perimeter has been secured."

Captain John Rogers pushed his helmet back a little on his forehead and regarded his subordinate. "Casualties?"

"Jamison took a bullet in the calf; medic's with him now. Otherwise, no casualties on our side. Three dead, twelve injured on the enemies' side so far, not including the poor bastard hanging on the whipping post. Shit."

"What about among the hostages? Any injuries?"

"One of the men has what looks like a couple of broken ribs. Otherwise, bruises, a sprained ankle. Damn lucky."

"'Lucky' has been what this whole operation's been about, Lieutenant Pritzker." Rogers sighed.

"You're not kidding, Captain. It was a plain miracle that one of the Dutchmen had that experimental personal GPS transponder implanted. Best advertisement for his product you could ask for." The lieutenant pressed his fingers to his headset. "Barracks secured. Last building is apparently the commandant's headquarters. Had some fire from there earlier, but it's stopped; either the shooter's hit or fled."

"Or holding out for a more effective resistance," the Captain said cynically. "Everything's gone entirely too textbook for my liking. I'd like a team to circle around back; approach the building with maximum caution. I don't trust this luck." He glanced at the handful of enemy combatants kneeling a few yards away, their hands clasped on their heads. "Ask one of them where the camp commander is."

Pritzger went to stand in front of the one man that had been unarmed when they'd nailed him. "You. What's your name?" he asked in Spanish.

"Ernesto Camillo," he said dully.

"Where is your captain?"

The man jerked his chin at the far structure. "There, last I see of him."

"Is there anyone else in that building?"

The man laughed, a brief, humorless snort. "Just his little dog."

"What did he say?" Rogers asked. "I didn't get that."

"Perrito," Pritzger said. "It means 'little dog'."

"He's got a dog in there?"

"If he does, I doubt if it's little," Pritzger said dryly. "The camp commander's probably the type that likes Dobermans or Rottweilers. These paramilitary types usually do." He indicated the whipping victim, who was even now being eased down onto the ground by a pair of his fellow soldiers, their activities supervised by some of the combined American-Dutch forces who'd spearheaded this operation. "Fucking macho bastard. Let the teams know there's the possibility of a guard dog…."

The little man laughed and said something. Rogers said, "What? I don't understand this dialect."

Pritzger said, "He said it's not a guard dog."

"Still," Rogers said.

They waited until the teams had secured the building, and then went in. It was a simple two-room structure. The main room where they stood was an office; through the open door to the other room, Rogers could see a neatly made bed and another door already standing open from the other team's entrance a few moments before. The office contained a desk, a laptop computer, file cabinets, a chair, and a wire dog crate—the big kind, made for large dogs like the Rottweilers and Dobermans Pritzger had mentioned. It was empty. Near the window lay a body that Rogers assumed was the commandant; he had fake gold bullion on the shoulders of his uniform, also typical with these paramilitary types. He'd been garroted with a thin strip of leather. It looked like a dog leash. "No one else in the building, Captain," one of the guys who had been first in said. "Whoever did this must have cut out the back before we got here."

"Take the laptop and what you can get out of the file cabinets," Rogers instructed. "They'll have all kinds of data on funding, activities, links to other groups, contacts…. The boys at Bragg will be short-stroking themselves over this stuff. They love them some paperwork."

Pritzger nodded and detailed a couple of guys to start on the file cabinets near the desk. He himself moved around the dog crate to the file cabinets behind the cage.

And froze.

Rogers saw it and went on alert. "Lieutenant?"

"Shh," Pritzger said. "Everybody just… shh…." He moved slowly, going into a crouch.

Rogers shifted the crate and saw what Pritzger was looking at. He held up a hand to indicate that the others in the room should maintain their positions.

Wedged in between the far side of the file cabinets and the wall, beneath a shelf, in a space that should have been too small for it, was a bony, naked human figure with a thick mop of tangled black hair. It was curled up with its face hidden, its back arched, the spine and ribs sharply delineated and slashed with scarring. It was worse than thin; it looked like a skeleton with skin. Rogers wondered how long the body had been there—not long, he supposed, since there wasn't any smell of decay….

Then he saw the ribs expand in a tentative breath, and he realized the thing was alive.

"Shit," he murmured.

Pritzger said in Spanish, "Who are you? It's okay—we're not going to hurt you."

The thing made a sound. It sounded like a dog's whine. A dog….

Rogers looked back at the cage. "Fuck," he breathed. "Fuck, Lieutenant. The dog. The commandant's *dog*…."

The tangled mass of hair lifted. A gaunt, pale face looked up and whined again. Then it gave a soft bark and tried to cram itself deeper into the corner. "Jesus," Pritzger murmured, then, again, still in

Spanish, "We're not going to hurt you. Who are you? What's your name?" He put out a hand; the creature flinched but made no move to bite or resist, even when Pritzger put his hand on its shoulder. "Come on, come out. We aren't going to hurt you."

"Is that a *human*?" one of the men behind the desk asked in disbelief. The creature's eyes flicked in his direction. In the shadows, Rogers couldn't tell what color they were, but by the reaction, he saw that he understood.

"He speaks English," Rogers said flatly. The thing looked at him, a strangely steady, empty look. It was the look of someone who'd long ago forgotten how to care. "He understands English and I'll bet my left nut he's the one that killed the commandant."

"I doubt if he could strangle an overripe banana," Pritzger objected.

"Never underestimate the power of hate-fueled adrenaline, Lieutenant."

The thing sighed and put its head back down on the floor. Rogers touched his headset. "Randy?" he said to the medic. "I need you in here. Jamison okay?"

"Yeah," Randy said in his ear. "What's happened in there?"

Rogers looked down at the figure on the floor. "You are not going to believe this…."

THEY found a pair of sweatpants with a drawstring waist; the legs were too short, but the man couldn't stand up straight for more than a couple minutes anyway. He squatted in the dirt of the compound, his arms wrapped around his knees, staring into space. The T-shirt the medic had put on him hung in draped folds around his emaciated arms. Rogers had seen pictures of people like him coming out of Auschwitz or Bergen-Belsen after the liberation of the concentration camps in the forties. Pritzger knelt beside the kid, cutting off the studded collar with a pair of shears someone'd dug up. The buckle had been soldered shut. "I'd put his age at twentyish," Randy Josten said, making notes on his clipboard. "American or European—good nutrition in childhood, luckily for him—healthy bones, teeth loose from malnutrition but all still there, and signs of past dental care. Camillo says he's been here about five years, give or take. Once we're back at Bragg we can go through missing persons reports from about then and see if we can figure out who he is."

"Still not talking?"

"Barks. Whines." Randy frowned. "Kid's physically and mentally traumatized, Captain. He's a fucking basket case. He's been beaten; a couple of his ribs have been broken and healed badly; from what I can tell, he can't take a deep breath without it hurting. Had a couple of fingers broken, his wrist, and God knows what else. And," he said, taking a breath, "he's been raped. I don't know how often, but given that the last time was about an hour ago, I'd say pretty damn regularly. He's got scars all over his legs and ass from the damn wire of that fucking cage, and you can see yourself he can't even stand up."

"So figure he's been in that cage pretty much continuously for the last five years. Fuck." Rogers shook his head. "Let's get him back to Bragg and into the hands of the docs there; let the Dutch contingent handle cleanup of the remaining personnel. They know what's going on and have better contacts than we do locally. Load the kid with the hostages and the computer and stuff we took from the office on the first chopper out of here."

"Yes sir," Randy said. Then, "What?" at Rogers's suddenly arrested expression.

"Something," Rogers said. "Something about computers. Did you say five years?"

"Yeah, that's what Camillo said."

Rogers stalked across the compound to the kid. Crouching in front of him, he tilted up the kid's face to study it, narrow-eyed. Out of the dimness of the building where he'd been held, the eyes that looked back at him were a cold, crystal blue, their expression hard and wary. "Zach?" he asked.

"What?" Randy had followed him. "Do you know who he is?"

"Zach? Is that you?" Rogers asked the kid again. "Zach Tyler?"

The kid... barked. "Fuck," Rogers said. "It is. Zach Tyler."

"Holy shit," Randy said. "Tyler Technologies? But Tyler's kid got kidnapped from fucking Costa Rica. We're in eastern Venezuela— a couple thousand miles from there!"

"So tangos can't travel?" Rogers asked sarcastically. "But it's him. I remember the description, the pictures—hell, it was all over the TV, particularly after they paid the ransom and didn't get him back. Five years. Shit."

Zach whined. Rogers looked down at him and released his chin. "You said it, kid. You said a fucking mouthful."

I HAVE forgotten what kindness is. I keep waiting for something to happen, for me to wake up from this oh-so-pleasant dream, but I don't wake up. It can't be reality; I know reality—it's a cage, and table scraps and beatings and pain and rape and hunger. For so long I've known exactly what to expect; I've kept my sanity by being hard inside, meeting cruelty with indifference when I can, and hatred when I can't. I haven't had a lot to be proud of, but every day I was still alive after five years of Esteban gave me a kind of strength to keep going. Hate can make you strong; I know it did me.

But people who give me food and water, who are gentle when they put clothes on me and lift me and carry me to sit in a cushioned chair and even buckle me into my seat confuse me, and I don't know how to deal with them. This is not reality. It scares me, even if it's kind of nice.

When they first put the sweats on me, I finger the fabric endlessly, and rub my cheek on my knee. It's so soft, and clean. It smells as good as it feels.

I don't like the helicopter ride. I don't like the noise, or the vibrations, or the way it lurches in the air. It scares me, and I haven't been scared for a really long time. I'm out of practice. There are other people on the helicopter ride, the other freed hostages and the soldiers to protect them, but they're mostly excited and happy. I don't know what to think about them. They don't know what to think about me, either. A couple of them stare, like they think I'm some kind of animal. I lift my lip and snarl at them softly, just to let them know they're right.

It seems like I'm scared forever, but finally the helicopter touches down at an airport, then there's more noise and confusion, but there's also more of the unexpected gentleness, and pretty soon I'm sitting in the cabin of an airplane.

Again, I'm scared—not because I'm afraid to fly, I've been in planes lots before, but all I can remember is that last terrible flight to Costa Rica, landing and walking off the plane and looking for the driver my aunt would have sent to meet me and then nothing until I wake up in the jungle and Esteban is looking at me. I break out in a cold sweat and one of the soldiers nearby asks if I'm okay. I don't answer him, of course.

I shouldn't be feeling this way, shouldn't be remembering like this, because I'm in an Army troop transport, not first class in a luxury jet. The other hostages aren't on this plane. Just me and a bunch of soldiers; not the same ones as before except the lieutenant who cut the dog collar off back in the compound. He's standing up near the front of the plane, talking to one of the pilots.

My legs hurt, and my back. I rub my thighs through the grey sweats. It hurts, and I try to hold back a whimper. I've had lots of practice at keeping quiet, but for some reason this time I don't succeed.

"Hey, lieutenant," the guy who'd asked if I was okay calls. "Your passenger here's upset about something."

The lieutenant turns and comes back down the aisle. He smiles at me. "Hey, you doin' okay, Zach?" He hesitates a little before he says my name, like he's not sure if it's right. I'm not quite sure, either.

I rub my thighs again. He frowns, and then says, "You aren't comfortable in the seat, are you, kid?" He's more comfortable with "kid." "Bet your muscles are all wonky from that cage." He straightens, glances around, then goes in the back of the plane where I can't see him. A minute later, he comes back and unbuckles me. "It ain't exactly protocol, but I think you'll feel better here," he says, and lifts me out of my seat. "Damn, kid, you can't weigh a hundred pounds soakin' wet." He carries me back a few rows to where he's folded up some seats on the half-empty transport and put the cushions on the floor. He sets me down on the cushions. "There you are. Is that better?"

I look up at him, meet his eyes for the first time. They're brown. I feel my lips move, twist, and realize I'm smiling. I don't think it's a snarl because he grins back at me.

I curl up on the cushions, so soft and comfortable, and sleep for the rest of the trip. When I open my eyes again, it's to the lieutenant shaking my shoulder. "We're about to land, kid, and you gotta be buckled in for that. Sorry."

I experiment with that smile again and lift my arms for him to pick me up. He does so, laughing. "I got a little nephew does that, but he's three. What's your excuse?"

I rest my head on his shoulder. He's kind, and he smells good. I don't even mind him waking me from the first good sleep I've had in years. I didn't even know you could sleep in dreams.

He buckles me in and I wait for the plane to land, and stop, and for him to come and fetch me again. This time he only carries me to the front of the plane, where a couple of men in white are waiting with a stretcher. They put me on the stretcher, but when they start to move away, I reach out and grab his sleeve, and whine. He pats my shoulder and says, "I'll see you at the hospital, kid. Don't worry."

His smile is warm and makes me want to trust him. He's the only one so far, but I trust him. I let the stretcher men carry me away to the waiting ambulance, but now I'm scared again. I don't know what's waiting anymore. I knew, with Esteban, what was waiting, but I don't anymore, and I'm scared. I remember a saying: "Better the devil you know...." but Esteban wasn't better. Just... familiar.

Nothing is familiar anymore, and I'm scared.

RICHARD TYLER picked up the ringing phone on the desk in his cubicle. The number on the phone's screen was the receptionist's. "Tyler," he said absently, his attention on the computer in front of him.

"Rich, there are a couple of people here from the State Department," Abby said. Her voice trembled.

Richard's stomach dropped. This was it: the news he'd been expecting since the ten-million dollar ransom had vanished into the jungles of Central America five years ago. Numbly he replied, "Put them in the small conference room. I'll be right there." He set down the phone and stared at it a moment.

It could be just another one of the interminable interviews that he'd sat through off and on throughout the last half-decade, State Department suits looking for things that might lead to capture of the terrorists that had kidnapped Zach from the airport in Costa Rica, supposedly one of the safest spots in Central America. The abduction had shaken the business world and tightened up security in the little tourist-friendly country, but it had come too late for Zachary. Richard rubbed his forehead and took a deep breath. This time, though, it felt different, and Richard suspected he knew why. This was it. The end of the waiting. It wasn't as if he hadn't expected it. Best to get it over with. He closed down the program he was working on and left his cubicle.

Barry Genelli, his vice president in charge of research and development, was in the cubicle next to him—everyone worked on the floor; no corner offices in this company, one of the largest in revenue in the world, but one of the smallest in terms of officer perks—and he looked up as Richard went by. "What's up, Rich?"

"Another visit by State—probably on the Zach thing," Richard said dully.

"Maybe not: maybe they're looking for something like the locator chip Davey designed that that Dutch company bought. Gotta be at least thirty thousand State Department employees abroad; be a hell of a sale."

"Except that Dutch company bought the manufacturing rights, Barry. They'll have to deal with them."

Barry shrugged. "We still own the patents. We'd still make a killing in royalties."

"Yeah." Richard nodded disinterestedly. He raked his hand through his graying hair and walked through the maze of cubicles to the reception area and conference rooms.

The pair of men that waited for him weren't the usual suits. One of them was, with the obligatory briefcase, but the other was a man in an Army uniform with captain's insignia. Richard stopped in the doorway, his gut hurting. This was it. "Gentlemen," he said, and closed the door behind him, then leaned on it, his hands in the back pockets of his jeans.

"Mr. Richard Tyler?"

"That's me. What can I do for you?"

"It's regarding your son Zachary."

"Yeah. I kind of figured." Richard walked across the room to the floor-to-ceiling windows. They framed a spectacular view of the Colorado Rockies in the distance. "You found him, didn't you."

In the window, he saw the reflection of the two men as they glanced at each other. The suit said, "Yes, sir. You may have heard about the joint American-Dutch rescue of ten hostages from a Venezuelan paramilitary group last week?"

"Yeah. Yeah. Is that where he ended up? Venezuela?"

"Yes, sir."

Richard let out a breath. He could not deal with this, not now. He'd thought he could, but no. Curtly he said, "I suppose he's been positively identified?"

"Yes, sir," the captain said. "You had registered his fingerprints with that child-protection database some years ago…."

"Jesus," Richard said over his shoulder. "There was enough left after five years to match fingerprints? No"—he held up his hand to forestall an answer—"I can't deal with the details right now. Just tell me—when can we bring him home?" He didn't say "the remains" though that was what he was thinking. But it was Zachary. His pride, his brilliant boy, his loving child. Not some grisly "remains."

The captain said, "Well, there are health issues that need to be dealt with, both physical and emotional. You'll need to get a good physical therapist for him, and…."

Richard whipped around, staring at the captain. "Physi… are you saying Zach's *alive*?"

"Yes, sir," the captain said in surprise. "We found him in Venezuela, a prisoner of the same paramilitary group that kidnapped the group from Suriname…. Sir…?"

Richard bent over the conference table, his hands flat on the surface to support him. He fought to keep his breath even, to stop the hyperventilating that had become a regular occurrence in the last five years. But this time—this really *was* it. The real end of the nightmare. "Oh, my God," he said, weeping, and drew his hands across his face to wipe away the tears. "My Zachary—my boy...."

"Sir, please sit down," the suit said. "Can I get you a drink of water?"

"No, no, thank you," Richard said. He wiped his face again. "God. I've got to tell his mother.... Is he all right? You said physical therapy—was he hurt?" His eyes went from the suit's face to the captain's. They were holding out on him....

"He walked out of the camp on his own two feet," the captain said, "but I won't blow smoke up your skirt and tell you he's fine. He's in rough shape, Mr. Tyler. I saw the conditions he was in and they weren't pretty, plus he sustained some injuries that have healed kind of badly."

Richard sat down. "What kind of injuries?"

"I think you'll be better off talking directly with the attending doctor. I don't know all the details. Zach's at the civilian hospital in Fayetteville, near Fort Bragg. He's still undergoing tests; we want to make sure he's not hiding any bug we haven't dealt with before. After all, he's been in the jungle for five years in poor conditions, prime breeding grounds for all kinds of disease. There are psychologists working with him too; he's been through a lot." The captain drew a breath. "My name's John Rogers; I was the commanding officer of the joint American-Dutch task force that went in to rescue the hostages. My men were the ones who found Zach."

"Captain Rogers," the suit said, "recognized your son and had him sent directly to Fort Bragg, where he was positively identified by the database we mentioned earlier. Since then, his passport and personal identification were found in the files that were removed from the site. The Venezuelan government, although not on particularly good terms with the U.S. at this point in time, has nevertheless been very helpful in assisting us in tracking down the kidnappers...."

"But ironically enough, the real help was that one of the Dutch businessmen who was taken was implanted with that GPS locator you designed," Captain Rogers said.

"I didn't design it," Richard said shakily. "That was David Evans—my housekeeper's kid. He was working for us when Zach was taken. He did it for Zach, worked on it the whole summer after.... He was obsessed with it. Said if Zach had had something like this...." He stopped. David. After everything, it had been David who'd made the difference. "He did save him. David. David saved Zach."

"I'd say so," Captain Rogers agreed. "Or at least made it possible for us to. We were damned lucky this mission."

"Captain," Richard breathed, "I hope to God you're always so lucky."

"MR. AND MRS. TYLER? I'm Dr. Duffey."

The man held out his hand to Richard; he shook it, as did Jane a moment later. Duffey seemed competent; a man of small stature with a shock of brown hair standing up on his head, too thick to lie flat. "I've been working with Zach since his arrival five days ago. Most of that was just trying to get him to relax a little; he spent the first two days in the fetal position, terrified out of his wits. But he's shown vast improvement in the last couple of days."

"You're the psychologist?"

"Psychiatrist, yes. I specialize in trauma victims. Dr. McKinnon is the doctor handling Zach's physical condition. Zach's in poor shape, but it's mostly a matter of severe malnutrition. We're more concerned at this point with his psychological state. You'll meet Dr. McKinnon later this afternoon."

"When can we see my son?" Jane asked anxiously.

Duffey smiled at her. "Soon," he said reassuringly. "But I need to tell you some things you have to know before you go in there. To prepare you."

"Prepare us for what?" Richard demanded.

The doctor rubbed his forehead. "They didn't tell you anything about him, did they?"

"They kept telling us to wait to talk to you. What's wrong with Zach?"

"Aside from being very emaciated from malnutrition, he's severely traumatized and nonverbal."

"What do you mean 'nonverbal'?" Jane asked.

"He doesn't talk."

"We know what 'nonverbal' means," Richard said impatiently, "but what does it mean in Zach's case? He's got something wrong with his throat? He ignores you when you talk to him? Makes funny sounds? Doesn't make sounds at all?"

"He barks."

There was silence in the little waiting room, then Richard said quietly, "What the *fuck* do you mean, 'he barks'?"

"He barks. Whines, occasionally whimpers. He responds as if he were a dog." Dr. Duffey shook his head. "From what the lieutenant who brought him in says, he was treated as if he were a dog for the last five years. Kept in a cage, with a collar, fed table scraps, occasionally walked with a leash—though not often; his leg muscles are atrophied, and he'll need physical therapy for a good long time before he'll be able to walk more than a few steps unsupported."

"Oh, God," Jane said, her hand on her mouth. Under his breath, Richard said, "Fuck."

"There's worse," Duffey warned. They both looked at him. "I'd suggest you both sit down."

"Fuck," Richard said again, and they obeyed. He reached for Jane's hand and held it tightly.

"He was raped, wasn't he?" Jane asked. Richard blinked and looked at her. She looked back and said simply, "He's beautiful, Richard. Of course someone would hurt him that way. Evil people want to damage beauty—they don't understand it."

"Yes. Physical indications are that he was sexually abused over a long period; there is scarring in both the genital and anal areas. There is nothing to indicate permanent damage, though, aside from the scarring; there's no sign of STDs. Once he's recovered, he should function normally."

Richard snorted. "It's the recovery part that's the question, isn't it? How do you recover from something like that?"

"Slowly, I'm afraid." Dr. Duffey shook his head. "The fact that he's still not speaking after five days in care is not a good sign. I'm hoping that now that you're here, his condition will improve considerably."

"I doubt it," Richard said savagely. He stood and walked away from them, staring out the window much as he had in the conference room in the suburb outside Colorado Springs. The view was less inspiring here—just the hospital parking lot.

"Richard," Jane murmured.

"Well, Jenny, it's true. He has no reason to love us. He was in love for the first time in his life, and how did we deal with it? We put him on a plane and sent him alone into the hands of that bastard that raped and ruined him—all to keep him out of the hands of someone who loved him. Someone who fucking *saved* him. Jesus, Jenny. We should have let him be with David—at least then he would have been happy and *whole*."

"I take it Zach is gay," the doctor said delicately.

"I thought it was just being fifteen," Richard said miserably. "David thought so too. He said he cared for Zach, but that he was too young for a relationship; he had told Zach they'd have to wait. I thought it was just… just hormones or something, that he had a crush on David. He'd known him his whole life, he's older, more mature…. David was just out of high school, saving money for college, working with my company, but he's the housekeeper's son and lived on the estate, they saw each other every day. David used to drive him around until Zach was old enough to get his driver's license… Jesus. He doesn't even have a driver's license…." Richard buried his face in his hand and wept.

Jane went to him and put her arms around him, her cheek laid gently on his shoulder blade. To the doctor she said, "My sister lives in Costa Rica, and she'd been asking for Zach to come down and visit her. We thought it would be a good idea for him to spend some time away from David, if it was just a crush, you know? David agreed. He said Zach needed to know his own mind, that he needed to be older before he'd be ready for a relationship with anyone, male or female. We all sent him away. It was all our faults. Richard blames himself, but it was all our faults."

"It's not your fault at all," Dr. Duffey said. "Let's cast the blame where it belongs, on the shoulders of the man that did this, the so-called General Benito Esteban."

"Have they caught him? Is he in jail, that bastard?" Richard demanded, wiping his face irritably. "I want to see the face of that foul, stinking...."

"He's dead," the doctor said in surprise. "Didn't they tell you?"

"No. Was he killed in the raid?"

"No. Zach killed him."

THE hospital room door opens and I jerk, startled. I should be used to the abrupt comings and goings of the doctors, but after living so long with only the sounds of human voices and bugs in the trees outside— not to mention the occasional gunshot—I'm finding the banging and humming and squeaking and beeping disconcerting. No, scratch that— downright annoying, irritating, scary....

It's Fluffy Duffey, my personal shrink. He's little and unintimidating, with fluffy brown hair and nice, patient eyes. "Hi, Zach," he says. "How are you feeling this afternoon?"

Same as ever, Fluffy.

"How was your lunch? The nurse said you polished everything off."

And would have eaten the tray, too, if it had been organic. My stomach shrank, they tell me, so I don't have much capacity for food, but I'm hungry now. I wasn't hungry the first few days, but I'm making up for lost time.

He takes my hand and checks my pulse. He's a shrink, but apparently he's a real doctor too; he seems to understand the monitors and charts and whatnot. Whatever my wrist tells him he's apparently happy with. "You have visitors," he says.

I blink, not understanding at first.

"Your parents are here."

For a minute, I don't know what he means. What are parents? Then my heart starts pounding and I'm terrified. No, not *them*. Esteban told me that they didn't care about me, that they never sent the ransom he'd demanded, that they'd replied that they didn't care what he did with me, that they had sent me to him on purpose.... I start hyperventilating, and Fluffy puts an oxygen mask on my face. "Breathe slowly," he says over the hiss of the oxygen. I can't breathe. I'm so afraid. This is a dream and I know what happens next: they come in and they've got the faces of monsters and they slaughter Fluffy and start eating my feet and then I wake up and it's Esteban again, only this time he'll know what I dreamt about and he'll start telling more stories about my parents and the monsters they are and how they've eaten everyone I knew. I'm crying in fear now, when I haven't cried in years, and I can't catch my breath and Fluffy's upset; not as upset as he will be in a minute when they come in and tear his throat out....

They come in and they're just people, strangers with frightened faces. I suck in a breath and wait for them to turn into the monsters, but they just stand there. The woman is crying and the man has his arms around her. He's got black curly hair like mine, but there are silver strands in it; his eyes are dark and there are lines on his face that only get deeper when he looks at me. The woman has blonde hair, sleeked back in some fancy knot I used to know the name of, something French, but I can't see her face because she's got it buried in his shoulder. "Jane," he says, and then I recognize him. The silver and the lines confuse me, because my dad didn't have silver hair or lines on his face. He does now.

I stop hyperventilating; I'm still crying but it's just tears falling, the sobbing stopped. I take a couple of steady breaths and pull the oxygen mask away. Fluffy goes with it. "Are you all right?" he asks in an undertone. I just look at him, then over at the people. My parents. Dick and Jane. I wipe the water from my face. I'm calm now, that cold, empty calm I'm good at; I can look at them and hope that just this once they aren't going to turn into monsters and eat everyone.

"Zach?" Dad says uncertainly.

I don't answer, but I meet his eyes. They're red and tired-looking, but he's smiling a little. It hurts, somewhere deep inside, and I blink. I thought I was used to pain, but this is a different kind of hurt, one I don't know quite how to deal with.

The woman turns then, and I look at her. She has blue eyes, like me, but they're red and tired, too, like his. Right now, they look more like each other than either of them does like me. Both old and tired and sad. I feel old and tired and sad too. It hurts. I sigh and close my eyes.

Something touches my hand and I open my eyes again. It's Mom, Jane of Dick and Jane. She used to get so mad at me when I'd call them that. It's from the old reading books kids got in school years ago— "Fun with Dick and Jane" or something like that. Their dog was called Spot, though, not Zach. Mom's hand is cold and very small. I can feel little bird bones in it. I could crush those bones without thinking about it, even as wasted as I am. After a few days of food and rest, I'm feeling a lot stronger, stronger than when I choked the life out of Esteban. If I could do that, a few little bones is nothing. But I don't crush them. She's so little and frail, much smaller than I remember. I whine in dismay, and her eyes widen. She doesn't say anything, just stares at me in horror, as if I had been the one to turn into the monster and start eating people's feet. Maybe she's right. Maybe it's me that's the monster. After all, neither of them has strangled anyone with a leash lately, right?

She starts crying again. "Oh, Zach, my baby," she says, and she puts her arms around me and hugs me gently, as if she thinks I'll break. Her hand is cold but her arms are warm, and I feel like a bird in a nest.

God, I wish this wasn't a dream.

I KNOW what reality is, and it's not this.

Reality is cold, and hard. Reality is a place where all I know is pain and hate.

Reality is where I'll wake up.

Some people are happy to go from their nightmares to reality; when your reality *is* a nightmare, there's not much sense of improvement. I don't sleep well anyway, never more than a few hours at a time; there doesn't seem to be much point. I don't get any exercise to get myself tired, and besides, when you're asleep, you can't see what's out there waiting for you to let your guard down. Not that it matters; I know what's waiting. He's in the room behind the door a couple yards away.

It's early, not quite light out, and Esteban's not up yet. I creep up to the bars of the cage and piss in the bucket that's set on the floor outside. I don't need to do anything else, and that's good; though the wire that forms the bottom of this dog crate sits up a couple of inches off the ground, it might be an hour or two before Esteban's orderly comes around to move the cage on its wheels and clean underneath it. It's not often an issue—not much fiber in my diet. But I don't like the reminder that it's one more thing I don't have control over. I used to be a really clean kid. It bugs me that I'm not anymore.

The orderly and I hate each other with a sincere, almost cordial hate. He hates cleaning up after me, and I hate him because he can stand up straight. I haven't stood in probably three or four months, whenever the last time it was that Esteban took me for a walk around the compound. I try to keep my leg muscles exercised by doing stretches when no one's around, like now: reaching down to grab my toes and pull, stretching out the tendons and muscles in my back and legs and shoulders and arms. It hurts. It always hurts. The muscles burn and the bars of the cage floor grind against my naked butt and thighs and calves. But I keep thinking someday I'm going to have the opportunity to kill Esteban, and I need to be strong enough.

Who am I kidding?

The orderly comes in first for a change this morning. It occasionally happens, when Esteban is out raping babies, or poking the eyes out of old women, or cutting the wings off flies. There was a bit of fuss a couple of days or weeks ago—I don't know—and I think there's something going on. Esteban has been entirely too happy lately. I hate it when he's happy. When he's happy, he's horny, and it's my fucking ass that gets the dubious benefits. The only thing is when he's pissy— then everything gets the benefits.

The orderly's name is Ernesto; I call him "Che" to myself; not that he has a clue who that is, even if I'd said it out loud. He's that stupid. He calls me "perro," but then, everyone does. It's what I am: Esteban's dog. My own fault—when I first got here I was a smart-mouthed kid and called him a "dog-fucker." He decided to make that literal.

Che sticks the little kid's beach bucket of water in through the food door at the bottom of the cage. The bucket is pink, another commentary. As usual, there's a plastic razor and a rag in the bucket, but no soap. I think I remember soap. I scrape the razor over my face, shaving my sparse beard; I think I'm close to twenty, but despite having black hair, I don't have much in the way of whiskers, which is fine with me—I can't imagine having to shave a thick beard with a ladies' plastic razor and water. The orderly uses the ladies' razors because they've got even less actual blade exposed. I tried to slit my wrist with a men's razor once, years ago, and Esteban beat his ass because of it. But Esteban doesn't like beards on other people—none of his men have them—though he's got one. It's some masculinity crap. For a guy who fucks ass daily, he's got a big thing about masculinity. Guess a shrink would have a field day with that.

I shave and wash up with the rag using as little water as possible; whatever's left is my drinking water for the day, and I'd rather be naked and filthy than naked and thirsty. Then I throw the razor at Che, just on principle. The rag goes into the little pile in the corner of the crate. It's my hobby, collecting rags. Someday I'll make a quilt. Except that every few weeks when Esteban's got me bent over his desk with his dick in my ass, Che sneaks in and takes the pile of rags. I think that pisses me off more than the fucking. They're *my* fucking rags, asshole.

I don't talk to Che, though. I don't talk to anyone. Nobody here I want to talk to.

I hear Esteban outside, yelling at someone, and then I hear the crack of his whip as that someone gets what's coming to him. It's not usual—Esteban's not stupid—but it's not unusual, either. Just part of life in the jungle. Esteban likes his whip, and he likes discipline. But his men are well fed. Not me, but I'm just a dog. The beating depresses me, though—Esteban likes his whip—did I say that?—and that makes him happy, and when he's happy….

He comes in a while later, patches of sweat on his paramilitary uniform, a grin on his face and his dick making a tent at his crotch. He opens the crate, reaches in and grabs me by my collar, hauling me out onto the floor. "There's my good dog," he croons, "there's my little puppy," and he strokes my hair as he puts on my leash. "Puppy's fur's getting matted," he observes. "Ernesto, remind me to take him to the groomer's." And he laughs like he's said something fucking funny. A regular laugh riot, Benito Esteban. He's not fat, but he's big, muscular, with a thick neck. Next to his arms, my emaciated little sticks look like twigs. He shoves my face into the floor; I turn my head just in time to avoid a nosebleed, but my cheekbone cracks against the wood and it hurts. "Down, dog," he says, and I draw my knees up, my arms tucked under my chest and my skinny ass flapping in the breeze, the picture of canine submission. He lets me stay that way while he deals with the orderly, giving him orders I don't pay attention to anymore. I hear him say something about "hostages," but not what exactly. It isn't hard to figure out what's making him so cheerful, even discounting the fun of whipping some poor fucker's skin off his back. He has hostages, which means ransom, which means more funding of his little army. All is happy time in Esteban-ville.

Che finishes getting his instructions for the day, and Esteban sits down behind his desk, tugging at his end of the leash and snapping his fingers. I crawl over and sit down on my haunches beside him, waiting for his orders. I wonder if real dogs hate their masters as much as I hate mine. "Up," he says, snapping his fingers again. If I were a real dog, I'd bite them off, but I'm not, so I get up in a half-crouch, knees bent, elbows on the desk. There are papers there, but I can't read them; they're in Spanish and in his handwriting. I never did learn to read Spanish, and his handwriting is for shit. I hear him rustling behind me, then the blunt pressure of his cock at my hole and he's pushing it in, humming happily, no spit, no lube, just that fat prick. Fortunately, I don't feel it much anymore; the muscles are torn or dead or scarred or something, and once he's past the entrance it's just him filling me up again, and then pulling out. He gets into a rhythm and then it's just a matter of waiting for him to come. Once or twice years ago I reacted to him, physically, but my cock doesn't get hard anymore, not even if he plays with me. He says I've been neutered. Could be. What do I care?

I'm careful not to think when he's fucking me, though, because sometimes I suspect that he can read my mind, and when he's fucking me he's got me vulnerable. He's brilliant at finding things that hurt, at wrecking good memories, memories of my life before, of my parents, of anything. I'm especially careful to never think about Taff. Taff was the only person to ever kiss me, and I'd like to keep it that way, so I don't think about it or him when Esteban's around, which is pretty much always. My memory of Taff's kiss is clean, as nothing else is. Sometimes I have nightmares about Taff, but when you don't talk, you don't cry out in your sleep. Besides, I won't sleep when Esteban's in the room, and Che's never said anything as far as I know.

Esteban doesn't kiss me; occasionally he will make me suck him off, but he's not big on that, for some reason. Maybe because even though I'm scared shitless of him, I still have all my teeth. I haven't got the guts to bite him, but maybe he's just that little bit unsure. If anything makes me happy, I think that does.

While Esteban's fucking me, that prick Che steals my rags. Bastard.

Esteban comes loud, grunting and pounding the desk by my head, so I don't hear the noises at first. Then I do, hollow popping sounds outside, and then yelling. Esteban jerks out of me, dragging me by the leash and throwing me in the cage. He stuffs himself back into his pants and pulls out the pistol he keeps in the holster at the small of his back—he doesn't keep it anywhere I can get a hold of it—and crouches by the window. Swearing, he pushes the window sash up an inch or so and pokes the barrel of the gun out and starts shooting. Che's nowhere around.

I reach up and unhook the leash from my collar. Then I look up and I realize Esteban latched the cage, but forgot to lock it in his haste to go shoot people. Very carefully, I unlatch the cage. He's still shooting. I freeze when he pauses to pop the empty cartridge from his pistol and slap in a new one, but he's forgotten that I exist.

The leash makes a handy garrote; just slide the end through the hand loop and drop it over Esteban's head. And pull. Hard. I can't stand all the way up, but with him in a crouch I've got enough leverage to yank him onto his back; he drops the pistol and I kick it away. Then I shove him back over onto his stomach and I stand on his back, pulling on the leash like some circus bareback rider. I don't know where I get the strength. He's got to outweigh me by a hundred pounds, but he's down, and the leather's thin but strong, and I find the stamina to pull. And pull. Until he stops fighting me. Until he's lying perfectly still. Until the stench of voided bladder and bowels fills my nose, and I know he's dead. Then I let go and stumble off him, falling exhausted onto my knees.

The popping noises outside stop. I don't know who's out there, but I figure it's probably a rival paramilitary group; Esteban's been complaining about some locals lately. I giggle a little hysterically to myself—no more complaints from that corner. But no matter who wins that little battle out there, I'm dead. Esteban's men will kill me for what I've just done; a rival group will kill me because I'm here. It doesn't matter, really, but something makes me drop the leash and crawl into the corner on the other side of the dog crate, cramming myself into as small a space as I can get into. Then I curl in on myself and wait to die.

Chapter
Two

Two years later

DAVID had the cab drop him off at the east gate of the compound, the private gate. The arch still displayed the twisting initials GK, belonging to the cattle baron who'd originally built the house and outbuildings back in the early twenties. The stone structure beside the road, though, had been put in about ten years ago to shelter the remote access to the computer that now managed the big, wrought-iron gates. David ducked into the shelter and keyed in his security password.

"Hello, David," the tinny voice said from the speakers on the panel.

"Hey, Andrew," David replied. "How they hanging?"

"They aren't hanging at all," the computer replied. "I possess no sexual organs, as you well know. It's been a long time since you've been home."

"It sure has," David sighed. "Just the foot gate, Andy."

The computer didn't answer; it had acquired sufficient voice recognition patterns to activate David's security access, and the smaller gate inset into the larger one swung open.

"Thanks, Andy," David said.

"You're welcome, David. Welcome home."

It was all preprogrammed text; even the comment about sex organs. David had programmed it into his access codes years ago, in his smart-assed teenage years. But even preprogrammed badinage made David feel like he had been welcomed back. Too bad he wasn't as sure of his welcome by the flesh-and-blood residents of the Tyler compound. He picked up the duffel he'd dropped on the ground and went through the small gate, giving it a push to set it back on a close trajectory. Then it was just a quarter-mile hike up the asphalt road to his destination, the two-story stone gatehouse.

Before he went in, though, he paused and looked out over the panorama, a sight that had been as familiar to him as his own face once upon a time. It had been more than three years since he'd set foot on the land where he'd grown up—he might have only been the housekeeper's son, but the Tyler family was part of his own, and this the only home he'd known. Now he wasn't really sure what it was, except for the place where his mother lived and worked. It looked the same, though. A half mile to the south sprawled the low buildings of Tyler Technologies, with their wood and adobe walls and tile roofs showing red through the surrounding aspens; a half mile north and west of there was the main house, a hacienda-style mansion with extensive gardens, a swimming pool, tennis courts and stables, all the amenities of the fabulously wealthy, amenities David had always been welcome to share. Before. Further north and west were the woods and in the distance, the mountains where he and Zach, and sometimes Richard and Jane, had hiked and explored and skied in the winters. He had to admit it had been pretty damn idyllic.

He hadn't done any of that after Zach had disappeared. If he hiked or skied, he did it somewhere else. Every inch of Tyler land echoed with Zach's laughter, every bit of shade sheltered his ghost. It was too damn lonely here without Zach. He'd lived here and worked for Richard until he'd scraped up enough money to go off to college, and then only came back occasionally, when he felt tough enough to last a few days. Every moment he was here he felt like there was something missing, something vital. And there was.

He'd had relationships in college, and since, but none of them ever lasted, not even this last one, the one he'd thought was It. His partners, to a man, accused him of being "emotionally unavailable," whatever the hell that meant. But none of them had ever been able to fill the hole that Zach had left. Zach, with whom he'd shared exactly one kiss, instigated by the inexperienced fifteen-year-old boy. Who'd vanished a week later, right out of a crowded airport.

David turned his back on the grandeur that was the Tyler

compound and the Rocky Mountains, and went up the steps to the porch of the gatehouse and let himself in. He dropped his duffel and set his laptop case down more carefully on the polished wood floor of the entry, and called, "Hello? Mom? You home?"

Silence greeted him. Not unexpected—it was the middle of the afternoon and she was probably at work. He went into the kitchen, got himself a drink of water, and called her cell phone from the kitchen extension.

She picked up on the second ring, her voice puzzled. "Hello?"

"Hey, lady," David said.

"Davey!" she cried in delight. "Are you at home? I was wondering who'd be calling from there."

"Yeah, just got here."

"You should have told me you were coming to visit! I'd have taken the day off."

"It's not really a visit, Mom. I—well, I sort of got a job here. At the community college. Teaching art."

There was a moment of confused silence, then Annie said, "But I thought you loved New York. You were so into the art scene there, and that internship at the Museum of Modern Art—I thought you were going to stay there.... Not that I'm not happy you're home, oh, Davey, that's wonderful, you'll be home...."

"Actually, I'm just looking to stay here a couple of days, just 'til I can find an apartment in town—either Wesley or the Springs. I think it's better that way."

"But...."

"Mom. Really, it's better. I'll be closer to work and everything. Maggie's selling me her old car, so I'll have wheels, and I can come up and visit anytime, but I think it's best if I'm not all that close, you know?"

"Yes, honey," Annie said quietly. "I know."

He swallowed. "You'd better tell Rich and Jane that I'm here. I'll try to keep out of sight, but I don't want them pissed at me. I'll be out of here as quick as I can."

"Davey, they don't blame you one bit, you know that. They're so grateful...."

"I don't want their"—he almost said "fucking" but remembered whom he was talking to—"gratitude. I know they're not mad or anything, but it's hard, Mom." He swallowed again and closed his free hand into a fist. "Nobody's mad, nobody's blaming anybody, nobody hates anybody, but it's the elephant in the kitchen, Mom. I can't deal with that. That's why I stayed away so long. I liked New York, sure, but I only ever really wanted to be here. I'm tired of being away from home. I'm tired of being alone. I want to come home, but this is as close as I can get, okay?"

"Yes, honey," Annie said again. "Look, Richard and Jane are going out to dinner tonight, so I'll be home early. How about some of my chicken fajitas for supper tonight?"

"I've been dreaming about your chicken fajitas, mamacita," David said. "Hey, I'm tired. It was a long trip, and I'm ready for a nap. Can I have my old room?"

"Of course—it's still the same. I rattle around in that big house. It'll be nice to have you home, even if it's only for a few days."

"It'll be nice to be home." David hesitated, then said carefully, "How is he?"

Annie didn't answer for a moment, then said, just as carefully, "He's fine. We'll talk more when I get home. See you then, love, and welcome home."

He hung up the phone and stared at it a long moment, then went to get his duffel bag and his nap.

HE WOKE to the smell of onions and peppers frying and shook himself fully awake before stumbling sleepily into the kitchen. Annie stood in front of the stove, singing cheerfully. David joined in on the chorus of "La Bamba." She turned around, and he caught her around the waist and danced her around the stone floor of the kitchen, singing and dripping olive oil.

Laughing, she tugged herself out of his arms, reaching for the paper towels. "Silly ass," she scolded, "now the floor's all slippery."

He took the towels from her hand and pushed her gently in the direction of the stove. "You cook, I clean up, okay?" in a mock-foreign accent, like Gilda Radner on the old *Saturday Night Live*.

"You'd better," she warned, grinning, "or you don't get any fajitas."

"You couldn't be so cruel," he said mournfully, and got down on his hands and knees to clean up the spilled oil.

She looked good, he thought, despite the fact that every time he'd seen her in the last three years her hair had been a different color. It was a bronzy-blonde this time, and it looked good. "I like the hair," he said. "It wasn't that color at Sandy's last Mother's Day."

"It was Sandy's idea, actually," she said. "Your sister thought the brown was too mousy, so I went and had it foiled. I'm about due for a touchup."

"Not yet, I don't think," he assured her, and tossed the greasy paper towels into the garbage can. Sliding up onto one of the barstools at the breakfast counter, he rested his chin on his hands and said, "So. How is he?"

She didn't answer, concentrating on turning the peppers and onions and chicken onto a platter. She set the platter in front of him, then got a plate of tortillas out of the warmer. "Sour cream coming up," she said, and got it out of the fridge, along with salsa and shredded cheese.

He let her putter, until she'd sat down across from him and started assembling her own fajita. "How is he, Mom?"

"He drinks too much and drives too fast, and if he kills himself it will destroy Jane and Richard," Annie said savagely, and she started to cry.

He reached over and covered her hands with his. "I'm sorry," he said. "I didn't mean to upset you."

She wiped her eyes with her napkin and said, "It's not your fault, Davey. It's just been so tense for so long. It's not that he's mean to us or anything. In fact, he's too nice. He's so polite and sweet, but it's all a front, you can tell that. He smiles but it's not real. And Jane and Richard smile, and they don't mean it. And it's gotten to the point that I don't mean it, either." Her fingers tightened on David's. "He moved into the chauffeur's old apartment over the garage two months ago, but it isn't any easier. Richard hasn't had a live-in chauffeur since Alan retired; he uses the firm's drivers, so it's not like he needs the space...."

"You're babbling, Mom," David said gently.

She took a breath. "Yeah, I am. Shit."

"I'm sorry," he said again.

"I told Jane and Richard that you'd be staying with me until you got someplace else and they both looked so sad. Jane asked if you'd mind if they came to visit while you were here."

"I wasn't the one who shut them out," David said bitterly.

"Well, honey, what would you have done if it had been you in their place? He was so fragile and he just freaked out when they asked if you could see him."

"I know how it went," David cut her off. "I heard him. I was there, remember?" He got up, appetite gone, and started to wrap up the rest of his fajitas. "I'll finish this later, okay?"

"I'm sorry, love," Annie said quietly.

"I've had two years to get used to it," David replied, "you'd think I would have."

"How did Jerry take your coming back here?"

"We broke up a few weeks ago, just before I got the job. Timing was pretty good, wasn't it?"

"Oh, love, I'm sorry...."

"It wasn't working out, anyway. I'm just shitty at relationships." He put the plate into the refrigerator and closed the door, thumping his forehead against the cool white surface. "Shit. Shit. Shit."

"He and Jane and Richard have been in therapy since he got back," Annie offered.

"What is that, ten months?"

"Nine, really. But they started even before that, while he was still in the rehab center." She hesitated, then went on. "Richard asked if you wanted to come back to work. They've got a whole new graphic arts division...." She trailed off when she saw David shaking his head.

"No, too close. Besides, I like teaching. I put in my time at Tyler Tech—I don't need to do it again. Community college doesn't pay much, but I don't need much. Besides, I'm still painting. I can make enough money to live on from that, even if I didn't have the interest from the investments. I'm flush, Mom. I can do what I want. Not too many twenty-five-year-olds can say that, huh?"

"No, love."

"And Maggie's been talking about me doing a show at a gallery in Colorado Springs. Seems she's friends with the owner, and showed him some jpegs of my stuff."

"It's nice you're still friends with her."

"Yeah, not a lot of girls would still hang out with a guy who dumped them the week after graduation because they were the wrong gender," David said dryly. "She told me once that if I'd busted up with her over another girl, she'd have been pissed, but that I couldn't help being gay. Then she tried to set me up with her cousin."

Annie laughed. "That's Maggie."

"She's apartment hunting for me. Since the college is here in Wesley, I'm trying to stay this side of the Springs, maybe one of the suburbs. I don't want a long commute, and I want to stay near the mountains." He turned and leaned back against the fridge. "I spent too long on the flats. I need me some hills."

"You and Richard," Annie said. She sighed wistfully. "I wish you would stay here, Davey. Jane and Richard wouldn't mind, and it's time…."

"Hell, no," David said brusquely. "No way in hell am I going to stay here a minute longer than I have to. I love you, Mom, but I just can't take the chance. He'll go postal, and Dick and Jane will blame me."

"Oh, don't call them that," Annie scolded. "It irritates the shit out of them."

"Zach was the one who came up with it," David said, then winced. "Shit."

"Besides, I told you, they don't blame you. It's something Zach has to get through, not you or them."

"Well, he's not, now, is he? That's assuming he even gives me a thought. For all I know, he doesn't even care if I'm alive or not."

"He asked me about you a few weeks ago," Annie said quietly.

David looked up, his heart aching. "He did?"

"Oh Davey," his mother sighed. "You still love him, don't you?"

"Shit," he said again. "I never stopped, Mom. But he's not the same kid I knew before... before all this happened. I know that. You said I don't have to get through this, but I kinda do. What did he say? God, I feel like I'm in high school again."

"He just asked, sort of, I don't know, quietly, if I ever heard from you. I said, 'Of course I do, he calls me all the time,' and he just said 'Good' and went back out to the patio. Never said another word. Of course, he doesn't talk much to me. Just please and thank you. That was the first time he said more than that, and it was just six words." She was quiet a moment, then said, "He doesn't say any more than that to his parents, except in their therapy sessions, and for all I know, that's all he says then too."

"He was always a polite kid."

She shook her head. "Polite, yes, but there's something... missing now. I don't know how to describe it. It's like he's polite because he thinks that's how he should be, not just naturally courteous the way he always was. It's like he's reading lines in a play he's not terribly interested in acting." Again, a head shake. "Well, I guess if he was normal he wouldn't be in therapy seven days a week, now would he?"

"Does he do anything except therapy?"

"Well, physical therapy too. And he has a couple of cars he works on. But usually he just disappears until suppertime, and even then half the time he doesn't eat with Di... Richard and Jane. He's got a kitchenette in the apartment and he'll cook something up there. I do his grocery shopping for him, and sometimes I clean up there, if he asks. He's very tidy."

"Quiet and tidy. Sounds like a serial killer."

"David!"

"Well, you know, that's how the neighbors always describe them. 'He was quiet, always kept to himself, but, boy, his yard was tidy.'"

David snorted. "Jeez, I hope the therapy works or they'll be digging up Dick and Jane's garden looking for bodies."

"David Philip Evans, I'm going to smack you so hard...."

He laughed at her. "Still want me to move in here?"

She softened. "Oh, honey, I wish you would."

He shook his head. "No, trust me, it's better this way. I promise I'll find someplace close, and we can visit all the time, okay?"

"If that's what you want."

"No, what I want is for things to go back the way they were seven years ago," David said with a sigh. "But that ain't likely, is it?"

"No, honey. It's not."

Chapter
Three

THE sun parlor where they had their therapy sessions was empty when Zach went in, but the French doors to the patio stood open, the gauzy drapes fluttering gently in the breeze. He crossed the room and looked outside to see his mother drinking coffee at one of the little white wrought-iron tables that circled the pool. She wasn't reading, although a book was open on the table in front of her; she was just sitting, drinking her coffee and looking out over the pool and the gardens beyond. Stray tendrils of fading blonde hair had escaped her neat chignon; she batted at them absently, tucking one strand behind her ear. She was so beautiful, Zach thought, his heart aching, and so sad. Even when she smiled, she never lost that little bit of sadness in the back of her eyes. He wanted to fix it, but didn't know how.

He didn't move, or speak, but suddenly she knew he was there in the sunroom, and turned, a smile on her face. This was her first smile of the day, the one that reached her eyes and made them shine; the one that said that for a moment she'd forgotten to be sad, forgotten what he was, forgotten everything except here was her beloved son, and she was glad to see him. He smiled back, kept the smile when hers faded to just lips, that ache back in her eyes. "Morning, sweetheart," she said cheerfully.

He nodded.

"Did you want some coffee? I think there's still some in the carafe."

He shook his head. "No, thank you," he said carefully.

"Did you eat breakfast?"

He nodded again.

"Annie's calling in a grocery order today; did you need anything?"

He thought a moment, then said, "Milk."

"Okay, I'll have her order some for you. Anything else?"

"No, thank you."

They gazed at each other across an unbridgeable gulf, then Zach heard the door open behind him and turned in relief. His father and the therapist came in together. Zach waited and saw the same smile curl his father's lips, brighten his eyes a moment. "Hey, Zach, morning."

Zach nodded at him in response. "Good morning, Dr. Barrett," he said politely to the therapist.

"Good morning, Zach."

Jane came into the sunroom at Zach's back, saving him from having to say anything about her whereabouts. "I'm here," she said gaily, and Zach flinched. She used to talk that way all the time, and he had loved it; now, it was so patently artificial it scraped his nerves. "Shall we get started?"

They sat in their usual spots: his parents on the wicker loveseat, the therapist in one armchair, Zach in the other. Zach folded his hands in his lap and waited.

After a moment of silence, Jane said, "There's something we need to tell Zach."

Zach's head came up and he stared at them expressionlessly. Inside, his guts had gone tense. She looked so solemn, so worried; he ran over in his head everything he'd done since yesterday, everything that could have possibly pushed them over the edge, made it too difficult to keep him. Were they going to send him away, maybe back to the nursing home; or worse—was he on the verge of getting committed? That's what they did with wackos, locked them up so they couldn't hurt anyone else…. A fine sheen of sweat beaded on his upper lip. He didn't think he could tolerate being locked up again….

"It's about… it's about David."

Zach went blank. Then fear roared through him and he grabbed the arms of his chair to steady himself. "What about him?" he asked, his voice shaking. Was he hurt—was he *dead*?

"He's home," Jane went on, and Zach realized he hadn't said the last few thoughts out loud. "Annie told me yesterday he's staying a few days here—well, at the gatehouse—until he gets an apartment. Apparently he's got a job teaching art at Wesley Community College. But she says he'll stay away. Zach won't have to see him—he'll stay away from us." She gave Zach a bright, fake smile; she'd seen the fear on his face. "So there's nothing to worry about, honey."

Of course he'd stay away. Just as he'd stayed away for the past two years. He had no reason to want to see Zach. Not if he figured Zach would freak out like the madman he was, just like he had when he'd been in the hospital, still thinking he was dreaming.

Sometimes he still thought he was dreaming.

"How do you feel about David being so close, Zach?" Dr. Barrett's voice was calm and soothing.

He shrugged.

"Does it frighten you to know he's here?"

Zach thought a moment. "No," he said. Broke his heart, yeah, to know that David was so close, just up the road at the gatehouse that had been his own second home throughout his childhood. Home in that warm little place with the fieldstone fireplaces, the polished wood floors, the cheerful curtains and overstuffed furniture. Was he even now sleeping late in that twin bed under the hand-pieced quilt his mother had made him years ago? No, David had always been an early riser. He was probably out on his mountain bike right now, or running, those long tanned legs flashing as he sprinted uphill, laughing back at the child Zach, who'd tried so hard to keep up with him…. Zach swallowed hard and turned away. "No," he said again. "I'm not afraid."

"Then how do you feel?"

Three months ago, Zach had snuck into the gatehouse when Annie was working up at the main house and crawled into that twin bed, bundled under that quilt. It had been clean and smelled of laundry detergent, and the sheets of bleach, but there was a scent of David there too. It had been so comforting that he'd fallen asleep there and only woke up when he'd heard Annie's car in the drive. He'd had to sneak out the back way so she didn't see him there. "I don't know," he said dully.

He felt more than saw the exchange of glances between his parents.

"What about you, Jane? How do you feel about David being here?"

Jane glanced nervously at Zach. He gave her his best blank face. "Well," she said hesitantly, "Richard and I have always been fond of David, so it's not easy, I mean, it's not *comfortable* to have him here and not feel like he's welcome.... Not that he's not welcome, their house is part of his mother's compensation, and she has every right to have whomever she likes there. But Zach is our priority, so we have to accommodate Zach's feelings...."

Zach was shaking his head. "No," he said. "No, you don't. I'm not the one in charge. I don't *want* to be the one in charge."

"Do you feel like your parents are trying to put the responsibility on you, Zach?"

"No," Zach said. He shook his head again. "I don't know. Ta... David can do what he wants. I don't care. He's nothing to me. I'm not afraid of him."

"You wouldn't mind if your dad and I went to see him while he's here?" Jane asked cautiously.

His head jerked up, his throat thick with betrayal. *They* wanted to see David, when he couldn't? That was unfair. That was so unfair.... "Do whatever the fuck you like," he said coldly.

"Zachary," Richard said reprovingly, "don't swear at your mother."

"I'm sorry," he said, drawing in on himself. "That was inappropriate."

"No, I think that was important," Dr. Barrett said thoughtfully. "Jane, Richard, one of the things that we've discussed in these sessions is that you don't feel that Zach expresses his emotions in a healthy way. He's never sworn before in any of these sessions. Does he swear outside them?"

"No, of course not," Jane said hurriedly. "Zach is always polite. It's just... just that he's stressed out because of David. You know, Doctor, you know how he hates and fears David."

"Do you hate and fear David, Zach?" the therapist asked curiously.

"No," Zach said.

"What do you feel for him, then?"

So *not going there,* Zach thought, and just shook his head.

"Would you like to see him again?"

"No." The answer was quick and sure. A knot of nausea soured his stomach at the thought of seeing David. "I don't hate him," he said dully. "I just can't see him, that's all. I don't care if you see him"—he glanced at his parents—"or anything; it's okay. I mean Annie sees him, right? I don't, like, freak out over her, do I?"

"Annie is not your mother," Richard said carefully. "Do you feel like we would be betraying you if we chose to be friends with David?"

"No." Zach shook his head. "I used to be friends with him myself."

"Would it hurt you if they did?" the doctor asked.

"No." That was a lie, but it didn't matter. He sat through these sessions for his parents, not for him. They thought they did some good, helped him reintegrate or whatever the current catchphrase was for trying to get a crazy person back among the sane. He thought it was rather pointless, but if it made them feel better, put him that much further from the loony bin, he'd play their games. It didn't mean he had to be honest. Just careful. He'd had a shock when Jane had brought up David, but he was back in control now. He smiled at the therapist. "I don't expect Mom and Dad to be friends with all of my friends, so why should I object to who they want to be friends with?"

"Do you have friends, Zach?"

He gave the shrink that careful false smile again. "Of course I have friends. I go out. I don't sit in my room and rock, you know."

"Where do you go?"

"A couple places in town." Zach shrugged. "I play pool, have a few drinks, same thing everyone else does when they go out."

"Do you have a boyfriend, or anyone special you go out with?"

"No. Just a bunch of people."

"Why don't you invite them over sometime, honey?" Jane asked with a smile.

He gave her the same smile back. "I don't think so. They're not that kind of people."

Her smile faded. His didn't. "What do you mean?" she asked carefully.

"They're just not," he said dismissively. "They're club people, not home people. Just because they're my friends doesn't mean I want them involved in every aspect of my life. They're not that important."

"Friends are important," Richard said.

"Not these." Zach shook his head. "It's okay. I've only been home ten months—"

"Nine," Jane said softly.

"—and I haven't had time to build any relationships, okay?" Not any that mattered. "It's okay, really. I'm finding my way. It takes time, okay?"

"Of course it's okay, honey," Jane said.

Yeah, of course it was okay. Everything he did and said was okay, wasn't it? His jaw was starting to ache from the fake smile. He wondered if they'd be okay with what really went on when he went out at night, went to the clubs with the convenient little rooms and the convenient guys that went with them. It would make them sick. Hell, it made *him* sick. He said again, "I'm just finding my way."

"I just wish—" Jane started, then stopped.

"Wish what?" Dr. Barrett asked.

"That I would do something constructive," Zach said. "Like go to school. What about it, Mom? Should I sign up for art lessons at Wesley?"

She flinched, but said only, "If that's what you want, honey, of course."

"Or maybe go to work for Dad," Zach said, still smiling. "I'm a shitty programmer, but hey, if the boss's kid can't get a job at the company, who can?"

"You know it's not just programming," Richard said carefully.

"There are other parts of the company that you'd enjoy working at."

"Thanks," Zach said gently. Careful. They were oh, so careful. Like handling a bomb. Not sure if it was armed, not sure if it was going to explode in their faces. So careful.

"But as long as you're going out and socializing, making friends...." Jane began.

Fuck it. Still in that gentle tone, Zach said, "They aren't really so much friends, Mom. Just people I fuck."

There was dead silence in the room. Then Jane said, "You are being safe, though, right?"

He stared at her a long moment, then started to laugh. Somewhere the laughter turned into tears, and he leaned his head down on his arm and cried. Jane went to her knees beside him and stroked his hair; Richard came around behind the wicker armchair and rubbed his T-shirted back. Finally, he raised his head to take the tissue his mother handed him and blow his nose. "Sorry about that," he muttered. "Didn't mean to go all stupid. Guess I kind of over-shared."

"That's the whole point of these sessions, Zach," the shrink said. "To share. I think this is a good step, because this is obviously an emotional issue for you."

"Ya think?" Zach said dryly.

"If this isn't a comfortable subject to discuss with your parents present, we can talk about it later, if you like."

Zach said, "It's not a comfortable subject, period. I'm not...." He shook his head. "It doesn't.... It isn't something I want to talk about."

Richard said, "It's usually the ones you don't want to talk about that you need to talk about. Trust me, I know." He rubbed Zach's shoulder again. "But if you don't want to talk about it with your mom and me here, that's okay. We're good with that, you know."

"I know. I appreciate it."

"We went through a lot of therapy when you were gone; we know the rules." Richard took Jane's hand and raised her to her feet, then led them back to the loveseat. Once they were seated, he gave Zach a long, steady look, and then said, "I'm just glad that you're... I don't know... exploring your sexuality, after what happened. We've been worried about that. It's an important part of life and relationships, and we were afraid you would end up cutting yourself off from that."

Zach returned his look with an "I-don't-believe-you-said-that" one of his own, then said to Dr. Barrett, "Do all your patients have ex-hippie parents that talk like this?"

Barrett laughed. "Some of them do. Does it embarrass you?"

"It's not comfortable," he said. "It doesn't...."

"Doesn't what?"

"Doesn't help. Doesn't make things easier." He turned and said to his parents, "I *appreciate* your trying to help. To let me know you care. I *know* you care. But in the end it doesn't matter. I mean, not that your caring doesn't matter, because it does, I know. But this"—he waved his hand—"it's not real, you know. It's like I'm still dreaming. Everything is nice and sweet and happy and I'm just waiting for the other shoe to drop. I'm dreaming."

"You're not dreaming, Zach," Richard said fiercely. "This *is* reality. This isn't perfect; it's not, as much as we want to make it so. We're not trying to cut you off from life or anything. We haven't locked you up here; you go out, and we don't even ask you where. We're trying to let you build your life again, however you want to do it, but we also want to support you. To be here for you. Damn it, Zach, why won't you *ask* us for anything? We're here trying to guess what you want, what will make you happy, but you don't ask. You don't give us a clue."

"I don't want a fucking thing!" Zach shouted. "I live in your house, you feed me, clothe me, practically wipe my ass for me, and you want me to ask for *more*? Jesus, Dick, I'm enough of a fucking parasite!"

"You are not a fucking parasite, you're our *son*, God damn it!" Richard yelled back.

Zach barked at him.

Richard nearly hit him, but froze with his fist an inch away from Zach's face. "Go ahead!" Zach yelled. "Hit me! You know you want to! You want to, go ahead!"

His father lowered his hand, flexing the fingers. "God damn you,

Zach," he said in a low voice. "I don't know what the hell you want."

"Sometimes," Zach said, "I want the cage." With that admission, he got up and walked out onto the patio, staring down into the pool. He heard the shrink talking in an undertone, and his mother crying. *Good job, asshole,* he told himself viciously. *Good way to alienate the only people in the world who give a shit about you.* How the hell had this gone so quickly downhill? Their therapy sessions had never exploded like this one before.

He knew what it was. He'd let David in.

Dropping to his knees, he dipped his hand in the pool and rubbed the water over his face, trying to cool himself down. He was still kneeling when he felt someone behind him and knew it was his father. "Yeah, I know," he said dully. "I upset Mom. I'll apologize." He sat back on his heels, still gazing down at the water. His father's silhouette quivered in the little wavelets from Zach's hand.

"I'm the one apologizing," Richard said wearily. "To you. I'm sorry, Zach. I didn't mean to go off on you like that. I'm just…."

"Yeah," Zach said. "I know. Frustrated. I don't blame you."

"You've got a lot of anger bottled up inside you, Zach. Well, so do I. I know you think we're being all patient and crap, but I'm not patient. I've never been patient." He sat down cross-legged on the edge of the pool beside Zach. "I hate this crap," he said savagely. "I hate that you lost so much of your life. I hate that *I* lost so much of your life. I hate the therapy. I hate not being able to talk to you the way we used to. I hate what happened to you and knowing that I probably don't know the half of it. I hate that you've shut us out. I hate that you can even say what you just said and *mean* it, because I know you do. It breaks my fucking heart, Zach. And I don't know what the fuck to do about it."

"I think, sometimes," Zach said, sighing, "that maybe I need to be gone. That maybe I shouldn't have come back. Not that I mean I should have stayed in Venezuela, but maybe instead of coming home from the rehab center I should have just gone into, like, an institution or something." He waited, his heart pounding.

His father's response was instantaneous and violent. "No *fucking* way, Zach! You aren't crazy, you don't belong in an institution. Jesus Christ, Zach, why the hell would you say that? You belong here!"

Zach didn't answer. Finally, Richard asked, "Do you *want* to go away?"

"No," Zach muttered. "No."

Richard's hand closed around Zach's forearm, his fingers digging into the taut muscle. "I don't want you to go away. Neither does your mother. Yeah, it's hard on all of us, and I know you feel guilty as hell for that. Well, we feel guilty as hell for what happened. That's why we're in therapy, remember?"

He ducked his head in a nod. "Yeah. I remember."

Richard released his arm, but not before giving it a good solid rub. "Forest service says the last of the snowpack's melting and they're opening the trails around the Peak. You want to go hiking this weekend?"

Zach was quiet a moment, then said, "Maybe a short one. It's been a long time."

"You need to add some aerobic exercise to your weights program. You should start using the gym at the office instead of just the one here—it's got a track…."

"No, I can't," Zach said. "I can't work out in public yet." He rubbed the base of his throat, where the scar tissue circled his neck. "Not yet. It's not like we don't have a pool, you know."

"You should use it more." Richard stood, and ruffled Zach's hair—or rubbed his head, since it was cropped way too short to ruffle. "That's what it's there for."

"Sure, Dad," Zach said.

Chapter Four

"IF YOU were a guy, I'd marry you," David said.

"Alex would have something to say about that," Maggie retorted. "So, you likee?"

"I likee," David replied, running his hand over the doorframe. "Just what the doctor ordered."

"It's not new—it's a 2004, but it's the old version of the Saturn before GM completely took over, so it's a fiberglass body—no rust. And those old Saturns lasted forever. I know someone who's got a '93 that has almost 500,000 miles on it, and it's still running." Maggie patted the car's roof. "She's got about seventy-five thousand miles on her, but Alex made sure she was maintained well, so she's just a baby, engine-wise. I've hardly driven her at all since we bought the urban assault vehicle—it's just a little awkward getting the mondo car seat in the back. I think the damn car seat is bigger than the car." She patted the roof again. "I'm just glad she's going to a good home. Now if we can only find *you* a good home, we'll be set."

"Bless you, child," David said. "Were you able to find any candidates before I got here?"

"Well, there are plenty of places where you *can* live," Maggie said, and followed David back to the porch, where he'd put a couple bottles of Sam Adams on the railing. The condensation steamed gently in the late afternoon sun. "But whether you'd *want* to live there is another story. High concentration of new construction, you know, from the cardboard-box school of architecture...."

"Little boxes on the hillside, little boxes made of ticky-tacky, little boxes on the hillside and they all look just the same...." David sang softly.

"Another hippie song from your mother's misspent youth?" Maggie asked, and took a swig of beer.

"Of course. I was raised on hippie songs. They formed an integral part of my psychological development. That and Warner Brothers cartoons."

"God bless Warner Brothers," Maggie intoned, and they clicked bottles in salute. "I've been looking for something a little more culturally significant as a habitat for you, but so far I am failing miserably. Though, frankly, why you'd ever want to live someplace other than this, I don't know." She sat on the porch steps and looked off into the distance.

David watched her serene face in amusement. "Gorgeous, isn't it?" he said.

"Yep."

"I know. And it was hard to leave. Almost as hard as it was to come back."

Maggie cocked her head. "Do tell."

"Nothing to tell." David drank some of the Sam Adams. "Got home yesterday, on schedule. Back in my old bedroom, just like always. Nothing's really changed."

"Nothing and everything," Maggie said wisely. "Have you seen him?"

"Nope. And don't plan to."

"What is the deal with that? You never said. I mean, you guys were like best buds. He worshipped the ground upon which you tread. It wasn't you who sent him off to hell. Unless you mean he blames you for the whole situation. But if I recall correctly, he kissed you, not the other way around. So...."

"I don't know. I guess he must blame me. He freaked out when his parents asked him if he wanted to see me." David swallowed the hurt, still vicious after two years, and went on. "I guess he does blame me. It might not make sense to you, but you didn't spend five years as a hostage in god-knows-what conditions."

"No, guess I didn't," Maggie admitted. "Is it true he didn't talk for months after he got back?"

"From what I hear, it's true enough."

They drank in silence. Finally, Maggie said, "That's the reason for the moving out, right? So you don't accidentally run into him again."

David sighed. "On the one hand, I kind of wish I could get it over with. You know, have the big confrontation, screaming match, fistfight, whatever the hell it's going to be, and be done with it. But I really don't want that. I can't see fighting with Zach. I still see him as this gangling little kid with big eyes and all that hair. Plus I don't know how a fight would impact Mom and her relationship with Dick and Jane. I mean, she works for them, but they've been friends a hell of a lot longer than that. They gave her the job when Dad died so she wouldn't have to go back to her family, not because she needed the money or anything. But her folks were pressuring her to move back home, and this gave her an excuse not to. Not that my grands are anything but nice, but Ohio's not Colorado, you know?"

"I know," Maggie said, and raised her bottle toward the mountains. "That sight gets in your blood. Which is what I suppose is the real reason you decided to come back here, all my superior blandishments aside."

"Yeah, much as the offer of a gallery show and the job at Wesley appealed, you know it was this place that got me back here. Only place I ever lived that could compete with this was New Zealand, when I had that internship with Weta. It was fucking gorgeous. But they all talk funny there."

"But those Maori tattoos are hot," Maggie said.

"No question."

"So Weta internship, ILM internship—and you *still* want to stick with painting over computer graphics?"

"For now. Mom said Dick asked if I was interested in coming back; if the teaching thing doesn't work out, then maybe I'll change my mind. I guess they're getting into some graphic arts software-building. I like that part of it more than the actual design end, anyway. I'm doing a couple of things with that in my spare time—working with some of the new 3D technology. Did you ever notice some of the effects that Disney got with his early full-length features, using multiple layers of painted cells? You got some really artistic results with that. I'm trying to design a program that will automatically build those layers, but in a way that reflects specific artists' styles—like Renoir, or Rembrandt, or the individual draftsman—"

"Which sounds pretty damn promising," a new voice interrupted. David and Maggie looked up toward the end of the porch.

Richard came around the house, hand-in-hand with Jane. "Sure I can't talk you into coming back to work for me?" he asked with a grin.

"Hey, Rich," David said, grinning back. He bounded down the steps to grab Richard's hand for a violent shake, then gave Jane a hug. "No thanks, but thanks! Hey, Jenny, how goes the battle?"

"Endless, as you well know," Jane replied, hugging him back. "Welcome home, Davey! We've missed you!"

"Missed you too," David replied.

"Hi, Maggie," Jane said with a smile. "Isn't it nice to have our Davey home again?"

"I think so, but my husband says I've got a screw loose anyway," Maggie said cheerfully. David pretended to hit her with his beer bottle.

"Behave, or I won't buy your beater."

"'Beater'? I'll have you know that's a classic!"

"Are you buying Maggie's Saturn?" Richard asked. "Good car."

"Well, you should know, you've had what, five? Six?" David grinned.

"Only four, counting the convertible."

"Guy's a gazillionaire and he drives Saturns," David said to Jane.

"I'm practical," Richard said.

"It's a change from Volkswagens," Jane told David. "And we *do* have the Rolls for showing off."

"Now *that* is a classic car," David agreed. "A '36 Silver Ghost? They don't come any more classic."

"I thought Alan was going to cry when he retired," Richard said. "We had to give him visitation rights. He comes by on Sundays and polishes her just for old times' sake." He was silent a moment, then said carefully, "We've got a few cars in the garage that when they're restored could probably compete with the Rolls. Zach's working on the engines—auto shop was always his favorite class in high school—and then we're going to see about getting someone to do the body work. Right now, he's working on a '71 Dodge Charger convertible. It's a beauty."

"So how are you getting home?" Jane asked Maggie brightly.

"Oh, Alex is going to swing by on his way home from work."

"He's a bright kid, Alex," Richard said. "His team leader likes him, and George doesn't like many people."

David laughed. "George doesn't like anyone."

"Okay, well, then," Richard said, "George doesn't hate him."

"That's about the best you can expect with George," Jane said.

"You guys want something to drink?" David offered. "I've got more Sam Adams in the refrigerator. Or you can have juice, soda, whatever."

"Sam Adams sounds good. Jenny?"

"Sure," Jane said, and sat down on the porch steps next to Maggie. Richard sat up a step or two, his long legs tucked around his wife. After David came out and handed them their beers, he swung up onto the porch railing and linked his feet around the slats. "Been hiking yet this year?" he asked.

"We're thinking of going up to the Peak this weekend with Zach. He hasn't done any hiking since he came back; at first he wasn't physically able, but now he's in pretty good shape. He needs new boots, though; he outgrew his old ones while he was away."

"He outgrew everything when he was away," Jane said. "It was silly to keep all his stuff for so long, but I had it in my head that when he came home he'd be just the same as he was when he left. But the difference between fifteen and twenty is pretty substantial. He's as tall as Richard is now, and his feet are bigger."

"You never gave up hope that he would come home, did you?" Maggie asked gently.

"No, never," Jane said with a smile. "I always knew he would."

"I didn't," Richard said bluntly, and he lifted his beer to his lips. When he brought the bottle down, he went on. "I figured he was dead the minute the kidnappers didn't release him after the ransom. Shit," he said, "I really didn't want to get onto this subject. So. David. What does teaching have to offer that working for me doesn't?"

"Um, let's see," David said. "Pathetic salary, lesson plans, staying up all hours grading papers and/or projects, crappy coffee in the teachers' break room, paperwork...."

"Sounds great," Richard said. "Sign me right up."

David laughed. "At least it's not grammar school. I did student teaching at a grammar school once and it was the longest freaking six weeks of my life. That pushed me toward my master's more than anything else. As for getting the job at Wesley—I think it was probably more my background at Tyler Technologies that got me the job, rather than my education. They're really pushing the electronic graphic arts programs there, rather than the traditional forms. But it's a community college, so they're going to go for the more economically feasible programs. Doesn't hurt either that they got a grant for their computer department from a prominent local businessman." He saluted Richard with his bottle.

"And before you ask, I had nothing to do with you getting the job. I didn't even know about it until Annie told us yesterday."

They went on talking about the job, the state of Tyler Technologies, Maggie and Alex's baby daughter Annabel, and inconsequentials, until Alex pulled up to pick up Maggie. They chatted a bit with him, then the younger couple drove away, and Richard and Jane bid David good night and another welcome home and started their walk back to the main house, hand in hand like a couple of teenagers. David watched them go until they crested the hill beyond the house and vanished from view. *Well,* he thought, *that wasn't bad.* Apparently, whatever grudge Zach had against him didn't bleed into Dick and Jane's opinion; they treated him the same as they always did.

He sat on the porch a while longer, watching the light fade. The sunset was spectacular, as usual; the white clouds stark against the blue gradually turning all shades of pink and purple and orange. He remembered that it was just about sunset the night the world changed, too. Dropping Zach off after a soccer game, the kid all sweaty and excited in his dusty, muddy shorts and uniform T-shirt.... He'd left his game shoes on the floor of David's Cavalier, and David had thrown the car into park and gone after him with them.

Zach had stopped and turned, grinning—no, *glowing*—with triumph from his team's win, his eyes bright and his face alight with the soft colors of the sunset, and David froze a half a dozen steps from him, holding the shoes out wordlessly, shattered by a sudden, unexpected realization. He'd never thought of Zach as anything other than the little tagalong, the kid that he schlepped to baseball practice and soccer practice and football practice, that he'd taken on hundreds of hikes, shepherded through skiing lessons, beat in video games, shared the big events and the little. But suddenly he realized that Zach was nearly as tall as his own six-foot frame, and broad-shouldered and strong, with the faint beginnings of a five-o'clock shadow, and the notion shook him. Zach wasn't a kid any longer.

Still smiling, Zach stepped forward and took the shoes, then dropped them on the ground. "I've been waiting for you to look at me like that," he said, and kissed him, his mouth soft and warm on David's.

For an instant, David fell into the kiss, barely feeling Zach's hand curling around the back of his neck, only aware of the scent of Zach and sweat and mud and the taste of his mouth, peanut butter and chocolate from the candy bar he'd eaten after the game. Zach's tongue licked inside, teasing his.

Then he jerked away and stared at Zach in disbelief. "What...?" he stammered.

Zach laughed delightedly. "The look on your face!" he chortled. "What's the big deal, Taff? You're gay; I've known that for a long time. Well, so am I."

"You aren't gay," David said. "You're *fifteen*."

"Since when are the two mutually exclusive?" Zach asked. His smile faded. "So—what? You're not interested?" He swallowed. "Gee, sorry. Didn't mean to infringe on your personal space or anything."

"No," David said, putting out a hand. "Zach... Jesus, Zach, you're fifteen. It's—it's like hero worship, or a crush, or something. You're too young—fuck, Zach, you're *jailbait*."

"You're only three years older than me," Zach retorted. "And I'll be sixteen in two months. I'm not stupid, Taff. I'm not imagining things. And I didn't imagine the way you just looked at me. Hell, the way you're looking at me now. You want me, Taff. I can see that." He reached down and palmed the thick, heavy ridge of David's erection through his jeans. "You want me like I want you. It's okay. It's okay."

"It *ain't* okay," David snarled, grabbing Zach's questing hand. "You're fucking jailbait, Zach, if nothing else." He took a deep breath, but that didn't help; all he could smell was sweet, sweaty Zach, all he could feel was the taut muscles of his wrist under the silkiness of his young skin, all he could see was the beautiful curve of Zach's cheek and the arch of that wickedly sweet mouth. "Christ," he muttered, and despite himself reached up to stroke that silky cheek. "You're so fucking beautiful, Zach. Yeah, I want you, but you are too. Fucking. Young. And here I am perving over you. Jesus."

"'Perving'? Is that what you think? Like you're some old man and I'm just some kid?" Zach's voice was hurt.

"Not 'just' some kid," David said miserably. "But you are a kid, Zach. You got time… Jesus, think about it. Just—think about it."

"I've *been* thinking about it for two fucking years," Zach snapped. "Ever since I figured out that girls just don't do it for me. You know what my wet dreams are about, Taff? Dicks."

David covered his ears. "I can't hear this. Fuck, Zach, your parents are gonna go berserk. They're gonna blame me for this. I am so dead."

"Fuck you," Zach had said, and walked away. David had walked back to the car but hadn't gotten in; he just stood beside the driver's side door and rested his forehead on the warm metal of the roof.

Richard's voice had come out of the gathering twilight. "David."

David looked up to see Zach's father standing with Zach's forgotten soccer cleats in his hand. It didn't take a genius to see that Richard knew exactly what had just gone on between David and Zach. "I'm going," David said curtly. "I won't talk to Zach again."

"That's not necessary," Jane said from behind Richard.

David groaned. "I take it you heard everything?"

"Enough," Jane said. "Enough to hear you discouraging him. David, we've known—or suspected—that Zach was gay for a long time, but he never seemed to think of you as anything but a big brother, and so we didn't worry about it. He never seemed interested in sex of any kind...."

"Which in itself was a little weird for a teenage boy," Richard said, "but Zach is hardly your average teenage boy."

"We meant to have this talk with you sooner or later," Jane said uncertainly. "We just thought we had a little more time."

"So, what?" David asked, looking from one to the other. "You want me to leave, right? Take that scholarship you offered me? And go—where, someplace like the Sorbonne? University of Moscow? Is that far enough?"

"We're not asking you to leave, Davey," Richard said. "Particularly after hearing what we did."

"And what was that?" David asked in confusion.

"You said just what we would have asked you to. That Zach is too young for a relationship—with you or with anyone else—and that he should wait until he was older. Zach's brilliant, but he's still emotionally a kid. He's not ready for anything like that. And when he is—whether it's with you, or with someone else—we'll deal with it then as appropriate." He hesitated. "Zach was accepted by the early admissions program at MIT. We weren't going to let him go because he *is* so young, but we're reconsidering it. It would mean relocating to Boston for the school year, but there's no reason I can't work from there; it's just been more convenient to be so close to home. I'm not saying this because we plan to keep you two apart, but because hopefully the excitement of college will distract him from feeling resentful of us trying to rein him in a bit."

"I'm not in favor of the idea," David said bluntly. "At MIT, he's gonna be meeting and working with guys even older than I am, who are used to students who aren't as young as Zach. They'll think of him and treat him like a contemporary, particularly since he doesn't talk or act like your average fifteen-year-old. If you don't want him in a sexual relationship, keep him away from that kind of environment."

"You have a good point," Jane said, nodding. "Zach is not the only brilliant kid around here, Davey."

David shook his head. "Not brilliant. It's just common sense. I've visited friends at college and I know what kind of crazy-assed shit goes on. Jeez, guys—you aren't that old—don't you remember how it was?"

Richard actually flinched. "Shit."

"See?"

"Yeah. So we deal with it as is."

"Zach's upset, though," Jane said. "He's angry with David, and hurt."

"I'll apologize," David began, but Richard shook his head.

"No, don't. Zach needs to learn that he can't get everything he wants."

"I wonder...." Jane said thoughtfully.

"What, Jenny?"

"Well, my sister Alicia's been asking for Zach to come visit her. She's the one who's got a grant to study climate change at the Monteverde Cloud Forest Reserve. Zach was excited at first when she invited him, but then he lost interest." She glanced at David. "I think I know why, now. But maybe it would be good for him to go see her after all. It would be a distraction...."

AND how, David thought wearily as he watched the sun slip behind the mountains. *Quite a distraction for all of us, particularly after Zach disappeared from the San Jose airport in Costa Rica....*

Still, that was all over.

Right.

A wave of grief as strong as any he'd had during Zach's five-year absence washed over him, and he clutched the porch railing. The grief didn't care that Zach was home, safe, recovering. All it cared about was that Zach was as irrevocably lost to David as if he had died in that jungle.

"Shit," David said angrily, wiping tears from his face. "Shit." He slammed into the house, went to the kitchen, and turned on the little under-cabinet TV, switching channels until he found a loud, mindless game show to keep him distracted until his mother came home.

Chapter Five

HE MANAGED to make it through dinner with Annie without breaking down. Afterwards, they watched a movie on HBO; then when Annie announced that she needed to get to bed, he said, "You go ahead. I'm still antsy. I think maybe I'll take my new wheels out for a drive."

"Don't drink," Annie said automatically, then yawned.

"Maximum one beer," he promised. "I just need to reconnect with the old neighborhood. I won't be late."

"You're an adult, Davey," she said, then dimpled. "Okay, that's a bullshit line. You're still my baby, so don't be late, don't talk to strangers...."

"And I've got on clean underwear in case I fall off my bike and need to go to the hospital. Yeah, Mom, I know the routine." He kissed her cheek. "It's good to be home, Mom. Even if you're a total whack job."

She smacked his butt. "What a way to talk to your mother. Go. Have fun. Don't be late."

"I won't, he said, and kissed her again.

HE DROVE around for a while, seeing what was new and what had changed in his old stomping grounds. After an hour, that wasn't helping anymore, so he pulled into a Wesley bar he used to hang out in occasionally. It looked pretty much the same—more or less a local pub, but friendly to the gay community in Wesley and the Springs. It didn't have the little back rooms some of the more blatantly pick-up places did, but David had met a guy or two he'd liked here.

It being a Wednesday, the lot wasn't as full as it would have been on the weekend, but there were still more than a few cars parked there. Cars, and an amazingly hot-looking Ducati motorcycle. The sodium lights in the lot didn't give a true impression of the color, but David thought it might be red. Wow, he thought, looking the bike over. He didn't know much about motorcycles, but he knew that Ducatis were the top of the line, and kind of rare here in Harley country.

He picked out the owner the minute he walked in. The guy stood with one foot on the brass rail, leaning forward on the polished black surface of the bar. He was tall; taller than David by a couple of inches, from what David could see. He paused a moment to admire the way the broad shoulders tapered into a lean waist, a taut, fuckable ass, and long legs in black denim. A black leather jacket was thrown on the barstool beside him. *Ducati guy,* David thought. *Only a biker would wear leather in this weather.*

The guy had his hair buzzed, but what was there was thick and black as the T-shirt that stretched over those wide shoulders and muscled arms. There was something entirely too sexy about the way the shirt bagged loosely where it brushed the narrow waist of the jeans. The T-shirt and buzz cut left his neck bare, and David frowned as he came closer and saw the ridge of scar tissue that marred an otherwise perfect view. It looked like the guy had been strangled or something.

Then he was standing at the bar next to the guy ordering a beer, and when he turned he saw the man's profile, the strong jaw set and the face expressionless. "Holy shit," he breathed. "*Zach??*"

"Fuck off," the man said, and took a drink of his Scotch.

"Jesus, it is you," David said. "Zach...."

"What part of 'fuck off' don't you understand, *David?*" Zach replied, still looking straight ahead, still expressionless.

"Zach, can we talk? Please?" Here it was, his chance to make amends, his chance to find out what was going on in Zach's head. "I've been wanting to see you...."

Zach's eyes closed briefly, then he set his Scotch back down on the bar, picked up his jacket and turned to leave.

David stepped in front of him. "No, Zach, please. I just want to talk...."

Pale eyes flicked up to his, cold and empty. "I don't talk. You want to fuck, that's another story. But no talking. No kissing. No follow-up phone calls. I don't suck dick, and I don't bottom. Interested?"

David stared at him, uncomprehending.

Zach smiled thinly, humorlessly. "Didn't think so." He brushed past David and out the door. A moment later David heard the roar of the motorcycle.

"What did you do to piss off the Ice Queen?" a voice said behind him.

Dazed, David turned to the young guy, a stranger. "What?"

"The Ice Queen. He's cold, but he's always polite. Helluva fuck, though."

Rage roared through David and he grabbed the guy's shirt. "What. The. Fuck?"

"Hey! Don't get all pissy, dude!" the guy protested. "I just asked what you said to piss him off. He don't get mad, ever. Never saw him react like that to anybody." The guy relaxed as David released him, and gave him a once-over. "You look like his type," he said meditatively. "Mine, too." He broke into a grin. "Lemme buy you a drink."

"Got one," David said curtly, and walked back to the bar.

The guy followed. "I'm Brian," he said. "And you're David? I heard the Ice Queen call you that."

"Yeah."

"I figured when you walked in that you'd walk out with him," Brian said thoughtfully. "Like I said, you're his type. But you guys, like, know each other, huh?"

"What do you mean I'm his type?" David asked. His fingers closed hard around the glass of beer in front of him.

"Blond surfer dude." Brian waved his hand to indicate himself. "Like me."

"You met him here?"

"Nah, at the Goose. You know it?"

"Gray Goose on Sheffield? Yeah. I know it." Shit, David thought.

That place was a meat market. Zach was hanging out there? Some of the patrons referred to it as the Dirty Duck—or Dirty Dick, as the case may be.

"He's there a lot. Doesn't do repeats too often, though—more's the pity." Brian ordered a beer.

"Do *not* tell me he's a helluva fuck again," David snarled. He stared at the beer in his hands, wishing he had the nerve to get wasted, to forget what had just happened. Jesus. He hadn't expected this. Hadn't been ready to run into Zach, hadn't known what to say, hadn't expected to start burbling like an idiot. And he sure as shit hadn't expected to see Zach not only all grown up but looking older than David himself. Older and harder. He shuddered and he didn't know if it was fear, misery… or arousal. Shit. If he held the beer glass any tighter it would shatter in his hands.

With an effort, he eased his grip, finished his beer and said, "Well, thanks for the talk. See you around."

"I hope so," Brian said with a grin.

I don't, David thought, but only nodded and left the bar.

ZACH took the south gate too fast, the opening barely wide enough for the bike when he shot through going way too fast, as if he could outrun the acid bite of panic burning the back of his throat. Going up the hill toward the garage at about eighty, he skidded to a stop beneath the overhang of the upper porch, shut off the Ducati, and raced up the outside stairs, slamming into his apartment and stopping, finally, his chest heaving as if he'd run all the way from the bar. He pulled off his leather jacket and threw it over a chair, then flung himself onto the couch and let the panic attack take over. The shrink had always told him not to fight it, to let the anxiety go, wash over and through him, but it was easier said than done. The damn shrink probably never had a panic attack, never knew what it felt like to be convinced you were dying, that the incredible pain in your chest was a massive heart attack, that the turmoil in your brain was a stroke or you finally falling over the edge into insanity…. He shivered violently, sweat pouring from his clammy skin and tears from his blurred eyes, sobbing and shuddering and crying hysterically.

It was perhaps ten minutes later that the terror finally loosed its grip, leaving Zach limp and exhausted. He lay still, tucked up in a fetal position, waiting for his heart to slow. Finally, he unclenched his fists and stared at the red half-moons his nails had bitten into his palms. "Fuck," he whispered, and got up, going into the bathroom to wash his face with cold water.

He had only had one Scotch at the bar, so he poured himself another and sat at the kitchen table, holding the glass in both hands and searching the golden depths as if the liquor held answers. He wasn't even sure of the questions.

No, he knew the questions. What the hell had David wanted? And why the hell had Zach been such a dick to him? He couldn't seem to stop fucking things up. First losing all control during his therapy session this morning and upsetting his parents, now this. If he'd ever had any remote hope of rebuilding his friendship with David, that hope was as dead as... well, as dead as Esteban.

Zach rubbed the scar circling his neck from the dog collar he'd worn for five years, a habit he'd been unable to break. Feeling the rough dead skin somehow always helped him focus, help him settle. *Stupid,* he thought wearily. Like a toddler's favorite blanket or teddy bear—only his was scarring from five years of misery. How wacked was that? Still, it was familiar. Almost comforting.

The Scotch slid down his tear-roughened throat, the burn cauterizing his emotions. He was sitting debating whether he should have one more or just drink himself into unconsciousness like he did most nights when there was a sharp rapping at the door. *Shit,* he thought, and glanced at the clock on the stove to see that it was barely past eleven. Had his parents heard him coming home and were wondering why he was so early? He left the Scotch on the table and went to answer the door.

To his shock, David stood there. He reached up and pushed gently on Zach's chest; Zach stepped back automatically and David came in and closed the door. "Hell yes," David said.

"What?" Zach stammered.

"Hell yes I'm interested. If it's the only way I can get you to spend ten seconds in my company, hell, yes." He pushed Zach back another step. "So what's it to be? You want me to suck your dick, or you want to fuck me?"

The breath whooshed out of Zach's lungs. "What the fuck?" he gasped. "Are you *crazy?*"

"Yeah, I think so," David said. He dropped down onto the arm of the sofa and looked up at Zach. His eyes looked as tired as Zach felt. "I have to be fucking crazy to be here. I just—shit, Zach, I just need some closure." He looked away. "But I'll settle for whatever I can get." His lips quirked in a humorless smile. "Sorry. Forgot. No talking."

Then to Zach's shock, he dropped to his knees in front of Zach and reached for Zach's fly.

Zach batted his hand away. "No," he said roughly.

"Oh, okay," David said. He got up, moving stiffly, and unbuttoned his own jeans. "Where do you want me? I gotta warn you—I've never bottomed before, so I'd appreciate it if you'd take it easy...."

"No." Zach shook his head. "No fucking way, Taff. No. Just... just get the fuck out, okay?"

Slowly David rebuttoned, not looking at Zach. His face was white and his hands shook. "Right," he said numbly, and left.

Zach stared at the closed door a long moment, then hissed, "*Fuck,*" and shot out the door, intending to chase David.

He didn't have to go far; just to the top of the stairs. David sat on the bottom step, his face in his arms and his shoulders shaking. "Taff?" Zach said uncertainly.

David stood, wiping his forearm across his face. "I'm going," he said in a muffled voice. "Sorry."

"No. Wait."

Shoulders slumped, David turned to look up the stairs at Zach. "I just need to know," he said wearily, "why you hate me. That's all. I just need to know why."

"I don't hate you."

David's face closed down and he turned away. "Whatever," he said bitterly.

"No. Wait," Zach said again.

He watched David's shoulders sag before he turned back. "What?"

"I'm fucked up," Zach said. He swallowed desperately, his mouth dry and his voice rough. "I'm completely fucked up, Taff." Then he sank down onto the top step of the stairs, his eyes on David, waiting.

David considered his words a moment, then looked up to meet Zach's eyes. "Yeah. I guess you would be."

"I'm in fucking therapy, you know. Twice a day, every day of my life, including Sundays. I can't imagine what my folks are paying the shrink to come in on Sundays," Zach babbled. "I go 'cause it makes them feel better. Makes them feel like they're doing something, you know? But they can't do anything. Nobody can do anything." He met David's eyes. They were patient and a little sad. And wet. "You want a beer?"

David considered, then nodded.

"Okay." Zach shot to his feet. "Wait. Wait right there." He patted the air, as if he were telling a dog to sit, then realized what he was doing, shook his hand roughly, and raced into the house. A moment later he came back with two bottles of Goose Island, relieved to see David still standing at the foot of the stairs. He came down a few steps and held out one of the bottles.

David came up a few and reached out to take the bottle. Zach retreated to the top step again; David sat down a few risers from the bottom. They opened their beers in silence.

After a few minutes of it, Zach said, "I really *don't* hate you, you know. I mean, I know you gotta think that, after what happened at Terry's just now—but it isn't like that. I don't—I don't know why I acted that way. I wasn't expecting to see you, I guess. I don't...." He took a sip of beer. "I don't respond well to unexpected things. Most people got a sort of, of, I don't know, buffer or something, helps them figure out how to respond to stuff. I just... I just flip out. Not very mature." He gave David a brief, humorless grin, and drank some more ale. "I'm a control freak. Things don't go the way I plan, I freak out."

"You didn't expect me to show up at Terry's."

"I didn't expect you to show up anywhere. Stupid of me." Zach shook his head. "I knew you were back in town, but I just figured you'd stick close to home 'til you moved out, and you'd probably be in the city, and I wouldn't run into you. You don't hang out in dumps like the Dick, or Fat Charlie's. I thought... I thought you wouldn't be at Terry's, either, your second night home only. Figured you'd be with DB, or Maggie and Alex."

"You still call my mom 'DB'?" David asked in amusement.

Zach shook his head. "I mostly don't talk to her," he admitted. "I mostly don't talk to anyone. It's... I don't know. It's hard."

"You've been talking a blue streak here," David pointed out.

"Sorry."

"No. It's nice. It's kind of like the old days. You never shut up then. You could talk the hind leg off a burro. But you weren't boring. You were never boring." He gave Zach a faint smile. "Annoying as hell, sometimes, but never boring."

Zach picked at the label on his bottle. "Yeah, I guess. It was a long time ago."

David asked gently, "Can you talk about what happened to you, or is that, like, too sensitive or something?"

"Something," Zach agreed bitterly.

"I met this guy tonight at Terry's. Brian something. You know him?"

Zach shook his head. "Maybe. I don't know. I don't remember."

"Blond surfer dude type. Like me."

Zach flinched. "Yeah. Maybe."

"He called you the Ice Queen. Says you never lose your cool. Always cold." David took a swig of beer. "Also said you were a helluva fuck."

There was dead silence a moment, then Zach said, "Yeah. I guess so. I try, anyway. I mean, I try to make sure they're okay, I mean, you know."

"That they come first, you mean?"

Zach's face was burning. "Shit."

David chuckled. "Sorry. I guess it is a little personal."

"It's okay."

"I mean, it's hard reconciling the kid I knew with someone called 'the Ice Queen'. It's weird."

"Yeah, well." Zach hesitated, then said tiredly, "I guess the kid you knew is pretty damn dead. There's just me left. The fucked-up crazy-assed cold-hearted Ice Queen. Battered, bruised and bewildered."

"But still fucking beautiful," David said.

Zach blinked. "What?" he asked in confusion.

"You're still beautiful," David repeated with a shrug. "Not a compliment, just a fact. You got great bones or something."

"I am *so* not," Zach shook his head. "Not really. The light here is pretty bad." He gestured up at the fixture over the door above him. "You're just projecting your memory."

"No, I'm not," David said dryly. "For one thing, you look way different from how you looked before. I mean, you were a pretty little kid the last time I saw you. You're a man now, with a man's bones and a man's looks. Does that scar hurt?" He indicated Zach's neck with the bottle he held.

"No. Why?"

"You keep rubbing it."

"Oh. Habit, I guess."

"Oh. Okay. What did they do, try to hang you or something?"

Zach shook his head. "No. It's from a collar."

David sat up and stared at him. "Like a fucking dog collar?"

"Exactly like a fucking dog collar," Zach replied dryly.

"Shit," David said.

"Yep."

"Fuckers."

"Yep."

The silence this time was less strained and more companionable. They finished their beers and David held out his hand for Zach's. Zach dropped the bottle into his hand wordlessly, and he tossed them both into the recycling bin under the stairs. Then he stood at the foot of the steps, looking up at Zach.

"Taff?"

"Yeah?"

"I need to know… you said you just wanted to know why I hated you. Why do you think I hate you?"

"Well, maybe because I heard you screaming when your parents told you that I wanted to see you? I flew all the way to North Carolina from New Zealand when I heard you'd come back. I was waiting outside in the hallway. You scared the shit out of your folks." David picked at the paint on the banister rail. "Shit, you scared me."

"I'm sorry I hurt you," Zach said quietly.

"Oh, I wouldn't call it hurt," David said. "You can recover from hurt. But I didn't blame you, Zach. I knew that whatever had happened to you had wrecked whatever chance we might have had. That's okay. I get that. But what really wrecked me was that we couldn't even be friends again."

"I'd like to be friends again."

David looked up and met his eyes. "Are you serious?"

"Yeah. What happened at the hospital… there were reasons for that. Reasons I'm still kind of dealing with. But it was never you. I never hated you, never blamed you, never was afraid of you. It wasn't you. Dick and Jane don't quite get that—they still think I've got something against you but I never did. Even in the jungle… even then, it was never hate." He swallowed hard. "I don't know if I could ever be the person you wanted. Shit, I don't even know if I can really be your friend, or anybody's friend. I told you I'm fucked up, Taff. You can't even begin to suspect how much."

"You homicidal? A serial killer? Torture animals? Stalk kindergartners?"

"What? No, of course not!"

David shrugged. "Then you'll do."

"You're serious? You want to be friends?"

David grinned, all the weariness in his face vanishing. "Shit, yeah."

Zach smiled for the first time in forever. "Dad and I are going hiking up at the Peak next Saturday. You want to come with us?"

"Sure, but that's Saturday. It's only Tuesday. What about going running with me tomorrow? I haven't been on the trail yet since I've been back."

"I don't have much wind yet," Zach admitted. "I don't know how far I'd get."

"Then we'll take it slow and alternate running and walking. I've trained a few people in my time." David grinned again. "I'll meet you here at seven."

"Seven a.m. or p.m.?"

"Hardy-har-har. Seven a.m., dweeb. Just be grateful it's not six." He dusted his hands off and dug into his pocket for his car keys. "We'll take it slow, Zach. I just don't want to be afraid to run into you anymore. I don't want to feel so guilty just because I'm staying with my mom for a while. I just... I know things can't be what they were, but I don't want to keep them the way they are."

"No," Zach said. He stood up on the stairs and gazed down at David. "See you in the morning, then."

"Yep," David said.

Suddenly exhausted, Zach nodded and went inside, closing the door and managing to turn off the lights and get to the bed before collapsing. *Gotta get out of these boots,* he thought vaguely to himself, then fell heavily into dreamless sleep.

DAVID watched the lights go out, then dragged himself to the car, crawling into the driver's seat and resting his forehead against the steering wheel. Zach had looked drained, and he felt like that too. But beneath the exhaustion was a warm feeling of triumph and contentment, as if he'd gotten everything he'd wanted for Christmas. Zach didn't hate him. Zach wanted to be friends again. He would see Zach again tomorrow.

With a smile, he started the engine and turned the Saturn toward home.

Chapter Six

HIS parents were both in the sunroom with Dr. Barrett when Zach got there the next morning. He'd gone running with David, though it was more like walking with periodic bursts of speed than really running, and when they'd gotten back, he'd had to run up to his apartment for a quick shower before his therapy session. David had merely waved goodbye with a grin as Zach shot up the stairs, and took off at a quick jog toward his own home.

They hadn't talked much; but then, they hadn't needed to. A brief exchange of hellos, David's skeptical glance at Zach's tan fatigue pants with a grunted "Gonna get hot," and Zach's dismissive shrug; then they'd done some preparatory stretches and headed down toward the trail that circled the compound. The whole route was five miles, and Zach was wiped, winded and dripping by the time they got back to their starting point. David wasn't the least bit tired. Zach grimaced at the memory. His father had been right, yesterday; working out was all well and good and helping build back the muscles that had deteriorated during his five-year imprisonment, but he definitely needed aerobic exercise to build his stamina. If he kept this up, maybe in a few months he'd be able to keep up with David and still carry on a conversation instead of staying focused on dragging in each painful breath.

A shower helped, though, and a cup of coffee and a few minutes to breathe. Still, he was a little later than he normally arrived for therapy—not late, per se, but he was usually the first one in the room.

Dick and Jane were already sitting on the wicker loveseat. The shrink had apparently just gotten there and was about to sit down in his usual chair when Zach came in and closed the door behind him. "Sorry I'm late," he said apologetically.

"You're not," Dr. Barrett said, with a raised eyebrow. "How are you, Zach?"

"Good," Zach said. He went to his chair and dropped into it. He was already starting to ache a little from his exercise; he reached down and massaged a calf muscle. "A little sore—I went running this morning."

"You did?" Jane asked curiously. "All by yourself? Did you remember to take the cougar stick?" She referred to the heavy walking stick they took on the trails when hiking.

"No, I forgot, but we didn't leave the compound, just followed the running trail. Well, I didn't do much running. Just every once in a while. Besides, I wasn't by myself." Zach took a deep breath. "I was with Taff. I ran into him last night, and we talked, and, well, decided to go running this morning."

There was dead silence, then Jane said, "But I thought...."

"Yeah. Mom. I *said* I didn't hate Taff. I don't. And I'm not scared of him or anything stupid like that. I know I let you think that for a long time. It was just... easier."

"Easier?" his father echoed in confusion. "Easier than what?"

"Than... than explaining why I reacted the way I did." Zach shot a desperate look at Dr. Barrett. "Do I have to talk about this?"

"Of course not," Dr. Barrett said. "You and your parents direct these sessions, Zach—I'm only here to facilitate."

"I'd like to know, honey," Jane said quietly. "It's really bothered us, thinking that something had happened between you and David that might have caused you...."

"No! Jesus, no," Zach shook his head. "I didn't even *talk* to Taff before I left for Aunt Alicia's. No, David didn't do anything. It was all me. I mean...." He sighed and dropped his head into his hands. "Shit. You know how fucked up I was when I got back to the States. I didn't even fucking *talk*, for God's sake. I was afraid of *you* guys. I was afraid of everything." He took a deep, shuddering breath and raised his head. "Esteban used you guys to get to me. He told me shit, like that you'd sent me off on purpose, that you didn't want me to come home, that you never paid the ransom, that kind of stuff. You know all that. But he didn't know about David. Taff was safe as long as I never said anything, never even *thought* about him, never let him into my head. He couldn't talk trash about Taff if he didn't know Taff existed. So I had to keep it that way.

"You know from yesterday that I had—and still have—issues with reality. With belief." Zach met Richard's eyes. "I *know* things, but inside, I don't always *trust* them. When I first came back, I didn't believe anything was real. That was part of what made me afraid. I'd had nightmares about you in the jungle from Esteban's stories, nightmares that you would turn into monsters and eat me—"

"Jesus," Richard muttered.

"—and I was terrified when you first came to see me. I don't remember exactly, but Fluffy told me that I had my first panic attack then. All I remember is being scared that you would eat me after you got done ripping Fluffy to shreds.... And then you came in and you were just you guys and it was okay. I *knew* Esteban was lying all along, but I didn't *believe* he was. It's just how good he was at fucking me up.

"When Taff came to see me...." Zach paused, feeling the first bits of nausea that presaged another panic attack. He flexed his hands and plowed on. "When you came in and said he was there, all I could think about was that Esteban had found out about Taff, that he wasn't hidden anymore, that he wasn't *safe*, and I'd been trying for *five years* to keep Taff safe in my head." His breaths were coming quicker now, and he fought it, breathing slowly in through his nose, holding it, releasing it slowly from his mouth. It took a minute, but his heart slowed.

His parents were watching him, their hands clasped tightly together.

"That was why I started screaming. I was so afraid of what Esteban had done to Taff. I *knew* Esteban was dead, but I didn't *believe* it. And now he had Taff...."

He was shaking when he was finished, but at least he'd staved off the panic attack. It was a relief, to have that all done with, to have the truth about his craziness out.

"Oh, love," Jane said gently. He met her eyes and tried to smile.

"I know. It's really fucked up, isn't it? Thinking a dead guy could do anything to someone thousands of miles away he didn't even *know….* It's not even rational."

"Zach, if everyone was rational all the time, we'd be Vulcans, not humans," Dr. Barrett said easily. "It's very common for perception and belief to be 180 degrees from reality. You were in a highly unhealthy situation for a very long time. It's only been a relatively short while since you've been back, comparatively speaking, and you've made tremendous strides. But you have to accept that you're a human being. You won't *be* rational all the time—we're just not built that way. Humans are emotional, empathetic, superstitious, suggestible and infinitely flexible, and people like Esteban know how to manipulate others to do and *think* the way they want them to. He was a professional, Zach. He manipulated his followers, he manipulated local government officials, and he manipulated you." He smiled faintly. "It's a normal human desire to think of oneself as being smarter than the average, but in the end, we are none of us any *wiser* than the other."

"I killed him," Zach said abruptly.

"Yes."

"When we were in Minnesota last year, at that clinic for torture victims, they talked about Stockholm Syndrome?"

"Yes?"

"I didn't get it. I never empathized with him, I never identified with him. I hated his fucking guts and I fought him. I fought him until he broke me, but I never stopped hating him." His eyes met Dr. Barrett's, for probably the first time since he'd started working with the man. "Stockholm Syndrome, my ass. I fought the bastard, I hated the bastard, and I killed the bastard. And you know what? I'd do it again."

"And how do you feel about that?"

"It kind of bugged the therapists at the clinic," Zach admitted.

"I'm not asking about the therapists. I'm asking about you."

Zach didn't answer right away. He wasn't sure what the answer would be.

Jane said fiercely, "You did the right thing, honey. You absolutely did the right thing. It was, it was *war*."

He laughed. "You're such a mom, Mom. What happened to the pacifist?"

"She is a mom, Zach," Richard said. "Pacifism is fine until it's your offspring on the firing line. You should have seen her ripping into the Costa Rican officials we had to deal with in San Juan. Almost got your aunt kicked off her project."

"Well, Zach?" Dr. Barrett asked.

"Well. I feel—well, I feel like I should be sorry, but I'm not."

"Why do you feel that you should be sorry?"

"Because normal people don't kill people."

"Soldiers kill people. Cops kill people."

"Yeah, but in extraordinary circumstances...." Zach trailed off. "Jesus, I couldn't have gotten into a more extraordinary circumstance, could I?"

"I would say it was pretty much unique," Richard agreed.

"So you think I shouldn't feel bad because I *don't* feel bad?" Zach frowned.

"Let me put it to you this way." Dr. Barrett sat back and steepled his fingers. "Do you foresee any circumstances, any situation that you would be in, where you would feel the need to kill anyone, outside the extreme situation that you found yourself in? If you had had the chance to escape without killing Esteban, would you have taken it?"

"Hell, yes," Zach said.

"Why did you kill him?"

"I should think that was obvious!" Jane said indignantly. Richard hushed her.

Taking a deep breath, Zach said, "Because it was my only chance to end it. I knew...." He glanced at his parents. They hadn't heard this part and he was frightened of how they would take it. "Because I knew that either way it would end. If I didn't succeed in killing him, he'd kill me in self-defense. And it would be over. And I thought"—he swallowed—"I thought the shooting outside was one of the other paramilitary groups in the area, and that they'd kill me, but I would have rather been killed by them than gone on being Esteban's dog. So I figured I'd be dead either way and that would be okay."

His mother was crying softly.

"I'm sorry, Mom," Zach said. "I didn't want you to know about that. It was stupid. But it turned out okay, didn't it? I would have much rather it turned out the way it did, really. Even if I am a bit nuts now." He flashed Dr. Barrett a quick smile; the good doctor blinked in surprise. "So it's okay, what I did?"

"That's for you to decide," the doctor said.

"Then I decide it was okay," Zach said. He collapsed back in the chair, astonished at how relieved he felt. "It was okay. It was like a soldier, killing an enemy before he kills him. Or a cop, killing a… a murderer. Justifiable homicide." He grinned widely. "Shit, it was justifiable homicide, not murder. He was the criminal, not me."

"Not revenge?"

Zach blanched. "What?"

"You didn't kill him for revenge? Because of what he did to you?"

"No. I hated him for that, but I killed him to make it stop."

Dr. Barrett smiled. "Excellent session today, Zach, Jane, Richard. Zach—I'll see you this afternoon."

"Sure," Zach said.

He hung around waiting until Dr. Barrett had gone, then he said to Richard, "Dad, do you gotta go right back to work?"

"No, of course not," Richard said in confusion. "The place runs fine without me; they just keep my cubicle so I have someplace to go when your mother throws me out."

"Good. I'm almost finished with the Charger's engine block and I need some help getting it back in." Zach gave him a shy smile. "I thought maybe you could help?"

"Glory hallelujah," Richard said. "He asks for something!"

"Yeah. Well." Zach felt his face flush. "I did a lot of thinking this morning, about some of the stuff Taff and I talked about last night. He said something about we can't have things the way they were, but he didn't want to keep things the way they are. I feel the same way. You said yesterday that you and Mom hated the way things were just like I did, and when I was running this morning I thought that maybe we could change them. Make things not the way they were, but not the way they are now, either. Does that make any sense?"

Jane said, "It makes perfect sense, Zach. We're none of us who we were seven years ago, and it's foolish to try and be those people again. I know we've been trying to relate to you as if you had never gone away, but we can't, can we?"

He shook his head slowly.

Jane put out her hand. "Well, Zach Tyler, I'm Jane Tyler. Pleased to meet you. We've got the same last name—think we might be related?"

Zach laughed, rocked back on his heels and laughed. Then he shook her hand and said mock-seriously, "Why, that might be the case, Mrs. Tyler. We'll have to check into that."

"You two," Richard said dryly, "are lunatics. And I need my elevenses. Let's go get some bagels and then I'll help you with the Charger."

Chapter Seven

ZACH'S phone buzzed against his hip. He set down his drink and dug in his jeans pocket, but when he looked at the number, it wasn't familiar. Frowning, he opened the phone. "Hello?"

"Did you know that mallard ducks have a corkscrew-shaped penis?"

"I didn't even know ducks had penises," Zach said. "How'd you get my number, Taff?"

"My mother. I just called to remind you that you have a run at seven a.m., and it is now ten-thirty-six p.m., so put down the Scotch, and step away from the surfer dude."

"More like 'Put down the Coke and step away from the Big Mac,'" Zach said wryly.

"You're at Mickey D's? What the hell are you doing there at this hour?"

"Um—eating? I was hungry."

"My mother is the best cook in the world and you're eating at McDonald's?"

"Well," Zach said reasonably, "I went five years without a Big Mac or McDonald's French fries."

"Oh, my God," David said in horror. "I didn't realize it was *that* bad! Isn't that like against the Geneva Convention or something?"

Zach dunked the last of his fries in barbeque sauce and stuffed them in his mouth. Around the fries, he mumbled, "Well, I've got a lot of Big Macs to make up for, that's for sure. I'm done now anyway, and on my way home, Mother."

"Better be. You're going to have to put on a better performance tomorrow."

"Jesus, Taff, my thighs are aching already," Zach complained. "I'm gonna be stiff tomorrow."

There was a moment of silence, then David said, "Uh, yeah. Sorry, I got distracted."

"I'm not even going to ask," Zach said.

"Yeah, you better not. Well, um, I guess I'll see you tomorrow morning."

"Yep."

"Uh, Zach?"

"Yeah?"

"Um—be careful driving, okay?"

Zach grinned. "Yes, Mother."

"Well, it's raining and I know how dangerous motorcycles are in the rain."

"I'm driving the Jeep tonight. It was already raining when I left. You're a fussy old woman, you know."

"Well, I don't want you to get hurt."

"Aww. I feel so loved."

"You should." There was a click as David hung up. Zach stared at the phone blankly. Had David just said what he thought he'd said? Nah.... Must have said something else. *"You shit,"* probably.

It *was* raining pretty hard, so Zach ran to the Jeep and ducked in, shaking the water from his head. When he'd left the apartment an hour ago, he'd planned on a quick bite at McD's before heading over to Fat Charlie's or the Dirty Dick, but suddenly he was tired. Tired and bored with the idea of another evening of drinking, listening to loud obnoxious music, and anonymous pickups. Besides, David was right; he did have an appointment at seven a.m., and he wasn't used to getting up early anymore. He rested his forehead on the steering wheel a moment before putting the key in the ignition and starting the Jeep.

For some reason, he went through the east gate of the compound instead of the closer south gate. The remote gate control worked the same as at the south gate, but the response time was slower, so he sat and drummed his fingers on the wheel a minute before Andy got the gate wide enough for him to get the Jeep through. The last couple of years had made him hyperaware of his emotional state from moment to moment, and right now he was feeling anxious. He didn't know why; it was pouring rain, but it was coming straight down and visibility wasn't bad enough to make him worry, and deciding not to hit the clubs tonight took away his usual evening anxiety about hookups. Must just be the idea of getting up that early, or maybe worry about getting to sleep at such an early hour....

The gatehouse loomed up on his right, lights still on upstairs, though the downstairs was dark. Zach let the Jeep roll to a stop across the road and sat there, staring at the steering wheel. His heart was thumping hard, but steadily; nervous, but not panicked. What the hell was he doing? "Shit," he said, threw the car into park, and got out into the rain, standing looking over the roof of the car at David's lighted bedroom window.

David was sitting at the drafting table by the window, a pencil in his hand and an intent look on his face. The rain was pounding hard enough that he apparently hadn't heard the Jeep's engine or the closing of the driver's side door; his hand moved over the drawing before him without him raising his head. He was shirtless. Zach watched him, oblivious to the rain soaking him.

Finally, David got up and stretched, his back to the window, the thin cotton pajama pants he wore dropping low on his hips. Zach almost swallowed his tongue at the sight of the long, lean back, the upraised muscled arms, the light from the drafting table turning the skin gold and casting shadows on the curve of David's ass beneath the cotton. Zach swore softly and pressed against the doorframe of the car, feeling the pulse in his erect cock. God, David was beautiful, even more beautiful than Zach remembered.

Months ago, when he'd first come home, he'd started hanging around the gay clubs in Wesley and in Colorado Springs, trying to get up the nerve to actually have consensual sex with someone. He'd been approached, but turned down everyone. No one interested him enough to take the risk.

Then one evening, he was watching the dance floor at one of the clubs when he'd thought he'd seen David. His mouth had gone dry for a moment watching the man dance, his slim ass grinding against the man behind him, until Zach realized it wasn't David, just someone with the same general build as he remembered David having, and the same tawny, sun-streaked hair. Of course, the body had come from a gym, and the hair from an expensive salon, but when the guy—was his name Keith? Kevin? Something like that—had seen Zach watching him, he'd come over and invited Zach into one of the little private rooms. By then Zach had drunk enough Scotch to numb his panic and had gone with him, but he wasn't so drunk as to not know what he was doing, what he wanted....

What he wanted now was to be in that warm, lit room with David, his hands stroking down that long, smooth back, cupping the round ass, his mouth on the silky skin of David's neck. His hands tightened on the cold, wet doorframe.

David stretched again, then walked across the room to the door opposite. He rested one hand on the frame, reaching over with his right to lock the door. Zach frowned. Why would David lock the door in his own house? His puzzlement deepened as David stood there motionless.

No. Not motionless. His right hand was out of sight, blocked by his body, but his right elbow was moving, a tense, rhythmical motion. *Fuck.* David was jerking off. Zach's legs almost gave out on him. He pressed harder against the car door, sweat breaking out on his face and neck despite the damp chill, and watched in stunned disbelief as David's left hand curled tightly around the wooden frame of his bedroom door.

Then David turned around, leaning against the door for support, his head back and his right hand buried beneath the elastic waistband of his pajama bottoms. Zach whimpered, and in his mind, he was in the room with David, his mouth on that golden column of throat, licking, biting the tendon that stood out where David's neck met his shoulder, his hand wrapped around David's cock as he licked and bit and sucked the rose-brown nipples on that perfect chest. He watched the flutter of the loose cloth as David worked himself, every movement echoed by the pulse in his own cock as he rocked against the side of the Jeep, imagining David's hand on him, his mouth on his skin, the silk of that sun-streaked hair against Zach's throat.

David's face tightened; his rhythm stuttered, and his head went back with a thump as he came, his hand moving in long, hard strokes. Zach fumbled for his own zipper, battling it down against the heavy wet cloth of his jeans, and pulled his cock out between the teeth, wrapping one hand around the shaft and pumping it. He came hard, spurting onto the Jeep's tire and the gravel of the road; he turned and leaned back against the car, breathing roughly, and let the rain wash away the evidence before tucking himself back into his jeans.

Upstairs, David had vanished, but a light had come on in the bathroom adjoining David's bedroom. Zach stood in the rain until David had come out of the bathroom in fresh pajama bottoms and turned out the bedroom light. He felt like a voyeur, and wondered how he'd face David in the morning. *Fuck,* he thought again, and, dripping wet, got back into the car, putting it into gear.

Chapter Eight

"SOMETHING wrong?" David asked as Zach caught up with him, panting. "You're awful quiet today."

Zach shook his head.

"Well, if you're tired, blame the damn pants," David said, referring to the tan fatigues Zach wore again today. "I don't know why you just don't wear shorts. If you don't have any, I have some you can borrow."

"I don't wear shorts," Zach panted.

David didn't say anything, just ran in silence a while, then, "Psychological or physical?"

"Huh?"

"You don't wear shorts because of a psychological reason or a physical reason? Cuz I can tell you now I don't give a shit if you have scars or anything."

Zach eyed David's tanned, perfect legs. "Yeah. Whatever. I just don't like shorts."

"Then get some of those spandex bike leggings," David instructed. "Or sweats. Or those dorky track suits. I know it's not because your legs are fat or gross; I've seen you in tight jeans. So I figure you got some scars or something you're embarrassed about. Which is fucking stupid, but hey, they're your scars. But those pants increase wind resistance as well as friction and make it harder for you to run, so lose them, 'kay?"

"Up yours," Zach panted.

David stopped in the middle of the path and waited for Zach to catch up. "Seriously, Zach, if you really want to get in some real running, you can't do it in fatigues."

"They do in the army," Zach wheezed, bent over with his hands on his knees. "They have to run miles in full gear with full, eighty-pound packs, carrying ordnance."

"This ain't fucking basic training," David said irritably. "And you're having a hard enough time without making it more difficult. You need to build up your stamina, not give yourself a fucking heart attack. Okay. We walk for a while. We're almost back to the house, so we'll use this as a cool-down; then a few stretches when we get back there to work out knots so you're not as stiff as you were when we started. I don't want you pulling a muscle or getting leg cramps because you aren't getting proper warm-ups and cool-downs."

"Yes, Mother," Zach said. Which was a mistake, because it reminded him of their conversation last night, which led into his *other* memory of last night.

"Whoa," David said. "What just went on in your miniscule little mind?"

"What are you talking about?" Zach said defensively.

"The weirdest look just crossed your face and it shut down again. What's going on in your head, Zach?"

"I just remembered something unpleasant. I don't want to talk about it."

"Your call. Gonna talk about it with the shrink?"

"*Hell*, no," Zach said.

"Cuz getting a weird look on your face after saying the word 'mother' is kind of creepy, you know."

"Fuck off," Zach snapped. "It's got nothing to do with Jane. You know fucking well that Jane is a fucking saint."

"Hey, I didn't mean to cast any aspersions against her." David raised his hands in surrender. "I was ragging on you, not her."

"Thanks." Zach kept walking, not looking at David.

"Hey," David said after a minute, "seriously. Is everything okay?"

"Yeah, I'm fine. I just had a bad night."

"Wanna talk about it?"

Zach rolled his eyes. "What am I, a girl? No, I don't wanna talk about it."

David started to say something, but his cell phone buzzed. "Hold that thought," he said to Zach, and unclipped his cell from the waistband of his running shorts. He stopped walking, frowned at the display, then said questioningly, "Jerry?"

Zach stopped too, and watched David's face as his expression softened. "No, no, it's fine. What's up? ...No, I haven't found a place yet. I'm still staying with my mom.... No, it's not an issue. It's cool.... Most of it's still in storage. I'm thinking of just having it shipped to Mom's since I'm having trouble finding an apartment... Yeah. No, no, you were right, you really were.... Yeah, take it from me, it's hell being wrong sometimes too." David smiled, his expression gentle and sad. "Yeah. Yeah. I miss you, too, baby. Take care.... Thanks." He closed the phone and clipped it back onto his waistband.

"Boyfriend?" Zach asked, a hard knot in his throat.

"Ex," David said distantly.

"Sorry, but 'I miss you, too, baby' doesn't sound very ex to me."

"It's ex. Trust me, there is nobody in the world more ex than me right now."

"He dumped you?"

"Sort of. Doesn't matter—he's two thousand miles away."

"Were you in love with him?"

David shrugged. "I thought I was. We lived together for about a year. Just broke up before I came back here, so it's still kind of raw. I don't want to talk about it."

"Why not?"

"Look," David said, "For every one factoid you tell me about when you were in Venezuela, I'll give you one factoid about my personal life. Deal?"

Zach started walking. "It's not the same thing." He felt sick. He hadn't known that David had had a boyfriend—a serious boyfriend, from all indications—and now, thinking about last night made his gut roil. He'd fantasized something between him and David, and all along David had been dreaming about this guy Jerry. Zach hated the unknown Jerry with a sudden, vitriolic passion. This faceless stranger had loved David, done everything with David that Zach wanted: held that sleek, golden body, kissed him, made love with him. He was probably beautiful, too, with soft, unscarred skin and no emotional baggage. The opposite of Zach; Zach was Samsonite, Incorporated, after a bad day with the luggage handlers. He kneaded his gut with a fist and kept walking, not looking at David when he caught up with him.

"Hey," David said softly. "You okay?"

"I don't feel good," Zach prevaricated. "What do you want to know?"

"What?"

"What do you want to know about Venezuela?"

"Oh. Uh… I dunno. Anything. I don't know much."

"What do you know?"

They'd come up to the rear of the grounds, near the empty stables. Zach had always thought it was a pity that they had a ranch in Colorado but no horses; his mother was violently allergic to any kind of animal dander. They'd never even been able to have a dog, not even the hypoallergenic type. Not that Zach would ever have a dog now, anyway. He shuddered, but kept walking across the gravel stable yard to the stone wall edging the vegetable garden. He climbed over the low wall and sat on it, facing the garden.

David joined him. "I dunno. It was some paramilitary group working with drug traffickers. They killed the driver that was supposed to meet you at the airport. Your dad paid ten million dollars in ransom, but they never responded. You had your ribs broken at some point. You wore a dog collar that left a scar." He shrugged. "That's about it. That and they starved you and apparently did something that gave you scars on your legs you're embarrassed about."

"It was a wire cage," Zach said dully. "The floor of a wire cage."

David didn't say anything for a moment, then said in disbelief, "Like a fucking dog crate?"

Echoing his words of the other night, Zach said, "Exactly like a fucking dog crate."

"They kept you in a *dog crate?*"

"That's where you keep dogs," Zach said. He got up from the wall and dusted his butt off. "I gotta go. I have therapy this morning."

David reached out and caught his arm. "No, wait a minute."

Zach waited, his eyes on the ground.

"I thought I was in love with him," David said abruptly. "I really thought he was the one, but he wasn't. I loved him—he was a great guy. Still is. Smart, funny, loving, hot…. He called it quits because I'm 'emotionally unavailable', whatever the hell that means. I went from being 'a good listener' to 'emotionally unavailable'." At Zach's puzzled look, he smiled faintly. "A factoid for a factoid. That was the deal, wasn't it? Mine aren't much. Yours? Jesus, Zach. I need to know more."

"No, you don't," Zach said curtly. "You really don't."

They stood there in silence a moment, David's hand still curled around Zach's forearm. The fingers had turned gentle, not stopping him now, but holding him, connecting him with David like an extension cord to the heart. Zach closed his eyes a moment, feeling the connection, the warmth of David's skin, the strength of his bones.

"I'm sorry," David said unhappily. "I didn't mean to remind you."

"You didn't," Zach responded. He let his fingers brush David's before pulling David's hand away. "It's not like it's ever very far away. I really need to be getting over it, you know." He squeezed David's hand, then let him go.

"Zach, wait."

"I have therapy," Zach said over his shoulder as he walked toward the house.

"I just was wondering if you were busy this afternoon. I thought maybe…."

"I'm busy. I have a really full plate, Taff. I'm all kinds of busy." Zach broke into a trot, but was pulled up short by David's fist in his T-shirt.

"Will you stand still for one fucking minute?" David snapped. "I'm trying to talk to you, you microcephalic dweeb."

"And I don't feel like talking to you, *Taffy*," Zach snapped.

"Son of a fucking bitch, Zach, what did I tell you about calling me Taffy?"

"I'm not afraid of you anymore, Taffy," Zach sniped back. "I'm bigger than you are now… *uphm!*" He was suddenly on his stomach in the dirt, an arm and a leg twisted behind him and David pinning him to the ground.

"The bigger they are and all that," David said in his ear. "I had wrestling in high school, dweeb. You didn't. And I've had some martial arts classes since, so don't even think you can get out of this. To remind you, I told you if you ever called me 'Taffy' again I was going to club you like a baby seal, and that still stands. Got it?"

"Get the fuck off me."

"Not till you surrender. You remember the words, don't you? Say 'em."

"Fuck you."

"Wrong!" David was laughing now. "Say the magic words, dweeb!"

"Get *off* me, David! I swear, I'll kick your ass…."

"Doing a good job of it now," David snorted. "I'm trembling in fear."

Zach struggled, but not hard. David's weight felt good along his back, his breath warm and soft on his neck. "Say the words," David whispered, and his voice sent the hair on Zach's neck quivering. Zach blurted out, "David Philip Evans is God."

"And?"

"And I worship the ground he walks on!"

The weight and warmth was suddenly gone, and Zach clambered to his feet. "Prick," he muttered, dusting off his shirt and fatigues.

David hooted in laughter, and despite himself, Zach grinned. It was so much like the way they were long ago, before he'd gotten so lost. "I'm so gonna kick your ass," he said again, chuckling.

"Not if you can't catch me, and you'll never catch me in those damn fatigues. Come on. I know for a fact your therapy doesn't start until ten, and it's only eight-thirty. I'm hungry, and I'll bet we can talk Mom into making omelets."

"You go ahead," Zach said. "I need a shower."

"We could go for a swim," David suggested.

Zach shook his head. "No thanks."

David let that slide. "So, lemme ask again. You busy this afternoon?"

"Yeah. Today's the day I have physical therapy, then the shrink again at four."

Frowning, David asked, "What's the physical therapy for? You look in pretty good shape to me." He wriggled his eyebrows in an attempt to look like a dirty old man. The expression was so ludicrous on his golden surfer-boy face that Zach laughed.

"Right at this point, it's for my wrist."

"Ah. Carpal tunnel from jerking off," David said wisely.

Zach threw a swing, which David ducked easily. "No, it was broken and didn't heal right. Esteban—" He stopped, then went on. "It healed a bit crooked and I had to have surgery to fix it. Same with the ribs. But it's only twice a week now, and it should be done with in a month or two. I had a lot of physical therapy when I got back. That was brutal." He plucked at the fabric of the fatigues. "Running in these is nothing in comparison."

"Blah, blah." David waved his hand. "As your running instructor, I insist on something other than baggy old fatigues. How can I ogle your ass when I can't see it?"

"You aren't supposed to be ogling my ass."

"You ogle mine."

Zach stiffened. "I so do not." He so did, but how did David know?

"Not stupid. I know the real reason you run slower than I do."

"You are *such* a dick," Zach said.

"Yep. Come on. There's an omelet with my name on it."

"You go ahead. I'm going to go home and shower."

David folded his arms. "I thought we'd gone through all that."

"Well, maybe I'm just not ready."

"For an omelet?"

"No. To show up in Annie's kitchen with you, okay? I'm still tryin' to figure out why you even came over the other night after I saw you in the bar. I'm not ready to try and explain to Annie why I'm suddenly friends with you when I haven't so much as mentioned your name in all the time I've been back here."

"You did."

"What?"

"You mentioned my name. You asked Mom if she ever heard from me."

"Once. Okay, once in nearly a year." Zach blew out his breath in frustration. "Not the point. The point is I don't want to talk about it, okay?"

David gazed at him, a shuttered expression in his eyes. Finally, he said, "Sure. Right. See you tomorrow?"

"Yeah. If you want."

David shrugged. "I run every day. No big deal to swing by here. If you're ready, you can come with me."

"Thanks."

Again the jerk of the shoulders. "See ya, then," David said, and then jogged off toward the house.

Zach followed more slowly, turning off toward the garage and his apartment upstairs. By the time he'd climbed up, David had disappeared through the kitchen door. Annie would probably be delighted to feed him. To be honest, she would probably be delighted to feed Zach as well, but he wasn't ready to make any changes in his relationship with her yet. He'd always adored Annie, but his problems with David had put a barrier up between them that Zach wasn't ready to breach. Somehow he thought she would be less forgiving of his treatment of David than David was.

It didn't matter, anyway. Better to let David be. He'd keep running with him in the morning and try to avoid personal conversation, and just stay out of his way the rest of the time. It shouldn't be hard. Aside from their enjoyment of sports and physical activity, they really didn't have much in common.

Zach pushed open the door to his apartment and went out onto the small veranda over the garage. It looked out over the house and gardens toward the mountains. A small tarp protected the weights rack from the elements; Zach sat down on the bench and picked up his five-pound hand weights, thinking. David's demonstration had made it clear to him that it wasn't enough to lift weights; he already knew he needed aerobic exercise, but it looked like he also needed some self-defense training if he wanted to feel safe. David was right; he hadn't gotten to wrestling in gym since that wasn't introduced until junior year, and he had no idea how to get out of holds or how to pin an attacker. Add that to his To Do List, along with reviving his long-dormant shooting skills; he hadn't held a pistol since taking lessons with Dad when he was a teenager. Sometimes he thought it wouldn't matter how much he worked on himself. He'd never really feel safe again.

But he felt safe when he was running. Safe with David.

It was funny—he was taller than David by a good two inches, and probably outweighed him by twenty pounds, but David had been able to drop him without even breaking a sweat. He knew it had more to do with skill and balance than brute strength, but it reinforced the feeling that when he was with David, he was okay. That David wouldn't let anything hurt him. Stupid to feel that way—David wasn't any more competent than his parents were, and the idea of a skinny little surfer boy being able to defend a big tough biker dude, or someone who was working on becoming a big tough biker dude, anyway, was kind of ludicrous. It was probably just a holdover from his childhood, always looking up to David. He'd probably imprinted on him like a baby bird when he was born or something.

Zach shook his head and put the weights back on the rack, covered it with the tarp, and went back through the glass doors into the kitchen, where he had a drink of milk before heading for the shower.

Chapter Nine

"MOST of your classes will be here in the computer lab," the teacher liaison said, opening the door to the state-of-the-art lab. "Having Tyler Tech in our district isn't just a benefit at tax time—Richard Tyler contributes a lot to all the schools in this district, public and private, not just to the one his son went to. Wesley's very lucky to have him as a resident. I understand you worked for him for a while?"

"Part time in high school, then for a year or so between high school and college," David confirmed. "It was a good experience— very challenging, but they have a great environment to work in."

"I'm surprised you didn't go back there," Bill Hernandez, the administrator, said. "He had nothing but great things to say about you when we called him for a reference."

David shrugged. "I like teaching. But I like working with people with a little more interest than the average high school student. Teaching high school is like herding cats."

The administrator laughed. "No question. I understand you're also teaching a couple of real art classes?"

"Computer art *is* real art," David said, "but yeah, I'm teaching basic drawing techniques and an introduction to watercolors class. I wanted full time—I know most of the teachers here only teach one or two classes, but I like to keep busy." He glanced around the computer lab, then settled at the teaching console to pull up the programs he'd be working with. The majority, of course, were from Tyler Technologies, but they had a nice sprinkling of some competing programs. "This is good," he said. "There's what, three weeks before the summer session starts? I've got some preliminary lesson plans and syllabuses— syllabi?—laid out, but I'd like to come in and work a bit on my own to familiarize myself with your network, if that's okay."

"Sure, no problem. The school's got classes going all the time, but I'll get you a schedule for the lab so you can come in at a time when no one's using it. Same for the art department. By the way, they're having their quarterly cocktail party—I don't know why they call it a cocktail party when all they ever drink is beer and wine—on Friday night, and they said to make sure you know you're invited. Did you meet Jack Larssen?"

"The head of the department? Not in person, but I talked to him yesterday. He's supposed to be here today, so I said I'd look him up when we were done here."

"He's a good guy, but he'll probably try and hook you up with his daughter Janet. You're not married, are you?"

"No," David laughed. "I'm way too young."

"You are at that. I think Janet's thirty, anyway. Not that that would matter, if you were attracted to her. She is a pretty girl, and I think Jack embarrasses her with his husband-hunting."

"Thanks for the warning," David said. "How many people are in the art department, anyway?"

"Six, including some that also teach other classes," Bill said. "Wesley's a pretty big school, for all it's a community college, but then part of our district overlaps Colorado Springs so we get a lot of students from there. And there's a real active seniors population going back for classes; we probably have an equal split between the techies and the artsies. You, of course, fall right in between them." He followed David out of the computer lab and locked the door behind him. "Hey, can I ask you a question?"

"Sure."

"I understand that you actually live in the Tyler compound."

"Yeah, my mother's their housekeeper," David admitted warily. "Why?"

"I'm just curious. About their kid? Zachary? The one that was held hostage by that drug cartel all those years?"

"It was a paramilitary organization, not a drug cartel," David corrected, "and what about him?"

"I just wondered if you'd ever met him. They say he's kind of a recluse. He's kind of a mystery around here; no one even knows what he looks like. They say he was horribly disfigured…."

"That kind of gossip is for shit," David growled. "He's perfectly normal. He's just not very social, that's all."

"My kid went to school with him," Bill said. "He said Zach used to be really outgoing."

David frowned, thinking. "Frankie Hernandez? That your kid?"

"Yeah."

"I remember Frankie. He played soccer with Zach. I used to give him rides home. What's he doing now?"

"He's in law school at John Marshall. He was really excited when Zach came home a couple of years ago, but he sent him a letter and Zach never answered."

"Not my business," David said, "but I'm sure when Zach's ready to contact people, Frankie will be at the top of the list. I don't see him much myself."

"It had to be really hard, coming back. I've heard that people held hostage have all kinds of psychological issues. Not that it's any of my business," Bill said hastily. "I mean, I know it's not. I just feel bad for Zach. You see him, you tell him Frankie and I were asking how he was doing."

"I'll do that," David said.

ZACH ran his hands down the long, golden-skinned back, feeling the muscles moving beneath his palms as the spine arched in pleasure. His lubed thumbs traced the deep dimples in the apple-cheeked ass before sliding down the crease and pressing gently on the rosy opening. The muscle relaxed and he pushed his thumbs in, rubbing; then he slipped a finger in, probing for the magic spot. He felt the bump just as the owner of that perfect ass moaned, "Oh, fuck me, please. God. Fuck me."

"Not yet," Zach murmured, and put another finger in, stroking inside the tight, hot channel. He waited until the moaning was almost continuous before pulling his fingers out and pushing the head of his latex-clad cock inside the entrance, feeling the sphincter open willingly at the pressure. He slid deep, his fingers digging into the slim hips in front of him, pulling the guy's ass closer and higher so that he got exactly the right angle.

The guy whimpered faintly. "Oh, fuck, that's good."

Zach didn't answer, just started to move, his hips driving forward, his left hand holding the guy steady with a tight grip, his right hand snaking around to close around the dripping head of the guy's cock. He rubbed the head hard, then used the guy's own juices to lubricate the shaft as his hand slid down to pump him in rhythm with Zach's own thrusts. He felt the guy tensing and moved his hand up toward the head again, pressing into the slit with the ball of his thumb. The guy groaned and came, his ejaculate soaking Zach's fingers. Zach kept pumping, both hand and cock, until the guy started whimpering again; then he released the guy's now limp dick and moved his hand back to his hip to steady himself as he fucked him harder. Zach came with a gasped, "*Taff*," and leaned forward, resting his forehead a moment on the sweaty back before him. But only a moment. Then he straightened and reached down to hold the condom in place as he withdrew, tying it off and tossing it into the garbage can by the door before pulling his jeans back into place.

"Wow," his partner said, looking over his shoulder from where he still sprawled over the chair arm. "That was fantastic."

Zach looked at him. "Brian, right?"

"Yeah," Brian said. "I didn't think you knew my name."

Zach shrugged. "Does it matter?"

"No. But it wasn't what you said in the moment. Got it bad for that David guy that was at Terry's the other night, huh?"

"What?" Zach was stunned.

"That David guy. The one you had the fight with. Though it wasn't much of a fight, I guess. I figured you knew him. Then you said 'Taff' when you came, so I figured it was him."

Zach gave him a what-the-fuck look. Brian grinned. "My grandfather's named David too. He's Welsh. His brothers all call him 'Taffy'. It's a nickname for David. So I figure 'Taff' is Taffy for

David."

"Not Taffy," Zach said automatically.

Brian shrugged. "Whatev. Anyway, I figured it was him. Gimme the Kleenex, willya?"

Zach tossed him the box of tissues that the room came equipped with, and he sat up, wiping his stomach and groin before pulling his jeans back up and buttoning them. "Can't say I blame you—he's hot."

"It wasn't David," Zach said numbly.

"No?" Brian shrugged again. "Then it's okay if I go for him?"

Zach clenched his fists, but said only, "He's got a boyfriend."

"You, maybe," Brian said. "He's hot for you, you know."

"No, he's not." Zach picked up his jacket. "You don't know jack shit."

"Maybe not, but he got all hot and bothered when I said I'd fucked you." Brian snickered. "I think he was jealous. So, what? You two haven't done the deed yet? What, is he married or something? I doubt it."

"Shut. The. Fuck. Up," Zach said, and left, slamming the door behind him. In the dank hallway, he leaned back against the concrete wall and struggled for breath. He'd known coming here tonight was a bad idea, and it was just pissing bad luck that he should happen to hook up with someone he'd fucked before, let alone someone who'd seen him talking to David. Who'd talked to David. Who'd had the unmitigated brass balls to even mention David's name. He wanted to go back into that room and beat the shit out of the guy.

Instead, he turned and walked stiff-legged out the back door of the club and around the side where he'd left the Ducati. The Brian guy had said David was hot for him, but he hadn't seen David that night, sitting on the arm of Zach's sofa, his face tired and sad, willing for Zach to fuck him just to get him to talk to him. There had been nothing of desire in David's face that night. He'd just wanted them to be friends again. Zach swallowed hard against the pain in his throat. David didn't want him as a lover, just as a friend. He *had* a lover, the absent Jerry, who Zach knew would change his mind and want David back again. He had to. He couldn't imagine loving David and letting him go. It was okay. He and David were friends; Zach could live with that.

But this was the last time he was coming to the Dirty Dick, or Fat Charlie's for that matter. He could drink at Terry's if he wanted to go someplace to drink. As for the sex…. He felt the stirrings of nausea and shook his head roughly. No more sex. It wouldn't kill him to go without, at least not until he met someone who meant something, someone who didn't care about the mess that Zach was, physically and mentally. He didn't want any more anonymous hook-ups. He wanted a Someone, like David had. He wanted a Jerry.

He wanted David.

"Fuck," he said, and started the bike, shifting into gear and rolling out onto the streetlight-streaked road. He turned toward home, early for the third night in a row, but this time he wouldn't make the same mistake. He'd use the south gate, away from David's house with its warm lighted windows. They weren't for him. They would never be for him.

DAVID erased a few lines, then redrew the jawline, adding a deeper shadow beneath with cross-hatching. There. That looked more like Zach. He was working from memory, trying to reconstruct the expression Zach had worn that morning as they were joking around, the laughing face that merged the two Zachs, the grown man with the merry boy. For that instant, David had seen the man Zach had been meant to be, not the bitter, angry one he'd become.

He flipped back a page or two in his sketchbook to the drawing he'd been working on when he'd called Zach last night. It was a full-length study of Zach in his black jeans and motorcycle jacket, just a quick sketch, again from memory, of the way he'd looked in Terry's Bar, done in a few strokes of charcoal. The face was shadowed but the body almost quivered with suppressed energy—anger, rage, frustration—and how much of that was the feeling he'd gotten from Zach then and how much was himself projecting, David couldn't begin to guess. He just remembered the feeling he'd had when he was working on it—that Zach was in the room with him, watching him, wanting him…. Not bloody likely. When David had offered himself to

Zach the first night he'd seen him, Zach practically tossed him bodily out the door.

It was probably only natural, David thought as he closed the sketchbook. Today Zach had shown him that he wanted things to be the way they were, before the kidnapping, before the kiss—just the way they had been when they'd been kids. That was okay. He could keep it that way, even if his body chimed like a carillon every time he was near Zach. But despite Zach's apparent promiscuity, he seemed awkward when anything remotely sexual came up between them. He even seemed disturbed by the idea of David having had a relationship. David supposed it was because of their previous friendship; he'd been like a big brother to Zach their whole lives, and he expected that Zach wanted to continue that. Like parents, a big brother shouldn't project sexuality; Zach was probably squicked out by the whole idea. So he'd be the big brother to Zach again.

Even if he didn't feel like one. He flipped open the book again, to the second of the sketches he'd worked on last night. This one was different, done in pencil instead of charcoal, softer, more detailed, and unlike the previous drawing, purely imaginary.

In the drawing, Zach sprawled nude on a bed against a pile of pillows as if he'd just made love, his knees bent, his left leg on the bed, his right at a forty-five degree angle, and the soles of his long, high-arched feet touching. His face was soft, his lips parted, his body lax and his sex lying long and limp between his thighs. David hadn't seen Zach's penis since they were both little, but he knew they'd both been circumcised, so he drew it as he imagined it might look now. He drew Zach without his scars; he knew he had them, of course, but he couldn't very well draw them without knowing what *those* looked like. The rest of him, though, that part he knew. He penciled with delicate detail: the long legs, the shadows of the solid, muscled thighs; the tendons of the hands, one resting on his leg, one lying upturned on the bed, the graceful fingers curled up; the broad, square shoulders and the acute curve where they joined the neck. Here he did include the scar he knew, circling the long column of Zach's throat just where a pearl choker would lie on a woman's neck. And of course, the strange/familiar face, with its echoes of the boy David had known.

There was a tightness in David's throat, an ache different from the one he'd had when working on this picture. Then, he'd had some faint hope that maybe they'd be able to work through their issues, to find some common ground where a relationship would be possible. The secret fantasy of that had fired his blood, aroused him mercilessly until he'd surrendered and brought himself off with his hand.

This morning's conversation made it clear to David that his secret fantasies were just that: fantasies. Zach didn't want him.

He ran his finger down the ragged edge of the sketchbook's pages. So this was what Jerry meant. Jerry, and Steve before that, and Chris before that. "Emotionally unavailable." That meant being in love with someone he couldn't have, while failing the ones that were in love with him. Jerry. And Steve before that. And Chris before that. All great guys. All serious about their relationship with him. All of them—gone. Because of this. Because in seven years, he still hadn't rid himself of Zach. He'd backed off of Zach when Zach wanted him, and sent Zach into hell, because Zach had scared him. Now Zach didn't want him, and he wanted Zach. How fucked up was that?

But what Zach wanted, he could give him—his friendship. It was little enough to pay for what he'd done in sending Zach away seven years ago. He'd have to fake it for a while, but it was doable.

It would be okay. Sooner or later the attraction would ebb, and then he'd be able to really be Zach's friend. Maybe by the time they were in their eighties....

"Fuck," David said, and shut the sketchbook.

Chapter Ten

"SO WHAT'S on the schedule for today?" Annie asked two weeks later as she slid the plate of waffles across the kitchen island toward David. "You haven't got a lot of free days left before the semester starts, do you?"

"No," David said, taking a drink of coffee and pulling the plate closer. "Next Tuesday's orientation."

"Have you got your clothes ready?"

"Mom, I'm not going into eighth grade," David retorted. "Yes, I have clothes ready. I'm teaching at a community college, not fricking Harvard. I'm wearing jeans and a sports jacket. Not exactly difficult to put together. And even so, I'll probably be more dressed up than most of the teachers."

"Just checking," Annie said easily. "More coffee?"

"Please." David held out his cup.

Jane wandered into the kitchen. "Did someone say coffee?" she asked plaintively.

"Sit, Jenny," David said, getting up and pushing her into a chair at the table. "I'll get you a cup."

"Thanks." She yawned hugely. "These late nights are for the birds," she said, in between yawns. "I hope that's the last fundraiser Richard has to go to for a while. I'm exhausted. Why am I exhausted? All we do is stand around and schmooze."

"You don't like schmoozing," Annie said practically, piling waffles and bacon on a plate for David to carry to Jane. "It's exhausting because you have to work at it. God knows I'd be miserable doing it."

"Remember the old days, when we were going to open a health-food store, and you were going to write a cookbook with your recipes in it?"

"Yeah, and we'd support Richard and Philip with their pie-in-the-sky ideas about *computers* of all things," Annie laughed. "God, looking back we were such conventional types, weren't we? The guys all about technology and us wimmenfolk all about the nurturing crap. But we thought we were so cutting edge."

"We did what we wanted," Jane said. "Like your girls are. Like David is. That's what's important. And I don't mind the other stuff, working with the foundation or the charities, when it's *work*, and not schmoozing. Some of the other women I have to deal with just live for the socializing. I like being in my little office all alone."

"You and Zach," David said, handing her the syrup. "Happiest when you're by yourselves."

"Zach didn't used to be like that," Jane said, troubled.

"He's getting better," Annie reassured her. "He called me 'DB' the other day. And smiled at me."

"My son smiles," Jane murmured. "Alert the media." She shook herself and gave them a game grin. "He is better," she acknowledged. "He's been talking more in therapy, maybe not necessarily about what's bothering him, but he's talking more. He's reading some book on mechanical engineering or architecture or something, and he's really into it. Are bridges mechanical engineering or architecture?"

Annie shrugged. "I don't know. Both?"

"Anyway, it's about bridges. And it's good that he's getting interested in that sort of thing again—it always fascinated him when he was little."

"Structural engineering," David said, swallowing the mouthful of waffle he'd been masticating. "Bridges are structural engineering. Zach wanted to be a structural engineer when he was little."

"Does he still? I mean, he's only twenty-two—there's no reason why he couldn't get his degree. God knows he's bright enough; he could probably test out of a lot of his classes. Didn't he get that scholarship to MIT when he was still a sophomore?" Annie held up a plate. "More bacon?"

"No, thanks," Jane said. "Yes, he did. But we've talked about it and he doesn't have any interest in going to school. He doesn't seem to want to do anything except work on his cars. That's why we're so encouraged about him reading again, in a subject he was interested in before. At least...." She stopped and picked up her cup.

"At least what?" Annie asked, not put off in the slightest. She and Jane had known each other far too long for that.

"At least he's not going out drinking at night anymore. He's still drinking, if the bottles in his garbage are any indication, but he's not going out driving while he's doing it. Or"—Jane hesitated, biting her lip, then plowed on—"or hanging out with his so-called friends. I've been worried about that. But he seems to have gotten past that."

"He's not going out at night anymore?" David frowned. "That's news to me."

Jane shook her head. "No, not unless he's taken to altering Andrew's logs, which I don't think he has the chops to do, since Andrew's about as high tech as you can get, and Zach's just not that good at hacking. He's not leaving the compound at night. And there'd be no reason for that; we don't monitor his coming and going, aside from the gate records, of course, but that's everyone. He still goes out, but mostly during the day. I think it's physical therapy a couple of times a week, and sometimes the library. But hardly ever at night anymore, and if he does, he's home an hour or so later." Jane looked embarrassed. "I asked him about it yesterday and he said he has to be in bed early because you two go running at seven a.m. and it's hard enough keeping up with you." She smiled then, an expression of relief on her face. "I am so *glad* that you two are friends again."

"Yeah. Well." David got up and put his plate in the sink. "We're friendly, yeah. We run together, and we went hiking with you guys, and yesterday we got out his trail bike and started cleaning it up so that we can take it out on Saturday, but I don't know about being *friends*. We just hang out together, you know."

Jane's grin faded. Annie sat down at the table with her coffee. "What do you mean, you don't know about being friends? What else do you expect?" she asked curiously.

"Well, it would be nice if he talked to me," David said bluntly.

"He's gone monosyllabic again. For a day or two he was talking—he even told me a little about Venezuela—a very little. But then he shut up again. Closed me out. Oh, he's pleasant enough, not broody or anything. Even smiles every once in a while. But closed."

"Welcome to my world," Jane said unhappily. "Oh, David, I'm sorry. He's doing much better with us—maybe he can't manage on two fronts yet."

"It's better that he communicates with you rather than me," David acknowledged. "You guys have been working much longer and harder at it than I have."

"Maybe that's just what Zach needs," Annie said thoughtfully. "Someone undemanding who'll just 'hang out' with him, and not expect him to talk or anything. It might be the best thing for him. Hard on you, Davey, but it may be what he needs right now."

Jane gave David a worried look. "Is that okay with you, Davey?"

"Zach...." David took a breath and tried again. "I fucking love Zach, Jenny. He's family. More than family. I will do any God-damned thing he needs me to do, up to and including murder—present company excepted." He grinned faintly at Jane. "Now, if you ladies will excuse me, I'm meeting the subject of our conversation to plan our overthrow of the free world."

"They're going to play Richard's new video game again," Annie told Jane. "The megalomaniac one."

"I love that one," Jane admitted. "I'm just a frustrated Napoleon, I swear to God. It's so much fun being evil."

David laughed and let himself out of the kitchen.

HE LEFT quiet behind him. Annie got up and got the coffee pot, refilling their mugs, then put the pot back on the stove and sat back down.

After a long moment, Jane said, "Do you think he does? Love Zach, I mean?"

"I don't know," Annie admitted. "David's different, these days. Less brittle. Still tense, but more like he's waiting for something. I mean, for the last seven years he seemed to be waiting for something, but it was like the other shoe dropping. Or global apocalypse. Or nuclear winter. He didn't seem to be expecting anything good. But since he's been back, it's like he's… watchful. Not quite hopeful—just watchful."

"He's watching Zach," Jane said.

"Is he? I don't see them together very often. Zach doesn't come in with David in the mornings after their run. He waits for David to leave. Or like today—he'll be having his own breakfast in his apartment, then he'll come down and meet David in the game room. I think he's uncomfortable around me and David. Singly, he's okay. But not together. I don't know why." She frowned. "That's just the feeling I get."

"I trust your feelings more than I trust most people's facts," Jane said. "So tell me, do your feelings say he's in love with Zach?"

Annie sighed. "He's certainly *something*. What about Zach? Is he even capable of it?"

"Hell if I know," Jane said. She put her elbow on the table and her chin in her hand. "He's talking more, but he's not talking *much*, if you know what I mean. He talks about things, not feelings. He talks about Maggie and Alex's Annabel, or the car he's working on, or the book he's reading, or the games. If he mentions David, it's in relation to what they're doing, if they're doing anything that day, or if they did something yesterday, or if they're doing something tomorrow. You know, 'well, we're going fishing tomorrow' sort of thing."

"He never said they were going fishing!" Annie protested with a laugh.

"Well, no, not fishing. But you know what I mean."

"Yeah," Annie said with a sigh. "I know what you mean."

Jane sat quietly a minute, then said, "Richard and I had a fight. He says I'm obsessing over Zach, but I'm not, really. I mean, he's my only child and I've only just really got him back, and he's not even all the way back yet. It's like he's being born, only it's taking months instead of hours. But Richard says I've got to step back and just let it happen, that my hovering isn't going to help. I'm not hovering!"

"Men are different," Annie said.

"You can say that again," Jane said. "But I'm not, not really. I just want to make sure Zach has everything he needs."

"Some things you can't give him, Jenny. Some things he's got to get for himself."

"If giving him David would help him, would you give him David?"

"I can't 'give' David to anyone," Annie said reasonably.

"You know what I mean!"

"Okay, okay. Yes. If it would make *both* of them happy, I'd love to see David in a relationship with Zach. But I don't want either of them hurt, Jenny. They're both my boys, even if David is the one that I bore. So if them being together is going to hurt one of them, I don't want it. And I don't know that right now they wouldn't hurt each other. David's just out of a serious relationship himself, and Zach.... Zach hasn't ever been in one. Just give them time. If it's meant to be, it'll be."

"I don't *want* to wait," Jane said stubbornly.

"Oh, the 'God grant me patience and I want it now' syndrome?" Annie shook her head. "Go to work, Jane. Leave the boys alone for a day."

"You and Richard are in a conspiracy," Jane grumbled.

"Yeah, us and the CIA. Git."

Jane stuck out her tongue and left the kitchen. Annie shook her head and went to clean up.

"DAMN it," Zach growled as his character died a bloody, flaming death. He and David were playing against both each other and the computer, and the computer had managed to get through his avatar's high-tech defenses to take him and his bodyguards down completely. "I just can't get past this level!"

"Yeah, it's hard," David said absently, concentrating on his own defenses. "And with you dead I'm just that much more vulnerable...."

Hah!" he said triumphantly as his avatar weaseled out of a booby trap. "Just wait 'til this goes online and you're dealing with other players."

"It's been too many years since I've played these kinds of games," Zach admitted. "I'm way out of practice."

David shot him a teasing grin. "You weren't that good before."

"Shut up," Zach retorted. "I'm gonna get something to drink. You want anything?"

"Yeah, whatever you're having."

The game was getting intense. David's avatar was on the defensive now, with the computer focused solely on him. Although, he thought in the part of his mind that wasn't concentrating on the game, it probably didn't make any difference to the computer; it was probably his own perception that made it feel like the game was getting more challenging. His avatar made it up a level, racking up a few more points, and the pressure got worse. He skated through another booby trap, but just as his crime boss took over the munitions organization, the Feds burst in and pulled a St. Valentine's Day massacre, taking out not only David's avatar, but his entire hard-built organization. "Goddamn *dog-fucker*," David yelled at the computer.

There was the crash of glassware exploding on the flagstone floor of the game room. David whirled to see Zach standing empty-handed, his eyes black holes in a white face. "Zach?" he asked faintly in dismay. "Are you okay?"

Zach stared at him blankly. David got up and started toward him, but Zach took a step back, then held up a hand. "Don't come closer," he said hoarsely. "There's glass everywhere."

Annie came running in, broom and dustpan in hand. "Are you guys okay? I heard the glass break—did you trip, Zach, honey? Are you okay?"

"I'm fine," Zach said numbly. "I'm... I'm okay." And he turned and bolted out the door.

"Davey?" Annie met her son's eyes in confusion. "What happened?"

"I don't know," David said, his voice equally confused. "He went to get something to drink while I was playing the game. I just lost and yelled at the computer—maybe I startled him or something, but why did he run out like that?"

"Better go after him," Annie said. "He went toward the patio. Just make sure he's okay. I'll get this."

"Thanks, Mom," David said, stepping around the shattered glass and heading for the patio.

Zach was nowhere in sight. David stood a moment, looking around in puzzlement; then a flicker of movement drew his attention to a shadowy corner in the landscaped area on the other side of the pool. Zach was sitting on the low rock wall that edged the flowerbed there, half-hidden beneath the overhang of a yew bush, his heels tucked up on the edge of the bank and his arms wrapped tightly around his knees. "Hey," David said softly as he approached. "I'm sorry I startled you. It's okay, Mom's cleaning up the glass...."

"Is she mad?" Zach interrupted dully.

"No, of course not. Shit like that happens, you know. You didn't have to take off like that."

"Yeah, I did," came the muttered reply. "Sorry. I'm okay. You don't need to hang around."

"Hey," David said again, and sat on the wall, but in the sunlight. "I don't *need* to do jack, but I want to make sure you're okay. Did I scare you, yelling at the computer?"

"No," Zach said.

"Cuz I've been yelling at the damn computer all morning, so I didn't think much of it."

"You didn't do anything wrong."

"I think I did. I think I said something that freaked you out. Can you help me out a bit here? Just so I don't do it again?"

Zach swallowed and put his forehead against his knees. "You didn't do anything."

"You're full of shit. You looked like you'd seen a ghost."

"Guess I kinda did," he muttered.

David draped an arm over Zach's shoulder. "Wanna talk about it?"

"No."

"How did I know you were gonna say that?"

Zach didn't answer, but shifted a little so that his head rested against David's shoulder. David tilted his head so that his cheek rested on the top of Zach's head. Zach's hair smelled like coconuts and vanilla from the shower he'd taken after their run: warm and sweet and clean. "What did I do?" David whispered gently.

"I forgot," Zach said. "I forgot you said that when you were really mad. I didn't remember where I got that. But I remember now. When you were really mad, or frustrated."

"Said what?" David asked in puzzlement.

"The," Zach swallowed. "The dog thing."

"Dog thing?" Enlightenment dawned. "Oh, jeez, did I say 'dog-fucker' again? Mom is always yelling at me about saying that. She says it's not only rude, it's inelegant."

"Don't say it again," Zach said. He hunched his shoulders. "Please don't say it again."

David ran his hand gently over Zach's cropped hair. "I won't. Mom's right. It isn't cool. I should be able to come up with a more creative insult than that. I am an *artiste*, after all."

"Yeah. Just not the dog thing." Zach reached up and rubbed the scar on his neck again.

David froze. Suddenly things were frighteningly, terribly clear. He felt incredibly stupid. "Jesus," he whispered. "The dog thing—the collar, the cage.... *Fuck*, Zach...."

Zach was instantly five feet away, standing with his hands fisted. "It's *nothing*," he hissed. "Nothing."

"What did that fucker do to you?"

"None of your fucking business," Zach snapped, and stalked away.

David caught up with him easily, grabbing his arm. "Jesus, Zach, don't do this. Don't clam up on me like this. Please. I'm trying to understand."

"The only thing you need to understand is that my life is none of your fucking business, David. Why don't you give me a break and go back to New York and your boyfriend, okay? Because I don't need you here poking around in stuff that's *none of your business.*" Zach jerked away from David's grip and walked quickly away across the patio to the path to the garage.

David sat down on the rim of the pool and pulled off his running shoes and socks so he could dunk his feet in the water. Stupid, he berated himself. He knew better than to push Zach, knew Zach would take refuge in anger whenever he felt threatened. But the whole dog thing freaked David out to no end, and what he was thinking—the terrible things he was suspecting.... He felt sick.

A shadow fell over the sunlit water. David looked up.

"Hey," Zach said wearily.

"Hey," David replied.

Zach sat, cross-legged, on the edge of the pool beside David. "How's the water?"

"Cool, but pleasant." David kept his voice neutral.

"Uh-huh."

Silence, broken only by the soft plash of the water against the tiled pool wall. Finally Zach said, "I'm sorry about the New York comment."

"You had your reasons," David said. "But for the record, there is no boyfriend."

"Uh huh."

More silence. David gazed down at his feet, pale and quavery beneath the surface of the water.

"You got the whole dog thing," Zach said.

"Uh-huh."

"That's what he made me. His dog. When I came back two years ago, I didn't talk. I barked."

"Fuck."

"Yeah." Zach reached down and stirred the water.

"Put your feet in. I promise I won't look," David said.

"Okay." Zach pulled off his shoes and socks and rolled his jeans legs up to mid calf, then put his feet in. "Feels good."

"Yep."

Zach blew out a sigh, a short, quietly explosive sound. "He took the 'fucker' part of 'dog-fucker' literally."

David closed his eyes. "*Shit.*"

"Yeah."

"I was afraid of that. I was just sitting here thinking, God, I hope that what I'm thinking happened didn't happen, but it did, didn't it?"

"That's pretty convoluted, but I think you got the point." Again, that softly explosive sigh. "I wasn't just his dog. I was his whore."

"Fuck."

"Yeah." Something in his voice made David look at him. There was a tightness in his face, white lines around his mouth, and his lips had gone thin, as if that "yeah" had been the only thing he could have gotten out at that moment. David looked away, giving him time to collect himself.

It took a while. Finally, Zach said, "That's done. I was kind of freaked to tell you, but it's done."

"Was it as bad as you thought it would be?"

"Yep." Zach tilted his head back and closed his eyes. "But it's done. I don't have to worry about telling you anymore."

"Out of the dark, into the light," David said.

"Huh?"

"Things. Secrets. They're always worst when they're kept in the dark. They grow, like mushrooms and mold. But you put them out into the sunlight and they wither up. It's like Vitamin D for the soul."

"Poetic…. What are you thinking?"

"You sound like a girl," David said. "But I guess under the circumstances you've got the right to ask. What am I thinking? I'm thinking it's too bad that bastard got killed because as mild-mannered as I am, right now I think I could take him apart barehanded. I'm thinking that I want to go throw up. I'm thinking that if it had happened to me I'd be fucking catatonic and the fact that you aren't just fucking amazes the hell out of me." He reached over and took Zach's hand.

"You are fucking amazing, Zachary John Tyler. You are God and I worship the ground you walk on."

"You aren't disgusted? You don't think I'm a coward because I let him do that to me?"

"You didn't 'let' him do it. He just did it. 'Letting' wasn't involved. I know that much about rape, Zach." He looked at Zach's white, strained face and his heart broke. God, he loved him. He wanted to hold him tight and safe and never let him out of his arms, but instead said, "So let's go finish cleaning up your dirt bike so you're not hauling around fifty pounds of mud when we take them out Saturday, okay?"

Chapter Eleven

THEY drove out to Mueller State Park at the crack of dawn in David's Saturn, their mountain bikes hung on the rack David had added to the back. The sky was a bit overcast when they got there, but by the time they biked up to the higher altitudes, it was blue with a vengeance. The last two miles were ridden in silence, both of them focused on getting to their destination: a small, sheltered alpine meadow off the beaten track, far away from the campgrounds and regular hiking trails. Zach practically fell off his bike, crawling over to the little creek that bisected the meadow. "Don't drink," David called from where he was pulling both bikes off the trail and onto the grass.

"Not," Zach panted back at him, and splashed a handful of water on his heated face. The water was one degree away from frozen, and he gasped at the shock.

"Bugger, it's hot," David said.

"Uh huh," Zach said. He sat up and gave the meadow a once-over. "Looks the same. I don't remember the trail being that long, though. My legs are killing me." He rubbed his thighs through the knit fabric of the bike tights he wore. The tights were more form-fitting than he was comfortable with, but he'd put a pair of gym shorts over them so he didn't feel quite as exposed, and at least his legs were covered. David, of course, was wearing shorts; ragged denim cutoffs that looked like they'd seen not only better days, but better decades. "You've been living in fucking New York for over a year—how come you're not hurting?"

"You kidding? I rode *everywhere* in New York. It's the worst place in the world for driving. Yeah, okay, it was taking your life in your hands every time you got on the bike, but it beat taking the fucking bus." David pulled off his T-shirt and wiped his face with it. "You thirsty? There's more water in the panniers on my bike. And sandwiches too—you know Mom."

"DB's the best," Zach acknowledged, carefully not looking at David's bare chest. He staggered to his feet and limped over to the bikes, pulling out a couple bottles of water and the bag of sandwiches. "You hungry?"

"I will be in a few minutes," David said, flopping onto his back in the mossy grass. "I just need to cool off a bit." He rolled the T-shirt up and tucked it under his head.

"Don't stay that way long," Zach said, "you'll burn to a crisp."

"Yes, Mother," David said sleepily, and yawned.

Zach took a drink of water and sat cross-legged beside David, his back to his friend, and looked out over the valley. A long way away, he could see the trailhead with its service buildings and parking lot; it was distant enough that people only appeared as small, brightly colored dots. Up here, it was peacefully silent except for the sough of the wind in the stand of trees a half-mile away, the trickling sound of the water, and the faint cries of birds even farther off. And, behind him, a soft, sporadic snoring. He grinned to himself. This had been one of his favorite places when he was a kid; at least two or three times a summer he and his family had hiked or biked up that trail to picnic here. He couldn't have pinpointed why; there were plenty of places just as peaceful, just as beautiful as this one on his own family's land. But something about this meadow called to him. No, not called. Spoke. Whispered. Here, it seemed to murmur, in the sound of the wind and the trickle of the water, here was Someplace. Long ago, before he'd stopped believing, he'd thought this place magic, and somehow it still felt that way. Magic. As if the wind and the water and the sunlight were all ingredients in some mystical spell.

The breeze skated over his skin, drying the sweat and cooling him enough that he could lie down in the grass without the blades sticking to him. A few feet away, David snored, his left arm flung over his head and his right sprawled out on the grass beside him. Zach rolled up on one elbow and watched him sleep. The sunlight shot tiny sparks off the little golden hairs on his chest and belly; David was too blond to be hirsute, but in the sun Zach could see what was invisible in lesser light. The hair beneath his arm was thicker and darker, more cinnamon than gold; impulsively, Zach leaned forward and drew in a breath, testing the scent. Sweaty, true, but a clean sweat, not the sour, unwashed stench of Esteban; clean sweat, and the green aroma of grass, and some faint spice that was the smell of David. Zach closed his eyes and breathed in the scent again, then jerked back, thinking, *Shit.* "Taff?" he called softly, worriedly.

David snored on.

Zach breathed a sigh of relief; he hadn't woken him with his weird, obsessive *sniffing*. Jesus. David would really think he was psycho.

Still, he didn't move away from David. Instead, he shifted around so that he sat beside his friend, unable to make himself move away, his eyes exploring what his hands couldn't. God, David was lovely, lying there like a sleeping prince in a fairy tale. A prince in ragged denim cutoffs that had slipped low on his narrow hips, a cinnamon-colored line of hair running from below the elegant dip of his navel to vanish beneath the loose edge of the shorts…. Zach swallowed, and was glad for the baggy shorts over the snug bike pants he wore; it would be embarrassing as hell if David woke up just then to see Zach sporting wood. But David slept on, the occasional soft snore fluttering past those silky, rosy lips. Lips the same color as the perfect, rosy nipples on that perfect golden chest. "Taff?" he whispered again, then at the silence leaned forward, his hands braced on either side of David's chest, and laid his mouth gently against the perfect right nipple. It tasted of David, sweet and spicy and sweaty, and he needed more of the taste, so he touched just the tip of his tongue against the softly pebbled surface, feeling the skin tauten and grow stiff against his mouth. He licked again, tasting him. Then he leaned further forward to brush his lips over the curve of David's shoulder, the hollow at his throat, the thin skin overlaying his jaw, tasting him, tormenting himself.

The shoulder beneath his lips shifted, and warmth and weight settled at the back of Zach's head; he looked up to see David's dark eyes watching him from beneath shuttered lids. The pressure cupping his skull drew him forward but he turned his head at the last minute so David's lips skittered across his cheek. He closed his eyes. "Zach?"

David whispered.

Zach pulled away from David's hand, sitting up and turning his back to David. "Sorry," he said gruffly. "Didn't mean to wake you."

"I should always get woken up that way," David said. He sat up, too, and put his hand on Zach's back, rubbing gently through the knit of his T-shirt. "Why did you stop? That was nice."

He shrugged David's hand away and reached for the sandwiches. "I was hungry," he said.

"So am I, but not necessarily for PBJs."

Zach didn't answer. David reached past him and he stiffened, but it was only to grab one of the sandwiches. "You know," David said, a minute later, his mouth sticky with Annie's gourmet homemade cashew butter and home-canned grape preserves, "you keep up with that sort of thing and I'm going to think you want me after all."

Zach turned, frowning. "What?"

"Well, you want to be friends, I get that. So I wasn't exactly expecting you to make a pass at me."

"You weren't supposed to be awake," Zach muttered. "I kept checking, but you were still asleep. I thought, I didn't want...."

"You thought you could make love to me and have me *not* wake up?" David chuckled.

"I wasn't making love to you. I was just...." Zach trailed off. "Curious," he said finally.

David cocked his head and studied him thoughtfully. "Curious."

"Yeah." Zach thought fast. "I fuck a lot of guys and I just wondered if you felt any different just cuz I don't, like, have a thing for you."

There was dead silence in the meadow. Even the wind had stilled. Finally David said, "Oh. Guess that's why you didn't let me kiss you."

"I don't let anybody kiss me," Zach said curtly. He finished his sandwich and washed it down with half a bottle of water. "Are you rested? Because we should probably start back."

"Right," David said.

ZACH took the lead on the way down, and David let him, figuring he probably didn't want to have to look at David after he'd caught Zach experimenting. Zach was probably embarrassed; he hadn't expected David to wake up and misinterpret the whole thing the way he had. *Curious.* Right. Of course he was curious—David had never been into the pickup scene; he'd only ever gotten physical with guys he had a relationship with, but he'd heard about the kind of sex that went on, and it wasn't the kind that encouraged exploration of the sort that Zach had been about. *Well, tough shit,* David thought angrily. He wasn't some kind of blow-up doll that Zach could use to explore his sexuality or whatever he was doing. Zach's sexuality was his business, and David's was his own, and never the twain shall meet and all that crap.

But for a moment, when he'd drifted awake to the sensuous pleasure of Zach's tongue on his nipple and lay silent beneath Zach's questing mouth, he'd let himself dream. Let himself fantasize that this was what Zach wanted, that his soft tastes would lead to soft kisses, then harder and hotter ones, until they were naked together here in this sunlit meadow. But he should have known better. Romantic as making love like that would have been, it wasn't Zach's style. Hot and hurried and anonymous fucking in a dark room, that was Zach. David's eyes stung. *Shit.*

"I'm sorry," Zach's voice came from beside him. He'd slowed his frantic pedaling and was riding parallel to David.

David blinked away the threatening tears and said gruffly, "For what?"

"For being a dick. I...." Zach hesitated, then went on, "I shouldn't have done that to you. It wasn't—it was rude. Personal space and all." He was silent a moment, then said bitterly, "I've always had a problem with personal space where you're concerned. I guess it's cuz I must have imprinted on you like a baby bird when I was little or something. I know you're your own person and I don't have the right to just push myself into your life like that, and I'm sorry. I don't have the right to touch you like that."

"No, you don't. Not unless you're serious," David said acerbically. "Only my lovers touch me like that, and you're not one of them."

"No. No, I'm not." Zach's voice was very small.

Relenting, David said, "Just don't 'experiment' with me anymore, dweeb. I'm your friend, not your fucking guinea pig."

Zach flashed him a quick, embarrassed grin, then sped up. "Come on, Taff. Beat you to the bottom."

David chuckled. "You wish," he said, and put on some speed.

THERE was a strange car in the long drive in front of the house, and as David drove the Saturn past on the way to the garage to drop off Zach and his bike, he saw that Jane and Richard were standing on the terrace talking to a tall man in olive-drab T-shirt and cammies.

"Mike!" Zach said delightedly, then, "Stop, Taff. Stop here. It's Mike...." and he was out of the car and running across the patio toward the house. He stopped short of throwing himself into the man's arms, skidding to a halt and thrusting his hand out for the stranger to shake. Numb, David put the car in park and got out slowly, watching as Zach started talking a blue streak, waving his hands in illustration while the stranger, a handsome, dark-haired guy in his late twenties, and Jane and Richard all grinned at him. Well. That explained a lot of things, particularly Zach's penchant for fatigues, his frequent comments about the Army, and the buzz cut.

He unlocked Zach's bike from the carrier on the back of the Saturn and walked it toward them, watching the group on the terrace. The guy looked up and met his gaze, then said something to Zach.

"Oh, yeah, Taff! It's Taff, Mike. He's, like, my oldest friend. I grew up with him. Taff, this is Mike Pritzger—Lieutenant Mike Pritzger. He's the guy who found me."

David's world crashed and burned. He stood amidst the flames, smiled, and held out a hand that was amazingly steady and unblistered. "Lieutenant. Pleased to meet you." *Well,* he thought. *Now you know why Zach only wants to be friends.* "Thanks for bringing Zach back to us."

"Well, it wasn't only me," Pritzger said, a grin lighting his handsome, olive-skinned face. "It was our whole team. I just happened to find Zach where he was hiding after all the shooting was done."

"You also stayed with me all the way back to the States," Zach objected. "You took care of me the whole way. And you cut the collar off me."

"Yep, regular hero with the pinking shears," the lieutenant said, laughing.

"So how long can you stay, Mike?" Zach asked enthusiastically.

"Just overnight. I've got a flight back to Bragg Monday afternoon and I promised my sister in Gunnison I'd stay tomorrow night with her."

"Great! I gotta show you the Dodge Charger I been working on— she's cherry. And Dad's grilling steaks tonight, right, Dad?"

"I am indeed," Richard said.

"And this new video game. Dad, can I show Mike World Domination?"

"Sure."

Zach turned to David. "You're gonna stay for dinner, aren'tcha, Taff?"

David froze, then said gently, "No, thanks, Zach. I... have a date." He shot Mike an insincere grin. "Gotta get home to shower yet."

"A date, Taff?" Was it his imagination, or did Zach sound a little... off? "With who?"

"I don't know if you remember him... Brian? From Terry's?" Into the silence, he flashed a quick smile. "See you all later. Nice to meet you, Lieutenant," he said, then he turned and walked back to the Saturn, making sure to put a little extra swing to his hips as he sauntered away.

ZACH watched him go, shock blocking any possible response to David's statement. Brian? The guy he'd fucked just a week or two ago? What the hell interest could David have in someone like Brian? Just cuz the guy was hot, and kind of bright, with a little bit of a sense of humor, and hot.... He pressed his fist to his stomach.

"You okay, honey?" Jane asked in concern.

"Yeah, fine. I think I'm a little tired out from the ride."

"How was it?"

"Good. We got up to the meadow and ate our lunch there before coming home." He turned to Mike, who was watching him thoughtfully. "It's this high alpine meadow people hardly ever go to, so it's pristine, you know. But it's a long ride. I'm gonna hurt tomorrow for sure."

"You look like you're in pretty good shape," Mike said clinically. "Better than the last time I saw you, anyway. You were still pretty skinny then. Though a' course nothin' compares to what you looked like in Venezuela. Crap."

"Yep," Zach acknowledged. "I've seen the pictures."

"You boys have about an hour before dinner," Jane said, "so if you're going to look at the Charger, go do it now. The only way I'll know you'll ever leave the garage is if you're looking for food."

"Aye, sir," Zach said, and snapped her a salute. Pritzger laughed.

"You're not supposed to salute a civilian, Zach."

"I'm a civilian myself," Zach said. "Come on, the garage is this way."

Chapter Twelve

"*FUCK!*"

Zach burst out laughing. "I *told* you you'd get pissed off. Isn't it a great game?"

"Fanfuckingtastic," Mike admitted. "I can't wait 'til it gets on the market. It just sucks you right in. I've never seen graphics like this before. The only thing I can imagine that would be better would be VR."

"Oh, Dad's already working on a virtual reality version," Zach said, nodding. "But his developers are worried about people having heart attacks."

Mike laughed. "Yeah, I can see that."

"He's got a big VR division—he's been doing a lot of work for the military, for simulations and stuff," Zach said earnestly. "There's a really great one they're working on with aliens—not like illegal aliens, but *alien* aliens, you know? And the weapons are real, well, not *real* real, but they look and feel like real futuristic weapons. I wish I could show them to you but it's all very hush-hush. You know, the whole 'but I'd have to kill you' crap? The feds are interested in using it to test and train next-gen infantry."

"Yeah, I bet your dad gets a lot of that, government stuff and all." Mike checked out the stats on the game. "Hey, DPE—who's that?"

"Taff. His real name's David. David Evans."

Mike raised his eyebrows. "That was David Evans?"

"Yeah." Zach gave him a quizzical look. "You sound like you recognize the name."

"Uh, yeah, kinda. Captain Rogers told me he was the one that developed the software for the locator chip that Dutch businessman had. The one we used to track him and find you." Mike tapped himself behind the ear. "Our unit's testing them for possible purchase by Uncle Sam. I gotta say, he don't look much like a software engineer. He looks more like a surfer boy."

"Yeah, he does. He's not a software engineer—he's mostly an artist. Got a Master of Fine Arts from UCLA. But he's fucking brilliant. He worked for my dad back a while ago, but he's been writing code since he was a kid. Now he's teaching computer graphics and programming design at a local school here." Zach pulled another beer from the bucket of ice. "You want another beer?"

"Sure. So," Mike said as he accepted the bottle and twisted the cap off, "Taff is David Evans. Interesting."

"Why?"

"Well, Captain Rogers said your dad said David Evans worked like crazy to develop the chip, like it would have made a difference to you. You know, more emotional involvement than is normal in stuff like programming. Can't say as most programmers I know are emotional about other people." Mike studied the beer in his hand a moment. "Kind of explains it."

"Explains what?" Zach was puzzled.

"Well, I don't get the whole gay thing, but that guy is totally into you."

The background music of World Domination ran uncontested a long moment. Then Zach said, "Taff is not into me."

Mike hooted in laughter. "He *so* is. My God, I thought he was going to punch my lights out."

"He's got a boyfriend in New York."

"He *said* he was going on a date tonight."

"Well, yeah… I think he thinks he's broken up with the guy in New York, but I don't think he really has."

"I think he's lyin' about the date tonight." Mike took a swallow of beer. "Seriously. He just said that because he's jealous."

"You're full of shit," Zach said.

"Nope. I bet he's sittin' at home with your picture in his hands, snifflin' into his hankie."

"He doesn't have a hankie, you ass." Zach reached over and shoved Mike playfully. "You're just jealous that he gets to live here near me and you don't."

"Honey, you lack several significant attributes and possess something I don't particularly find appealing in a lover, namely tits and a dick, in that order." Mike took another drink of beer. "Like I said, I don't get the whole gay thing, but as long as you ain't trying to put the moves on me I don't care if you fuck guys, girls, sheep, or little green men from Vulcan."

"You're too ugly to fuck," Zach said absently. "Seriously, you think Taff's into me?"

"What is this, grammar school? Shit yeah, Mary Sue. That boy has it bad. I saw his face when you introduced me. And I'll bet you five bucks that he's sittin' home right now, thinkin' I've done stole you away from him."

Zach licked the condensation from the side of the bottle. "I bet he's not," he said sadly. "Someone like Taff could have anyone he wants."

"He wants you. Trust me on this. I may not get the whole gay thing, but I know want when I see it."

"You know, you keep saying that you don't get the whole gay thing and I'm gonna start thinking you protest too much."

"Don't ask, don't tell," Mike said with a grin, "but there's nothing to tell if you did ask."

Zach pursed his lips in a mocking kiss. Mike threatened him with the beer bottle. "Don't wave that thing at me," Zach said, "it's giving me ideas."

"That is so wrong in so many ways," Mike retorted, "that I'm ditching your sorry ass and going up to bed."

"Yeah," Zach yawned, "it's been a long day. What time is it?"

Mike checked his watch. "Eleven-thirty. Late when you get up at five like I did."

"Me too," Zach said.

"But not too late for you, kid. If I were you I'd go out and hunt down that fine surfer boy ass and fuck it through the mattress."

"I can't," Zach replied. He swallowed the last of the beer. "You know I can't."

Mike turned serious. "Kid, I know that prick Esteban fucked you up royally, but you can't let that stop you. If David Fucking Evans loves you like I think he does, he won't give a shit about a couple of scars."

"Philip."

"What?"

"David Philip Evans, not David Fucking Evans." Zach met Mike's eyes. "The scars matter, Mike. You've seen them. And you've seen Taff. He's so fucking beautiful, and he's an artist, Mike. Beauty matters to him."

"I'll bet you five bucks you're wrong." Mike drained his bottle and handed it to Zach. "Go find out. Then come morning I'll be ten bucks richer."

"You wish," Zach said. "Okay, you know where your room is, right? We usually eat a big breakfast on Sundays at about nine—DB's a hell of a cook—but she's here at six, so if you get up early she'll fix you something."

"I thought her name was Annie."

"It is. DB's just a nickname."

"For what, 'Dumb Bunny'? She seems like a bright lady to me."

"No, it's for Dreamboat. You know. 'Dreamboat Annie', that Heart song from years ago?"

"You listen to Heart? You really *are* gay."

"Fuck you," Zach said. "Their stuff is great. 'Barracuda'? 'Crazy on You'? 'Magic Man'? Those aren't gay songs."

"Yeah, I guess those were okay."

"Muwha-ha-ha," Zach said. "My eeeevil plot to turn him gay is beginning to work."

"Dream on," Mike snorted with laughter.

"Well, if my mind control begins to work, my apartment's over the garage." Zach saluted him with the empties in his hand.

"Don't hold your breath, gay boy," Mike said with a grin.

IT WASN'T working. David glared with irritation at his laptop screen and rewrote the line of code—again—before giving up and shutting down the program. He'd have to break down and call George on Monday to see if the crabby bastard could give him some help with the multiple-layer backgrounds he was working on. George would, of course, insist on Tyler Tech getting first whack at the finished results, but David had always planned to offer the program to Richard anyway. His loyalty had always been to Richard—well, to his dad first, but his dad had been dead since David was nine, and Richard was there, always there for him and his family. Richard and Philip had both gone to work for Richard's dad at Tyler Technologies when they'd gotten out of college, and after David's dad had died, Richard had insisted on giving Annie stock in the company, saying the company wouldn't have been able to move in the new direction that had brought it such success without the work Philip had put into it. David himself vaguely remembered his father first teaching him to write code and laughing about the awkward early programming languages like FORTRAN and COBOL.

He checked his phone, which he'd turned off when he'd started working on his project a few hours ago. There were a couple text messages from Maggie, and a voice mail from Jerry. He hesitated a moment, then sighed and played back the message from his ex.

"Davey, it's Jer. Yeah, I know, I know. I was right, blah, blah, blah, and I shouldn't be calling you, put it behind us, et cetera, et cetera. But I still miss you. Anyway, I just wanted to let you know that they didn't give your job to Dickhead Dennis; they hired the guy that they interviewed before you left. Hurray for the good guys. Dickhead is pissed; he's saying you sabotaged him, which you didn't have to do but if you did, good for you. Anyway, that's about it. Except that I miss you. I wish things had turned out differently. Hope that school goes well for you—you're starting next week, right?—and that everything else works out. You know what I mean. Anyway, talk to you later. Love you."

David turned off his phone again and tossed it onto the desk before dropping into his desk chair. *Fuck.* Maybe coming back here had been a huge-ass mistake. Zach had obviously moved on—maybe it was time for him to get a clue and move on himself, maybe go back to New

York, see if he could work it out with Jerry…. *Yeah,* he thought miserably. Finish out the semester, quit, and move on—again. By his own figures, he'd lived in no less than nine places in the last seven years, between college, internships, moving in and out of lovers' apartments… he was tired of moving.

But living here wasn't the answer, either—not so close to Zach. He booted his laptop back up and started going through the links Maggie had sent him for the apartments she'd looked at.

SON of a bitch, Zach thought. Mike was right.

The Saturn sat under the overhang beside the house, and the light in David's room was on. When Zach walked around to the front of the house, he could see David sitting at his desk behind the screen of the laptop. He stared up at him a moment, thinking.

By his cell phone, it was past midnight; the rest of the house was dark, but Zach knew they never locked the doors, so he went quietly up on the porch, inside and up the stairs to David's room. The door stood ajar. He pushed it open soundlessly.

David slouched back in his desk chair, his hand moving the mouse idly back and forth as he studied the screen in front of him. Again, he was wearing just pajama pants; as Zach watched, he scratched his bare belly absently, then clicked the mouse again.

Zach said, "Some date. What happened to Brian?"

He was gratified to see David jump and whirl in his chair, staring at him guiltily. "What? Who? When did you come in?"

Zach ignored his stammering and sauntered into the room. "Just now. What happened to your date? Or was your date with some internet porn?" He leaned over David to look at the computer screen. "Apartments? Not my idea of a fun Saturday night, but to each his own, I guess. Why did you lie to me?"

"I…. Shit. I'm sorry. I didn't mean to—I just didn't want… I…." David stopped floundering. "Sorry."

"Fuck, Taff, I thought we were friends," Zach said, sinking down to sit on the edge of David's twin bed. "And you lie to me. I don't get it. If you didn't want to stay for dinner, why didn't you just say so?"

"I don't know."

"And why are you looking at apartments? I thought you were going to stay here? I thought the whole reason behind the original apartment search was that you didn't want to be near... me...." Zach trailed off, going pale. "Oh. Yeah. So I guess that's still the reason, huh? Sorry." He got up and started for the door.

"No! Shit! Zach...." David bolted up out of his chair, across the room in a flash, grabbing Zach's arm. "That's not why I'm doing it. Okay, it kind of is.... Shit. *Shit.* But it's not you, really. It's me."

"Oh, fuck that," Zach said angrily. "Is that the line you give when you bust up with your lovers? The 'it's not you, it's me' crap? *This* is why I don't get involved with the people I fuck. Because sooner or later one of us is gonna say that line and it'll be bullshit, just the way it's bullshit now. Why can't you just admit it, Taff? You don't want to be friends with me—this was just your way of trying to keep the peace until you could move out again." He shook off David's restraining hand. "Well, fuck you very much."

"No!" David snapped. "That's not what this is!"

"Then what the fuck is it?"

"I don't know." David ran his hand through his hair in frustration. "I just know I couldn't stay and watch you with him without losing my mind."

"Shit," Zach breathed. "You *are* jealous. Mike was right about that too."

"What?"

"He said you lied about going on a date, and that you said that because you were jealous. That you were hot for me." Zach cocked his head and regarded him thoughtfully. "Are you?"

David turned and walked away from him toward the door. Shutting it, he said, "Keep your voice down; Mom's asleep."

"Are you jealous of Mike?"

David closed his eyes a moment, then opened them and walked to Zach. Putting a hand on Zach's chest, he pushed him gently backward until the backs of his knees hit the side of David's bed and he sat down.

David crawled into his lap, his knees resting on either side of Zach's hips. "Of course I'm fucking jealous," he said. "You greeted him like a long-lost lover. Me, first you screamed your head off, then you told me to fuck off. What can he do for you I can't? And why aren't you with him, anyway?"

"Because he's not gay, for one thing," Zach said reasonably, though his heart was pounding and he was as hard as a rock with David sitting on his thighs. "And for another thing, he's not gay."

David regarded him through narrowed eyes. "But you want him anyway."

"No. He's my friend, that's all. He's been my friend since I got back. You know, kept in touch, visited me in the hospital. We email a lot. But I'm not into him." Zach searched David's dark eyes earnestly. "I'm really not at all into him."

"Any more than you're into me. I got it," David said wryly, but before Zach could protest, he went on talking. "Okay. But before I let you up, I owe you one."

Zach frowned. "One what?"

David planted his hands on either side of Zach's face, turning it up toward his. "Return of a favor seven years late," he breathed, then touched his mouth to the corner of Zach's. Zach went still, feeling the soft brush of David's lips on his, first the corners, tenderly, chastely; then closer in, warmer and more firmly; then at last settling fully on Zach's, his tongue pressing gently at Zach's lower lip. Zach let him in, meant to let him explore at his leisure but somehow his own tongue was curling around David's, stroking and flirting, and his hands were on David's waist, feeling the taut, smooth skin under his fingers. David kept the kiss slow and exploratory, nothing touching but lips and tongue and the firm, gentle hold of his hands on Zach's face. His eyes were closed, as if he could better appreciate the territory he was investigating by touch alone.

Pushing beneath the waistband of David's pajama bottoms, Zach slid his hands over the bare skin of David's ass. David jerked back, his eyes glittering fiercely. "I am *not* one of your anonymous fucks," he snarled.

"No shit, Sherlock," Zach shot back. He stood up, lifting David with him, and turned around to dump David on the bed. Pulling the pajama pants off, he crawled up onto the bed between David's legs, pinning him down with his hands on David's upper arms. "None of that wrestling crap," he ordered. "I'm fucking serious, Taff."

"You God-damn well better be, Zach," David said.

"I have never"—Zach kissed him—"been"—kissed his throat—"more"—kissed his breastbone—"serious." A long tongue-lap, circling his navel, then sliding down his hip, across the tender paler skin of his groin, curling down around his balls and then back up the underside of David's rigid shaft. "God, you're beautiful," Zach murmured, licking the sensitive spot under the head. And he was, pale against the tan of his belly, sweetly curved, not too long, not too thick. Perfect.

"I thought you didn't suck… oh, *fuck*," David gasped as Zach's mouth surrounded him, taking him deep before sliding back up, his lips tight around him.

Zach released him and grinned. "I lied," he said, "but only where you're concerned," and bent to take him in his mouth again. His hand cupped David's testicles, his fingers playing with them idly. It was true: he didn't suck dick, because he hated the taste of latex, and he wasn't stupid enough to suck off his mostly anonymous partners without. But David wasn't promiscuous and Zach trusted him implicitly. He knew David would have said something before Zach had started this, if there were any problem. And besides, he tasted so fucking good; clean, with the faintest hint of soap and sweat and arousal, leaving the salty-bitter tang of pre-ejaculate on Zach's tongue. He swiped his tongue over the head again and sucked him down; David moaned in response. Good. It was so good. David's hands moved to cup Zach's head, not pushing, just holding him.

He stuck two fingers in his mouth and wet them, then slid them over the delicate tissue behind David's balls to the little opening and rubbed the muscle there gently. "Fuck," David whispered, writhing, and relaxed enough for Zach to slide one finger inside, stroking, searching for that little bump… then, "*Fuck!*" as Zach nailed it and David arched beneath his hands. He slid his finger out and replaced it with two, stretching him, crooking his fingers to rub the happy gland in rhythm with his mouth and tongue. David was moaning now, his hands hard and tight on Zach's head, holding him as Zach went as deep as he could without gagging, then back up, sucking all the way. "Zach!" David cried. "Zach—oh, *God*, Zach, coming…!"

And Zach kept sucking, kept stroking until David's body bowed in climax, and swallowed as David came against the back of his throat. He didn't release David until he'd collapsed bonelessly on the patchwork quilt, staring up at Zach through dazed eyes.

"I need to fuck you, David," Zach said harshly. "Let me, please, God, let me…."

"Drawer," David gasped, and flailed his hand limply at the nightstand.

Zach staggered to his feet and opened the drawer, finding an unopened box of condoms and a tube of lube; he tore open the box and fumbled for the first little packet. David reached up and pulled at the hem of his T-shirt. "Come on," he begged. "Come here."

"I gotta do this my way, David," Zach said, and pushed away his hand. "Just let me do it my way, okay?"

"What…?" David started to sit up, but Zach rolled him over onto his belly. "What the fuck, Zach?"

"Please, Taff," Zach begged. "Please just let me…." He unfastened his jeans and rolled the condom on, the latex cool against his heated flesh, then warmed the lube in his hands a moment before sliding his fingers back into David. David tightened against the intrusion. "I'm sorry," Zach said penitently, kissing the small of his back. "I'm sorry, I know you haven't done this before but please, Taff, please let me. I need you so fucking bad."

"Go ahead, do it," David went up on his knees and buried his face in his arms. "Do it before I chicken out."

"You won't chicken out," Zach said, his stroking fingers gentle and persuasive. "You like this part, right? It won't be much different."

"Fucking liar," David mumbled. "Don't bullshit me, Zach. Just… oh, fuck, that's good."

Zach kept stroking, adding a third finger and stretching the tight passage. When David started that soft moan again, he pulled his fingers free and pressed the head of his cock against him. "I'll be careful," he promised, and kissed David's back again, his shoulder blades and spine and neck, kissing him as he slowly pushed inward. David's breathing tightened. Zach kept kissing wherever he could reach. "Oh, God, Taff," he groaned. "You feel so fucking good."

"Good," David gritted out between clenched teeth, "'cause you fucking don't, Zach. What the fuck do you have there, a nuclear warhead?"

Zach laughed. "Sssh," he crooned. "Sssh, it'll be okay," and he slipped his free hand beneath David to curl around his limp cock, tugging gently. David gasped and arched his back, and Zach slid home, his balls pressing against David's ass, David's passageway tightening around him. "You okay?"

"Mmph," David mumbled, and Zach eased back. David's head snapped up and Zach felt his cock filling between his fingers. "Shit!"

Zach laughed in relief. "Hit the sweet spot, huh?" he said, and eased forward a little, feeling the resistance vanish. "Yes, God, yes," he hissed, and started to move, rocking his hips to plunge into David's sweet heat again and again. "God, yes...."

DAVID'S forehead was slick with sweat where it lay on his arms, despite the fact that Zach was the one doing all the work. The initial push had been awful, burning and painful despite Zach's careful preparations, but when Zach had started to move, he'd hit David's gland and it felt *way* different from when he'd had fingers rubbing it before, deeper, more intense. It felt fucking good, and when it felt good, David had relaxed, and when he'd relaxed, suddenly it hadn't hurt so much. He drew his knees up and apart and started rocking back against Zach, finding a good angle so that Zach hit that spot again and again. And Zach's hand on his cock was pulling in the same rhythm, just the way David liked it, and he knew he was going to come again if Zach could keep it up. It felt good. No, more than that—it felt *right*; even if he'd always been the one to top before, Zach felt so good inside him that he knew he wouldn't mind even if Zach never let him top again....

But, God, he was going to be sore in the morning.

Zach's rhythm had sped up, his slick fingers sliding faster and faster on David's cock, and David felt that tingling in the spine that said he was ready to shoot; but Zach came first, slamming hard into him, and then again, and again, groaning his name over and over again, "Taff—Taff—Taff—" His fingers dug into David's hip and around David's cock. "Don't stop," David gasped, "don't you fucking stop, Zach Tyler."

"Can't—got to—*shit!*" Zach's weight collapsed on top of David, but with his knees spread like that, David was able to keep from getting squashed beneath. To his credit, Zach didn't let go of David's cock, but kept jerking him off until David came all over the patchwork quilt and his muscles disintegrated. He lay panting and sated, Zach's weight like an unwieldy blanket: too heavy, but warm and comforting and familiar.

Chapter
Thirteen

EXHAUSTED, Zach lay breathing in the warm, musky scent of David's sweat, his head resting on David's shoulder. He'd sucked up a deep bruise at some point that darkened the skin of David's neck an inch or so from his face; he studied it ruefully, then realized with a shock that he was lying on top of David. "Shit," he murmured, "I'm sorry, Taff," and carefully eased himself from David's body. David murmured sleepily and sighed. Zach lay tight against him in the narrow bed, his arm around David's waist, his head on David's shoulder.

He drifted off for a little bit, but not so much that he was disoriented when he woke; he knew just where he was and with who. For a moment it felt good, right—and then reality sunk in and his stomach dropped. What the hell had he been thinking? This wasn't right. This was so not right that Zach didn't even have a word for how wrong it was.

Then he thought—why not? Maybe he and David would be able to work it out. Maybe Mike was right: maybe he was selling David short, that maybe the scars, bad as they were, wouldn't matter to David after all? He looked over at David, lying asleep in the dim glow of the lamp on the nightstand. Maybe David wouldn't get grossed out by the wreck of Zach's body. Maybe they had half a chance.

Zach shook his head. Maybe. Maybe. In the meantime, the condom was cold and slimy on his wrung-out dick and he needed to ditch it. He eased out of bed, careful not to wake David, and, tying off the used condom, went over to the garbage can by the desk and dropped it in, refastening his jeans automatically, without even being aware of it.

There was a sketchbook open on the desk, a half-finished drawing of Annie on the page facing. Zach glanced at it, then, out of curiosity, flipped back a few pages. There was a sketch of a dark-haired, vaguely Italian-looking guy, handsome and grinning out at him; as Zach paged through the book he saw a few more pictures of the guy, some against a backdrop of skyscrapers. The absent Jerry, he assumed, and his heart hurt just a little at the evident affection in the drawings. There were a few others he recognized—more of Annie, Maggie, Annabel—and then he turned the page to a charcoal sketch of himself. He swallowed. The other drawings were done carefully, lovingly; this one was rough, almost violent. Was that how he came across to David? The tough biker dude he tried so hard to appear to other people? He didn't think David saw him that way, but maybe he was wrong. Did David think of him as unfeeling, mean, *angry* like this picture? No wonder he'd thought Zach didn't want him....

And then he turned the page again and went cold.

The style of this drawing was more like the others; in pencil, detailed and careful. But the Zach in that picture wasn't anything like the Zach he was—it was a fantasy Zach, whole and beautiful. Yeah, David had paid lip service to the scars on Zach's neck, but even those were subtle, almost invisible. Zach felt sick. *This* was the Zach that David wanted, this imaginary, beautiful Zach. This was what David thought he had. Not the ugly, worthless piece of shit that had just fucked him.

"Do you like it?" David's voice came from behind him—too close behind him. Zach closed the sketchbook with a thump and glanced over his shoulder. David stood there naked, his body still shiny with sweat and his sun-streaked hair standing on end. He gave Zach a sweet, sleepy smile.

"It's okay," he said indifferently.

"Oh." David looked disappointed. Did he *think* Zach would get all googly over a stupid sketch like that? It wasn't even real. Then David went on and said, "Why don't you take your clothes off," tugging again at the hem of his shirt, "and come back to bed?"

"No, I don't think so," Zach said.

There was silence in the room, and then David asked quietly, the hurt plain in his face, "What's going on, Zach?"

"Nothing. This—this was just a mistake, that's all. It shouldn't have happened." Zach waved his hand. "I shouldn't have come here. I'm sorry. I gotta go." He brushed past David and went for the door.

David beat him to it, and slammed his hand on the door just as Zach started to open it. "What. The. Fuck?"

"Don't start anything, David," Zach warned.

"Start anything?" David demanded. "You come in here and *fuck* me and then you're going to just walk away like nothing happened? You fucking bastard."

"Yeah," Zach said icily. "Yeah, that's me. So back off and I'll get out of your life."

"I *told* you, asshole, that I wasn't going to be just another one of your fucks," David snarled, shoving Zach around and back against the door.

"No, you said you weren't one of my *anonymous* fucks," Zach temporized, "and you're not. I *do* know your name…."

"You fucking son of a bitch," David said, and punched him in the face.

Zach stared at him in disbelief, his hand coming up to cup his suddenly bloody nose, then slid down the door to sit on the floor, his eyes wide and shocked. David stood looking down at him, still naked, hands fisted, hurt and rage and frustration in his face. "You son of a bitch," David repeated, and Zach realized he was crying. "You fucking son of a bitch."

"I'm sorry," Zach said, and then he was crying, too, his bloody hands over his face as he sobbed heartbrokenly, weeping for David and himself and for mistakes and stupidity and lost opportunities and might-have-beens. "I'm so damn sorry, Taff, I'm so sorry…."

And then David was on the floor beside him, holding him, and Zach was in his arms and sobbing into his shoulder and bleeding all over him. David rocked him back and forth as he cried. David was crying, too, and that made it even worse, so Zach cried harder. It felt like all the grief and longing and despair he'd felt over the last seven years had suddenly decided to manifest itself. The sobs weren't just sobs, they were great, wracking things that threatened to tear him apart, and for a moment he wished they would, wished that he would just disintegrate into component atoms and that maybe then the hurt would *stop*....

But when he ran out of tears and was hanging limply on David's bare shoulder, wrung out and aching, he was still there, still in one piece, still hurting. David was stroking his hair gently, his other arm tight around Zach's waist. Zach lifted his head from David's shoulder. "I'm sorry," he rasped, his voice almost gone. "I'm so fucking sorry. I should have never come here, shouldn't have done this to you, should have never fucking come back from fucking Venezuela. *God*, I wish I'd died there like I wanted to instead of coming back to fuck up people's lives."

"Jesus, Zach, what the hell?" David drew back in shock. "What are you talking about?"

"Nothing," Zach said hurriedly, realizing he'd spoken aloud. "Nothing. I'm just babbling."

"No, no," David said. "Do you really feel that way? That you've fucked up people's lives—my life, your parents' lives, just because you aren't *dead*?"

"Yeah."

"You're a *moron*."

Zach choked out a laugh. "Thanks. You always make me feel so much better."

"Just telling the truth." David leaned forward and rested his forehead against Zach's.

"Look, dweeb, just because you fuck up occasionally—or in your case, constantly—doesn't mean that people don't love you or that they wish you were dead. Although it's not infrequently that people wish you weren't born, like me just a few minutes ago, asshole. But it doesn't mean we don't love you or that our lives were fucked up because something, God or fate or just blessed luck, brought you back to us alive. Fucked up, but alive. So shut the fuck up, apologize for being a dick, and come back to bed."

Zach raised his head and looked at him wonderingly. "Just like that? Just like that you're going to forgive me for being a complete soulless bastard?"

"No. But I'm going to give you the chance to earn my forgiveness. Shit. You're still full of blood. Come on, let's get you cleaned up." David stood and tugged Zach to his feet. "I hit you pretty hard. I'm sorry about that—I hope I didn't break your nose."

"You didn't. And besides, I deserved it."

"Grovel a little more and I'll start to believe you mean it," David said, and fisted Zach's T-shirt. "Get this off; it's all gory."

"I can't."

David stopped and drew back. Evenly he said, "You think I'll put up with you fucking me and then taking off, but that I'll go all girly at seeing your manly chest?"

"No," Zach said, pulling his shirt back into place. "It's just—scars, you know."

"Yeah. It's just scars."

Zach shook his head. "No. You don't get it."

"Not so far." David sighed. "I know you were flogged, Zach, and you have scars on your back. I've felt them when I touched you, and for them to be that noticeable, I know they're bad. But I can deal with it. It breaks my heart that you were hurt like that, but…."

"It's not the back," Zach said. "It's…." Then he realized it wasn't something he could explain. "Fine. You asked for it." He reached for the hem of the t-shirt and pulled it over his head.

"FUCK…" David breathed. He'd expected scars, but this… this was unexpected, an ugly mass of scarring that completely covered Zach's right pectoral muscle. Where the nipple should have been was a palm-sized knot of twisted tissue, purple and red and painful-looking. Other scars radiated out from the center, equally deep and violent, looking like a combination of cuts and burns. David swallowed hard.

"Yeah," Zach said bitterly. "Esteban kept trying to break me. He beat me, but I kept fighting him. So he whipped me. I kept fighting. He broke my fucking fingers, and wrist, and ribs, but I kept fighting. Then he did this." He indicated the scarring. "He broke me. I stopped fighting."

David reached up and touched the knot of scar tissue at the center. "Zach," he whispered, horrified.

"He used a knife. Dug the nipple out. It's amazing, the amount of pain a person can tolerate without passing out. I *wish* I'd passed out. But I didn't." Zach's voice was wooden, as if he were reciting a tale told about someone else. "He said if I kept fighting, he'd do it to my other one, and then my balls, and then my dick. I stopped fighting."

"Jesus," David said.

"It got infected; that's why the scarring is so bad. They did something with cauterizing it or something. I don't know. I wasn't exactly on top of things by that point. All I know is that it looks like shit. And that's not all." He turned around. His back was a mass of raised welts and slashes, still red and twisted and ugly. Over his shoulder, he said, "That wasn't a particularly accurate picture you drew, you know."

"I didn't know," David said.

"No. Nobody does. Dick and Jane saw some of this at the hospital, but I make a point of not letting them see anything I can hide." He turned back around and David saw more scars on his abdomen, leading down beneath the waistband of his jeans. He saw David looking and said, "Yeah, he was pretty... thorough. And besides, every once in a while I'd try to rebel, hoping that maybe I could get him to kill me, but he was too good at what he did. He knew just how far he could go without killing me. I should have expected it; he liked to torture people. So. Seen enough?"

David ignored the harsh tone in his voice, and laid a hand on Zach's left breast, which was unmarked except a thin surgical scar curving around the bottom of the muscle. "What's that from?" he asked.

"From when they fixed my ribs. They'd healed wrong, but when I got back to the States they were able to go in and fix them so I could breathe right again." Zach shrugged. "Eventually I'll probably have plastic surgery to clean up what can be fixed, but not yet. I'm kind of tired of being cut up, you know? It's not like these have an expiration date."

"No," David said. He leaned forward and laid his lips right where Zach's right nipple should have been. Zach said roughly, "I don't have any nerves left there, you know, so it's not like it's gonna turn me on or anything."

"I don't care," David replied. He moved his mouth, exploring the scars; they were rough against his lips and tongue and fingers. "Not everything is about sex, Zach."

He felt more than heard Zach's sharp intake of breath and looked up to see a strangely vulnerable look on his face. "Seriously. Now come on and let me clean you up, then I'll find a T-shirt for you so you don't feel so exposed, if that's what you want."

Zach let David lead him into the bathroom and sat obediently on the closed toilet seat. David ran water on a washcloth and wiped the blood from his face, then said, "Do you want to take a shower?"

At Zach's headshake, he said, "Do you mind if I do? You won't sneak out while I'm in there?"

Again, Zach shook his head. David turned the shower on and climbed in for the fastest shower he'd ever taken, just sluicing the blood and sweat and come off. He heard Zach running the water and figured he was taking the opportunity to wash up without David watching, but when he turned off the shower and reached for a towel, Zach was back sitting on the toilet. His T-shirt was spread out on the tank, obviously rinsed and wrung out, and the scars on his chest and belly glittered water, testimony to his hasty cleanup. "I was tempted to flush just to hear you scream, but then I remembered your mom is sleeping," Zach said solemnly.

"Wise decision, grasshopper," David said, and toweled himself dry before tossing the towel to Zach for him to use. "Come on, let's find you a clean T-shirt, and get some sleep."

"Huh?" Zach frowned.

"Well, I'm too wrung out for sex again, and you look like you're ready to drop, so I figured we can catch some shut-eye. Mom will wake us at six when she heads out; that'll get you back to your Army buddy before breakfast. I take it our run will be cancelled this morning?"

Zach, still a little confused, followed him out of the bathroom. It was so easy to fall back into the way their relationship had been years ago, with David as the leader and Zach his adoring follower, despite David being shorter and slighter than Zach now, or having let Zach fuck him. Well, that was the difference, wasn't it? David had *let* him fuck him. David was still in charge, would always be in charge. Zach didn't know quite how he felt about that. For the last two years, he'd been something of a control freak—make that *totally* a control freak. Why was he so willing to give up control to David now?

Answers didn't come to him, but he was tired, and took the T-shirt David handed him and pulled it on obediently; then David pulled off the damp quilt, and he crawled onto the warm sheets, laid his head on David's abdomen, and went to sleep.

Chapter Fourteen

ANNIE'S cell phone rang as she was making her bed; she glanced at the clock, frowning. It was five-thirty and she usually didn't get to the main house until about six, but maybe Jane needed something. She picked up the phone. Yep, it was Jane. "Hey, Jenny, what's—"

"Zach's gone," Jane gasped. "He's not in his apartment, and Andrew says he hasn't left the compound, but he's not there and he's not in the gym, and—"

"Calm down, Jenny," Annie said. "Did you check with his guest?"

"Yes, Mike's here, he's up and in the pool, that's why I went to see if Zach was up but he's not there."

"I got that," Annie said. "David's not down yet—he usually gets up before me—maybe he and Zach went running early. I'll check and see if he's gone, and if so, that's where Zach is. Calm down, Jenny. He's not going to do anything stupid."

"I worry about him drinking when he's on all those meds," Jenny said frantically. "He's not supposed to drink but he does anyway, and God knows what they can do to him and it makes me crazy."

"Calm down," Annie said again. "I'll run up and see if David's there. I'll call you right back." She closed the phone and went to the stairs, listening. It was true what she'd said about David getting up before her—he'd always been a morning person and it wasn't unusual for him to be in the kitchen frying eggs and making coffee when she stumbled down the hall from the master bedroom. He was usually up by now, but maybe since Zach had company they'd gone running earlier. There was no sound from upstairs, so she went up and knocked lightly on David's closed door. When he didn't answer, she opened the door and peeked inside.

David was still asleep, propped up half-sitting on a stack of pillows, as was Zach, who was crammed in next to him on the narrow bed, his head on David's stomach, one arm thrown over his hips. Zach was fully dressed in his usual jeans and t-shirt except for shoes; one of his white gym socks had a hole in the heel. David had on the Warner Brothers' Marvin the Martian pajama bottoms his sister Alison had given him for Christmas.

Or at least she'd thought David was asleep until she saw his fingers gently stroking Zach's hair. "Davey?" she whispered.

He turned his head to smile sleepily at her. "Hey, Mom. Sorry I overslept."

"No, honey, that's okay. Jane just called. Their guest is up and she went to look for Zach and panicked when he wasn't in his apartment. I thought maybe you two had gone running early today, but thought I'd check."

"It's okay. Zach came by late last night and we got to talking. He fell asleep."

"I see that. I'll let Jane know, but have Zach call her when he wakes up. She's so frightened for him, Davey."

"I know. He's kind of messed up. But he's still Zach inside, you know?"

"I hope so, honey." She hesitated a moment. There was a softness in his face that hadn't been there yesterday, a dreaminess in his eyes that was more than just mere sleepiness. "Honey," she said, her heart in her throat, "be careful with him."

He said in surprise, "I'd never hurt him, Mom!"

"He's not the one I'm worried about getting hurt, Davey." She leaned on the doorframe and cocked her head quizzically. "I love him nearly as much as I love you and Alison and Sandy, but Davey, he's still on the way back and has a long way to go. I don't want to see your heart get trampled."

"I know, Mom. I don't know what's gonna happen, but I know I want him to be happy at the end of it. That'll be enough for me."

"Will it, Davey?" she asked dryly. "It's easy to say stuff like that at the beginning of a relationship, but a lot harder at the end."

"I don't know if this is a relationship or anything. It's just—well, it's just me and Zach. I'm not making any assumptions." He looked down at Zach, his fingers moving over the dark velvety nap over his skull. "I'm not asking for anything."

"I just want you to be careful," Annie said.

"I'll be as careful as I can be."

"That's not much of a promise."

He shook his head. "It's what I can give right now. We'll see."

"I suppose that will do. I'll call Jane and tell her Zach's here and that he'll call her when he wakes up. I made coffee, and there are sweet rolls in the freezer if you want something to eat when you get around to it."

"Thanks, Mom."

"Hmm," Annie said, and closed the door quietly behind her.

ZACH was drifting in and out of consciousness; every time he started to wake up, he was lulled back to sleep by gentle fingers and the warmth beneath his cheek and hand. At one point he realized David was speaking in a low voice, but all he got out of it was a soothing rumble—no words, just David's diaphragm vibrating and a faint susurrus of sound—and he drifted back to sleep again. It was so restful, just floating like this, warm and peaceful and safe.

Eventually, though, he opened his eyes and peeled his cheek away from David's bare belly. "Ungh," he said coherently.

David chuckled. "I thought you were going to sleep all morning."

He shifted and sat up in the narrow bed. "Comfortable," he said, poking David's abdomen. "Your fault."

"Uh huh," David said skeptically, and sat up, draping his arms over his knees. "Mom stopped by. Your mother's panicking because she's lost you."

"Shit! What time is it?"

"Six-thirty. No biggie—Mom said she'd call her and tell her you were here. But she also said to call her yourself when you got up."

"Are we getting up?"

David smiled faintly. "It's only six-thirty, and it's Sunday. It's up to you; you're the one with the guest."

"Shit. Mike." Zach rubbed his face. "I gotta call Jane."

David reached over and snagged his cell phone from the nightstand and handed it to him. When Jane answered, Zach said, "I'm fine, Mom. I just fell asleep at Taff's."

"Annie told me," Jane said. "That's okay, honey. I was just worried when you weren't home. Mike got up and did some laps in the pool, but he said since he doesn't have to be at his sister's until tonight, he'd see you when—and I quote—you get your lazy ass out of bed." She laughed. "He also said he never gets the chance to sleep in so he was going to catch a couple more hours, so you don't have to rush home."

"That's good," Zach said. "Taff and I were talking into the wee small hours, and I don't think I got more than a couple hours myself."

"Well, go back to sleep for a while and come home when you're ready. Therapy's not 'til ten-thirty, so that should give you time for a nice snooze."

"Okay." Zach hesitated, then said, "I love you, Mom, you know that, don't you?"

There was silence a long moment, then Jane said, "Yes, honey." Her voice sounded funny, but Zach didn't know what else to say, so he just said, "Okay, then. I'll see you later," and disconnected the call.

David was watching him, his eyes thoughtful.

"What?" Zach asked defensively.

"Nothing," he said. "So. Sleep? Shower?"

Zach ran his tongue over his lips and tasted. Ecch. Morning breath. "Shower and mouthwash," he decided.

"Okay. Go ahead. I can lend you some boxers if you want clean UnderRoos."

Zach snorted. "Underwear?"

David raised an eyebrow, but said only, "It's your ass. There are some disposable toothbrushes in the cabinet; Sandy feels compelled to supply all and sundry with as many opportunities for brushing as possible. One of the problems with having a dentist in the family. On the other hand, I haven't paid for toothpaste in years."

Zach chuckled and went into the bathroom, closing the door. He brushed first and tried David's citrus-flavored mouthwash—not bad, better than that crappy mint stuff, or the mediciney stuff—then with a worried glance at the closed door, stripped out of his clothes and climbed into the shower, making sure the curtain was inside the tub so that the water wouldn't splash out onto the floor.

He was rinsing his hair when he heard the bathroom door open. "Taff?"

"You were expecting someone else?"

"No."

"Just brushing my teeth," David assured him. "I won't flush and make you scream. I owe you that from last night."

"And I'm grateful," Zach said. He heard the water go on in the sink and the sound of splashing.

There was a full-length mirror set in the back of the bathroom door; through the space left by the shower curtain Zach could watch David brushing his teeth, bending over to spit in the sink, the thin cotton of his pajama pants stretching over his round ass. Zach's mouth went dry and his hand slid without volition to his rising cock. Then David turned off the water and slid his pajama pants off. Zach's breath stuck in his throat.

"Zach," David said, and looked up into the mirror over the sink to meet his eyes. Too late, Zach realized David could see him watching, reflected from the other mirror. "Zach, I'm coming in there."

"No!" Zach breathed. "No, Taff…."

But the shower curtain was sliding back, its rings chiming musically on the rod, and David was there, facing him, the water sluicing over his tanned body. He pulled the curtain closed again and, before Zach could speak, put his hands on his face the way he had last night. "I'm here," he said softly, "looking at you," but never taking his eyes from Zach's. "I'm looking at *you*," he said again, and his mouth found Zach's, his tongue questing for entrance, and Zach let him in, let David's hands slide from his face to his neck, down his arms to draw them up and around David as he stepped closer, his body coming to rest against Zach's.

A moan broke from Zach's throat as he pulled David in tightly, his hands curving over the taut muscles of David's ass. David sighed into Zach's mouth and rubbed his pelvis lightly against Zach, his erection hard and hot.

Zach's fingers, still slippery with shampoo, slid over David's ass and down into the tight crease. His fingertips stroked the puckered opening and David bucked, his cock thumping against Zach's. He reached down and grabbed both his and Zach's cocks in one hand.

Zach froze.

"Sorry," David murmured, and reached past Zach to grab the bottle of shower gel. Pouring some into his hand, he reached down and smoothed the gel over both of them before taking hold again. "Better?"

"What the fuck are you... agghhh...." Zach trailed off, staggering back against the tub surround and closing his eyes at the phenomenal feeling of David's cock against his. "*Fuck.*"

David chuckled, and leaned in to lay his lips on Zach's throat, running his tongue over Zach's Adam's apple until Zach shivered. "Never done this before?"

"Shit, no," Zach gasped. He reached for David again, pulling him in as tight as he could, trapping David's hand between them. David eased him back to give himself room, but compensated by finding his lips again. Zach moaned into his mouth, his hands gripping David's shoulders for balance, letting David take control again. But it felt so good, so natural, David's hand on him, on them....

A second set of fingers settled on his balls, stroking and tugging gently; he whimpered in response. "Too much?" David whispered, and he shook his head, desperate for the feelings to go on. It was so different from fucking, different from the few times he'd dared let himself get blown. It was like jerking off, but so, so much more satisfying, with David's warm, wet hands and David's warm, wet body and David's warm, wet mouth.

Sensations more intense than he'd ever felt shot up his spine; he stiffened, cried out, and came in those warm hands. "Yes," David murmured against his throat, "just like that," and his mouth tightened on Zach's skin, sucking up a bruise as David himself came against Zach's belly.

They held each other up as the water washed them down. Zach found himself breathless, panting as if he'd run miles. David laughed weakly and kissed Zach just behind his ear, then bit the lobe gently. "Liked that, did you?"

"Uh huh," Zach acknowledged, reduced to grunts.

David reached behind himself and turned off the shower. "Come on," he said, "let's go back to bed. For a while, anyway." He kissed Zach's mouth again, tenderly this time, and climbed out of the tub. He tossed Zach a towel and got one for himself before padding back out into the bedroom.

Zach leaned back against the tub surround, drying himself off slowly. He could hear David in the bedroom opening drawers, then a wad of fabric flew in through the open bathroom to land on the floor beside the tub. "Clean T-shirt and sweats," David announced. "I'm not eager to get dressed just yet and your damn jeans are hell on my fragile, delicate skin."

"Pansy," Zach called back and put on the sweats.

David was sitting on the bed in his Marvin the Martian pajama bottoms and a red T-shirt that didn't match, that proclaimed "I'm with Stupid" with an arrow pointing upward. "Nice," Zach said. "Sandy give you that?"

"No, Maggie. The women in my life see it as their mission to totally destroy any self-confidence I might have."

"Is it working?" Zach sat down beside David, who immediately took his hand and laced their fingers together.

"No," David said, grinning. He didn't do anything else, just sat there, his hand in Zach's, smiling.

"So," Zach said after a few moments of silence, "what is this? We going steady or something?" Nerves put an edge to his voice, and David's grin faded.

"It doesn't have to be anything," he said neutrally, and started to release Zach's hand. Zach tightened his grip.

"I just want to know," Zach said hoarsely. "I'm kind of out of my depth here, Taff." To his acute embarrassment, his voice shook. "I don't know what you expect or anything, and I'm kind of afraid of fucking this up—whatever 'this' is, assuming it's anything. I mean— Jesus. I sound like a girl. Fuck."

David was quiet a moment, then said, "It's hard for me too, dweeb. I keep forgetting that you don't really know anything about sex or relationships. Just fucking. And that's the least part of it—the easy part. The part that doesn't require risk, or involvement. You should have learned about it the right way, relationships, emotions."

"Yeah, well, I didn't, did I?" Zach said, and let go of David's hand. Standing, he rubbed his neck and went on. "I don't know jack about relationships, Taff. I told you at the beginning that I was fucked up. Guess you know now just how fucked up I am."

"Sit down," David said quietly.

"Why? Come on, Taff, you know as well as I do that this is gonna go nowhere."

"You're fucking it up."

"What?"

"You said a minute ago that you were afraid of fucking this up," David said. "Well, if you don't sit down and kiss me, you will be fucking it up."

Zach rubbed numb palms on his thighs. *Shit,* he thought. *Not now. Not now.* "I gotta go," he said.

David frowned. "Jesus, Zach, you're sweating. What's the matter?"

"I gotta go," he repeated, and went hastily into the bathroom to retrieve his jeans and still-damp T-shirt from last night. David got up and followed him, grasping his arm when he went to push past him out the bathroom door.

"Slow down, Zach! What's going on?"

He jerked free. "*I have to go,*" he said fiercely. "I have to *go.*"

"No! Jesus, Zach, you're freakin' me out here. What the hell is wrong?"

"Nothing's wrong with me," Zach answered, then realized he'd said too much. His heart was pounding so loud he couldn't hear himself think. "I mean, nothing's wrong. I just gotta go."

"You're clammy and you're pale and you're scaring the shit outta me," David said anxiously. "Jesus, what's wrong? You're sick? Siddown and let me call your folks. Shit, let me call 911...."

"No! No, I ain't sick! It's nothing!" He had to hold it together until he got away from here. Outside it would be cooler—there'd be more *air* for God's sake—and he'd be able to breathe. He heard himself wheezing. Shit, he was already hyperventilating. "It's...." he wheezed, trying to speak, but the words weren't coming; his lungs were too busy trying to get air.

He saw David with his cell phone in hand and lunged for it, knocking it onto the floor. "No!" he managed. "Not...."

"You're having a heart attack or something. Jesus, Zach!" David grabbed him as he stumbled.

"No. No." Zach hauled in as deep a breath as his compressed airways could manage. "P... panic attack," he said, and sobbed for breath as the room spun dizzily around him.

"Jesus!" David breathed, but managed to shove him onto the bed before he fell. "Can I get you anything? Water... you got meds?"

"Jeans...." Zach waved at the pants he'd dropped when he stumbled.

David picked them up and went through the pockets, pulling out Zach's prescription meds and the inhaler. Zach grabbed the inhaler gratefully.

The adrenaline in the inhaler relaxed his bronchia, and fresh, sweet air flooded his lungs; using the inhaler focused him, and the hyperventilation eased as well. He was still shaking uncontrollably as he took the third puff, but not as hard as he had been. "Thanks," he said wearily.

"Valium?" David said, holding up the prescription bottle from his other pocket.

"Should have taken it earlier," Zach said. "Not much good in the middle. But I don't like it."

"You take this when you're drinking, you're gonna wake up dead," David said soberly.

Zach, still trembling, merely nodded.

David knelt on the floor at Zach's feet and put his hands on Zach's knees. "You're still shaking," he observed. "Anything else I can do?"

Zach shook his head. The hysterical crying that was the most embarrassing part of his usual panic attack seemed to be holding off for now, and he was grateful. Bad enough he was so humiliated in front of David without having to cry like a baby as well. But he was exhausted, so he lay down on the bed, not even caring that his head wasn't even near a pillow.

DAVID knelt beside the bed, feeling his own heart slowing. This panic attack had terrified *him*. He'd heard about them, but had never witnessed one before. He'd thought they were just nerves or something; he didn't realize that there were actual physical symptoms, let along such severe ones. He'd been certain Zach was having a heart attack; his skin had gone gray and clammy and he'd obviously been short of breath. It was weird. Worse than weird: frightening. "Does this happen a lot?" he asked Zach softly.

Zach didn't answer right away, and David was just beginning to think he'd fallen asleep when Zach said in a drained, exhausted voice, "Yeah, too often. Started when I was first in the hospital."

"It's scary," David admitted.

"Try being the one on the inside," Zach countered. He raised a trembling hand to cover his eyes. "Sorry. Yeah, it's scary. Scarier than you'd think. 'Panic' attack doesn't cover it. And 'anxiety' attack is way off the mark. 'Terror' attack, yeah. Maybe. And the worst fucking thing is that it's nebulous. I don't know what the fuck I'm scared *of*."

"It looks like a heart attack."

"Feels like one, too. Like your heart's about to explode." Zach rubbed his face again. "Sometimes if I'm quick enough, I can get out of wherever I am and away from whatever's causing the stress. And then it doesn't happen. But sometimes I can't, it happens too fast."

"Being here—being with *me*—triggered it?" David felt sick.

Again, a long moment of silence; then Zach said in a voice completely devoid of any emotion, "Yeah."

David turned and sat with his back against the side of the bed. *Shit,* he thought in distress. Maybe Zach was right. Maybe this wouldn't work. He thought about what Zach had said yesterday—Jesus, was it only yesterday?—that he didn't "have a thing" for David. But David had pushed it; even though Zach had *told* him that he didn't let anyone kiss him, he'd forced the kiss on Zach last night, and the sex on him this morning. Sure, Zach had gotten into it, had even blown David spectacularly, but shit, Zach was a twenty-two-year-old guy. Blowing David was probably just a friend's way of compensating for fucking a guy who'd never had anyone's dick up his ass before. He hadn't wanted David last night or this morning; he'd only wanted sex. He didn't want any kind of relationship; David *knew* that. It was David's fault Zach had had the panic attack, David who'd pushed him when he didn't want to be pushed, David who'd demanded more than Zach was willing to give. He felt like having a panic attack of his own.

So what if Zach said something about not knowing what he was doing in a relationship and not wanting to fuck it up? What he really meant was that he didn't want to fuck up his friendship with David— which was exactly what David was doing to him.

Fuck.

Then he felt gentle fingers touch his hair. "I told you I was fucked up," Zach said, his voice as raw as David felt. "But you know, lots of things trigger the PAs. Things that I eventually get used to. You know when I had my first one?"

David shook his head. Zach's fingers brushed his cheek. "When I first saw my parents again."

"Fuck."

"Yeah. Any time I feel trapped, or not in control of the situation, or when I don't know what's gonna happen next, or how I'm supposed to act, or feel... shit. Pretty much any time I'm not in absolute control—I freak out." He touched David's nose gently. "I was on the verge of one last night when you hit me. I hate to admit it, but it stopped it."

"So, what? Next time I see you start in on a panic attack, I punch your lights out?"

Zach said dryly, "Uh, no. I'd really prefer that you not. It hurt like hell."

"So, basically, if I want to avoid this, I just don't put you in a situation like that," David said. He reached up and drew Zach's fingers to his lips, pressed them lightly, then released Zach and got up. "I'm going to go down. Mom left sweet rolls in the freezer, and I'm going to put them in the oven and have a cup of coffee. You go ahead and sleep for a while more. You're tired. Can I get you anything else before I go downstairs?"

"You can do one thing."

"What's that?"

"Stop treating me like a fucking invalid."

"Sorry," David said, and bit back a smartass reply. Instead, he just gave Zach a vague smile. "Just come down when you feel like it."

"Yeah," Zach said, and closed his eyes.

David stood there a moment, then went out of the room and down the stairs to the kitchen.

Chapter
Fifteen

ZACH tried to get back to sleep, but despite his exhaustion, sleep evaded him. The pillows smelled like David, but he missed David's warmth. He remembered that day months ago when it had been enough to just lie here in David's bed, how it had comforted him then. It didn't comfort him now. Instead, all he could think about was the loss in David's voice when he'd asked if the panic attack had been because of him, because of what they'd done together. He should have said no, should have come up with some other innocuous reason for freaking out like that, but that "yeah" had escaped. He'd tried to soften it, to explain, and David certainly hadn't acted like he was mad, but had kissed his fingers gently and been kind.

Even yelling would have been better than kindness.

He got up and went into the bathroom. The face that greeted him in the mirror was certainly nothing to please a lover with: drained and ashen, except for his reddened eyes and the reddened nose that was already beginning to show bruising. Nice. No wonder David went running downstairs. No, to be fair, bad as they were, it wasn't Zach's looks that had chased him away, just Zach's charming personality. Zach washed his face with cold water, trying to reduce the redness, but it didn't do much good; he blotted himself dry and went back into the bedroom to skin out of the sweats and put his own grubby jeans back on. He left on the T-shirt David had given him and bundled his own still-damp one under his arm, then followed David downstairs.

DAVID was sitting at the kitchen table, drinking coffee and reading the Sunday paper. The smell of baking cinnamon rolls perfumed the air. He glanced up, a puzzled look on his face. "Up already?"

"Yeah," Zach said. "I couldn't get back to sleep." He laid the wet T-shirt over the back of a chair.

"The rolls'll be done in about five minutes," David said, and started to get up. "Coffee? Just cream, right?"

"No thanks," Zach said politely. "I don't need anything."

David sat back down again and regarded Zach with a serene expression that Zach hated on sight. "Do you want to read the paper?"

"No, I don't want to read the fucking paper," Zach said mockingly in the same serene voice.

David closed the paper and folded it, then looked up at Zach. Expectantly. Like he was waiting for something.

Zach swallowed. "I'm sorry," he said.

Whatever it was David was expecting, it apparently wasn't that. He looked surprised. "What for?" he asked curiously, his eyebrows raised.

"What *not* for?" Zach said. "For freaking out. For being a dick. For God-damned fucking you when I know that's not what you wanted. For all of it. For being born."

"Shut up," David said, still calmly. "You don't even know what you're apologizing for. Not a terribly effective method, or a convincing one."

"Is this how you do it?" Zach demanded. "Is this how you piss off your lovers? Just slide into this serene, untouchable thing? Act all superior over people who don't have your fucking emotional control? Cuz if that's how it is, I can see why they dump your ass."

David sat silent through Zach's diatribe, his eyes resting composedly on Zach's face. When Zach stopped, he said, "Well, that has to be the quickest relationship I've ever been in. From fucking to recriminations overnight. What's it been, about eight hours?"

"Fuck you," Zach said bitterly.

"You already did that," David replied. "Let me know if you want a repeat and I'll pencil you in."

"God damn it, Taff," Zach exploded, "I don't fucking want a

repeat, not if it's gonna turn out like this every time."

"Look, Zach," David snapped, his composure suddenly gone, "I didn't want this to begin with. You came over here spoiling for a fight. I kissed you, that's all. Where it went after that was as much your doing as mine, so don't fucking blame me for all of it. Yeah, I pushed you where you didn't want to go. I'm sorry. I didn't know, and I won't do it again. I know you didn't want me, you just wanted to fuck someone and I was available. I *made* myself available," he corrected, his voice as bitter as Zach's had been. "I pushed you too far and it's my own fault for that." He shook his head, hard, as if to scatter his thoughts. "Okay, I'm wrong. I *am* to blame. I should be the one apologizing, so here it is. I'm sorry. It won't happen again."

"*What* won't?" Zach demanded. "You confuse the hell out of me, Taff!"

David stood and rested his hands on the table top. "I won't kiss you again. I won't try to push you into a relationship when you're not interested. I won't make demands of you. Is that enough?"

"Yes. No. Jesus!" Zach shook his head. "God, you make me crazy."

There was silence for a moment, then David said quietly, "I don't mean to confuse you, Zach. I just don't want to hurt you and I don't know if I can avoid it." He swallowed and went on, his voice strained, not at all that calm, complacent voice Zach hated. Zach didn't like the strained voice much better. "I screwed up last night. I'm sorry. I shouldn't have kissed you—shouldn't have pushed you, should have just let you go right away the way you wanted to."

"I didn't want to go," Zach said.

David looked up, his face as lost as Zach felt.

"I didn't want you to let me go. I *wanted* you to kiss me. I wanted to do everything we did—except the panic attack and the punch in the nose, those weren't so much fun. But everything else…. Jesus, Taff, waking up next to you was the best feeling I've ever had." Zach clenched the back of the chair in front of him. It took an effort of will to look up, into David's solemn dark eyes. "I lied yesterday when I said I didn't want you. I want you. I want you so bad it's killing me. But I'm not what *you* want—I can't *be* what you want. God, you're so beautiful, you could have anyone. Why would you want someone like me who's as fucked up inside as I am outside?"

"Maybe because I love you?"

The words hung in the air between them. David waited for Zach's response, perfectly still, not even breathing.

Zach felt like all the oxygen had been sucked out of the air. He gasped for breath. "Fuck," he whispered.

All expression drained from David's face. He sat down again and opened the newspaper. "Yeah," he said flatly, not looking at Zach, "That's kind of what I thought. Don't worry about it—I'm not going to press the issue." He flipped over a page.

"Jesus, Taff, you're like hot and cold running boyfriend," Zach complained. "I'm not surprised your lovers dumped you—I'm surprised they didn't *murder* you."

"Yeah, well, maybe by the time they dumped me they didn't care anymore, either," David said indifferently, turning another page.

Zach reached out and grabbed the newspaper, yanking it out of David's hands and throwing it over his shoulder, so it scattered all over the flagstone floor of the kitchen. "God-fucking-damn-it," he yelled, "pay attention to me!"

David shot to his feet. "I don't *want* to pay attention to you!" he shouted back. "I don't want to stand here and listen to you if you aren't saying what I want you to say. And you're not going to say it, so why the *fuck* are you wasting my time?"

"What do you want me to say?" Zach demanded. "Just tell me!"

David stared at him, breathing hard. "I don't want you to say anything you don't feel," he said finally. "I don't want to hear it. I've had enough of people telling me what they think I want to hear, just to make me happy or make me stay or make me feel something I don't feel. Say what you want. I'm not going to put the words in your mouth. Or don't say anything. Just… go away."

"Do you want me to go away?"

"*Fuck!*" David screamed at the top of his lungs.

Zach burst out laughing.

David stared at him as if he'd lost his mind and dropped back down into his chair. "You fucking asshole," he said finally. "You louse. You *dick*. You did that on purpose to make me crazy."

"Just the last part," Zach chortled. He came around the table and leaned against it next to David. "No kidding, Taff? You love me? I mean, *love* love me? Not just cuz we grew up together or any of that shit. But like love, real love?"

"Like love I'd-marry-you-if-it-were-legal-in-Colorado kind of love," David said soberly. He leaned forward and rested his head against Zach's abdomen, curling his arms around Zach's hips and resting them on the table behind him. "I've been in love with you for seven fucking years, Zach Tyler, ever since you kissed me, and I don't care if you've got scars or cooties or the screaming heebie-jeebies, I love you and I want you. You can run and hide and pretend if you want to; I ain't asking for anything from you, but I want you to know what I feel. I know you aren't ready for any kind of relationship and that's okay. I can wait."

Zach ran his hands through David's tousled hair, toying with the streaky strands. "You're completely wacked, you know that, Taff? I don't know why the hell you'd want someone like me. I'm completely fucked up; I think you know that after last night. But Jesus, I want this. I really, really want this. I'm just kind of scared."

"I know. Me too."

They stayed in that position a long time, Zach playing with David's hair, running it through his fingers; David with his cheek pressed to Zach's belly, his arms tight around him, Zach's warmth solid and comforting beneath his cheek. Then the buzzer on the stove went off, and David released Zach to go and get the cinnamon rolls out of the oven. He set the baking sheet on top of the stove and used the spatula to slide the rolls onto the cooling rack before turning to put the pan into the sink.

Zach came up behind him and put his hands on the sink edge to either side of David's waist, trapping him there. His lips settled on the side of David's neck.

"Mmm," David murmured, leaning back against Zach.

"I do love you, I think," Zach said softly. "I'm not sure what it is. I mean, I want you and trust you, and like you, and…. Shit, Taff. I don't know what I'm saying. Am I screwing it up again?"

"No," David said, and turned in his arms, winding his own around Zach's waist. "Just—you don't need to say anything. Can I kiss you?"

"God, yes," Zach breathed and David did, fitting his mouth to Zach's. Zach put his arms around David, pulling him in close with a faint, contented sigh.

David explored Zach's mouth leisurely; Zach's tongue rubbed along his gently, with none of the hurried, anxious urgency of the night before. Oddly, Zach seemed almost hesitant, almost uncertain as he kissed back, always following David's lead eagerly enough, but never initiating. David drew back and rested his forehead against Zach's. "Are you okay with this?"

Zach flushed and bit his lip, then nodded. David smiled and kissed him again, his tongue soothing Zach's lip where he'd bitten it before seeking entrance again to Zach's sweet, soft mouth. This time he slipped his hands up under Zach's T-shirt, his fingers stroking gently over the ragged scars on his back. Zach stiffened a moment, but when David didn't react other than to keep caressing him, he relaxed again, his own hands motionless on David's waist.

"Take off your shirt." David drew back to whisper against Zach's lips. Zach hesitated, but David kissed him again. "Take off your shirt."

Wordlessly, Zach obeyed, pulling the T-shirt over his head and dropping it on the kitchen floor. David leaned in and licked Zach's remaining nipple, his tongue curling over it, tasting, teasing. Zach sucked in a breath in shock at the sensation; when David sucked on it gently, he moaned, his hands coming up to clench hard on David's upper arms. David chuckled under his breath, never letting go of the stiff, sensitive tissue, but sucking harder. Zach whimpered.

"Like that?" David said, releasing him and grinning up at him.

"I never... I didn't know...."

"Now you know why I woke up yesterday when you did that to me." David laughed again, and kissed Zach's chest just above the nipple before curling his hand over the rising bump in Zach's jeans. "Turnabout's fair play, love." He caressed Zach as he bent to suck again, then bit him lightly.

Zach cried out wordlessly at the nip, his hips bucking and his hands tightening on David's arms. David licked over the bite, then trailed his tongue over the nipple again, then up to Zach's throat, his hand still stroking Zach through his jeans. "Upstairs," he whispered against Zach's neck. "The guest room has a full bed—mine's too small to make love in properly—and we're not doing this in my mother's kitchen." He pushed Zach gently. "Come upstairs."

Zach pulled him close again. "Couch," he gasped hoarsely.

"Too small. No, this time we're doing it right."

That stopped Zach cold. "Wait. Wait." He released David's arms and rubbed his neck distractedly. "We can't. You've gotta be sore. I *know* I hurt you last night…."

"My beautiful dweeb," David said with a gentle shove toward the stairs, "there's more to sex than just fucking." He weaseled past Zach. "Beat you to the top."

"You wish," Zach said automatically, and took off after him.

THE spare bedroom had been Sandy's and was still a bit on the girly side, but the bed was a big four-poster sturdy enough for David to jump on, followed by a panting Zach. "No fair," he wheezed, "you kiss me breathless then challenge me to a race?"

"Shut up and kiss me," David said, shoving him onto his back and crawling on top.

Zach pushed back, rolling over and pinning him underneath. "You gotta get a king-size bed," he said, then kept David's mouth too busy to respond. David wrapped his legs around Zach's hips and rocked up into him, rubbing his pelvis against Zach's. Zach arched back, releasing David's mouth to throw his head back, his hands splayed on the mattress on either side of David's shoulders, his body grinding hard into David's, his eyes squeezed shut.

"Easy, boy," David laughed. "You in a hurry?"

He stopped and stared down at David. "What?" he asked in confusion. David lifted a hand and brushed away sweat from Zach's forehead.

"Ease up, Zach. It's not a race. You're working too hard."

"I'm hurting you," Zach said instantly, and rolled over, sliding off the bed. "Sorry."

David sat up and reached out a hand. "Come here." When Zach didn't obey, he patted the mattress. "Come on. Sit your butt down."

Zach snorted and sat on the edge of the bed. "What?"

"You've never had a lover," David said.

"Sure, I have—" Zach's words were cut off by David's fingers on his lips.

"You've had sex, but never a lover," David explained. "I keep forgetting that. I keep forgetting that this is all new to you."

"I'm not exactly a virgin," Zach said dryly against David's fingers.

"Sure you are. It's kind of exciting." David removed his fingers from Zach's mouth with a gentle caress. "To know I get to be the one, your first lover, the one who teaches you how to kiss, how to make love... I should have been, you know. Should have been the one to teach you all that."

"I wanted you to be," Zach said. He turned and lay down across the bed, his back to David.

"I'm sorry," David said softly. He lay down behind Zach and put his arm over his waist. They were close enough in height that his cheek rested against Zach's cropped skull. "I wanted to be, Zach. But you scared me. I was eighteen. I'd only ever even had one relationship, and that was the one I was sneaking around on Maggie with. I'd just busted up with him when everything happened."

"You mean when I came on to you," Zach said.

"When I realized that you were the one I wanted. Had probably wanted even before I knew what wanting was."

"You were just used to having me around."

"No. No." David came up on one elbow and looked down at him. "You know why you scared me so much? Because I was eighteen and I realized that you were the only person I wanted to be with. And I wasn't ready to commit even though I knew that it was always going to be you. And then you went off and died on me... or so I thought."

"Misplaced guilt," Zach said.

"Grief. None of my relationships after that lasted. Because none of them were you."

"Put a little pressure on a guy," Zach muttered.

David laughed and rubbed Zach's belly. "No pressure, really. What I feel is my business. I just wanted you to know that if you want me, I'm yours."

Zach twisted to lie on his back, looking up at David. "I don't know if I can do this, Taff."

"So let's just take one day at a time. I do have one thing I want to ask you to do for me, though."

"What?"

David swallowed. "Please stop going to those bars: Fat Charlie's, the Goose, any of those places. Not because I don't want you picking up guys—though I don't—but because it's dangerous." His eyes were dark and serious when they met Zach's.

Zach said soberly, "I'm always careful, Taff."

"I'm not talking about always wearing a condom and all that shit. Wesley's pretty liberal, but Colorado Springs in general isn't. There's still a lot of anti-gay sentiment around, and there was an incident at the Goose three years ago that was pretty ugly. A couple of people got really hurt. And…." He trailed off and just shook his head instead.

"And my dad doesn't need the bad publicity if people figured out who I was," Zach said. "Yeah, I've thought about that. I just… you know."

"I know."

"Security's pretty good around here and Dad's been pretty careful about not letting people know what I look like or anything," Zach went on. "No interviews, no photographs, nothing like that. He's careful about my privacy, and his security team and I have protocols *I'm* pretty careful about. But I don't think any of the guys I've been with know who I am. I mean, I never go anywhere where I see any of them outside the bars, anyway."

"Let's keep it that way, okay?" David kissed him gently. "I don't want you hurt. And neither do your folks. I don't think they give a shit about bad publicity or anything, but they do worry about you."

"Yeah." Zach looked up at David, and then curled his hand around the back of David's head. "I won't go there anymore, Taff."

"Okay," David said, and let Zach draw him down for another kiss. He eased onto his supporting arm and with his free hand, then trailed his fingers down Zach's muscled belly toward the button on his jeans, sliding them under the top of the waistband. Zach made a small noise that was swallowed up in their mouths, then another when David got the button open and fumbled for the zipper. Zach slid his hand down to help David unzip him, then David sat up and moved to the foot of the bed, pulling off Zach's socks and tugging at the hem of the jeans.

Zach flung his arm over his eyes, but didn't protest David's pulling off the jeans, just waited for the intake of breath, the expression of disgust or shock, but there was nothing. He waited.

Then it came, unexpectedly—the soft touch of lips, like a rose petal falling on his skin, on one of the scars on his thigh. Then another, then the shift in the mattress as David crawled back up on the bed between Zach's legs, his lips brushing each of the round scars as he crawled. It took a while. Then David laid his lips on the softer skin of Zach's groin, where there were no scars.

Zach let out a long exhalation of the air he'd held in his lungs from the time David had pulled his jeans off. Against Zach's hip, David whispered, "Burns?"

"From Esteban's cigar," Zach said in the same low tones, as if he might be overheard. He felt David's swallow, but then the soft mouth was moving again, exploring the hollow of his pelvis, then down to nuzzle his testicles. He sucked in a breath as David tasted him, tugging on the loose skin with gentle lips, then moved to lick the underside of his rapidly rising cock. *Oh, God*, he thought, David's mouth was on him, David's tongue on him, David was going... *oh, God....* "Condom," he gasped in protest, reaching down to cover himself just as David's mouth had moved to lick the rim of his glans. "Condom...."

David stopped and raised his head. Zach uncovered his eyes to look back at him miserably. "You test positive?" David asked gently.

"No, my last test was clean, but...."

"Have you ever barebacked?"

"No, never, not since Venezuela, I'm not stupid."

"Ever even gotten blown without a rubber?"

"No...."

"I'll take my chances," David said, and closed his mouth over the head of Zach's cock, his tongue stroking, lips tightening.

Zach almost shot off the mattress. The feeling was incredible, amazing, hot and wet and intense. His hands fisted in the coverlet as David took him deeper; then David swallowed and Zach felt the tightness of David's throat against him and he cried out wordlessly, his hips bucking as he fucked David's mouth and fist. The fingers of David's free hand dug into the taut flesh of Zach's ass, holding on.

David pulled away just as Zach started to come, cupping his hand over Zach's cock so that his come flooded over David's fingers. Then he moved up over Zach, dipping his head to kiss him. Zach tasted himself on David's tongue, then jerked in surprise as David slicked Zach's come on his own cock, then rocked forward, his cock sliding between Zach's thighs to rub against the sensitive skin behind his balls. Zach moaned, rousing again, or still, as David's hands and tongue and cock teased and soothed and tormented and pleased, until he was crazy with the sensation, wild with need and lust and love and hunger, so that when David's fingers found their way inside him and stroked gently, he barely even recognized the sensation, only the brush of beautiful pressure on that needy place, and he came again, burying his hands in David's hair and kissing him frantically as he cried his release into David's mouth.

And then he jerked back as he realized that David's fingers were deep in his ass, where he'd sworn no one else would ever go, and he stared in disbelief at his lover. "What the fuck?" he gasped.

The pleasure on David's face faded. "What?"

"Get your fucking fingers out of me. Now," Zach growled. David obeyed and Zach tried not to jerk away, not to overreact. It was okay. It was okay, he told himself fiercely. It was *David*, for God's sake.... He forced a smile and said, "Sorry. Reaction," and reached up to kiss David again, but David resisted, frowning.

"Are you okay?" he asked, pulling back against Zach's hand on his neck.

"Yeah. Sorry. I didn't mean to snarl at you. It was okay. It was good." Zach's mouth twisted. "Oh, God, tell me I haven't fucked up again."

"No," David said slowly. "No, I'm just... oh, shit. I'm sorry, Zach. I didn't think...."

The smile came a little easier now, still difficult, but more honest. "I hope you *weren't* thinking," he said, "cuz God knows I wasn't. It's okay. I'm sorry I overreacted. It's okay. It's okay." He kissed David again, this time desperately, wanting it to be the way it was, wanting to take away the tension that tautened David's body.

The tension eased and David moved to lie beside him, his waist in the curve of Zach's arm. He rested his chin on Zach's chest and said soberly, "You're okay, then?"

"Better than okay," Zach said. "Much better." He reached up his free hand and stroked David's hair gently. "That was awesome, Taff. I never realized you could do anything like that and have it be half as good as.... Well, you know."

"You're such a dweeb," David said, laughing. "It's called anal sex. And yeah, it's nice. It can be fantastic. But it's not the only thing you can do together, you know. Sex isn't just about fucking. And love isn't just about sex." He bent his head and kissed Zach's shoulder. "Though sex is a pretty good part of it. Can I ask a question?"

Zach blinked. "Sure."

"Why did you buzz your hair? Is it just part of the whole biker thing, or the whole Army thing?"

"Shit, Taff, that has to be the weirdest after-sex question I ever heard."

"So?"

Zach regarded him with solemn eyes. "Actually, I didn't cut it. About two months after I got back from Venezuela, it all fell out. The doctors said it was a weird after-effect of vitamin deficiency. I only ate crap for five years, but then when I got home and started eating real food again, my hair fell out."

"Weird," David agreed.

"It just started growing back in about six months ago, and it was really patchy at first, so I kept it more or less shaved until it started coming back in normal again. It's growing slow. I'm wondering if it'll be curly again; one of the doctors said that it might come back completely different from what it was. Though it looks like it'll still be black, anyway." He looked away and went on. "I didn't really mind not having any hair for a while, you know. Esteban used to drag me around by it, and pet it, and crap like that. So it's kind of nice not having it as a reminder. I'm thinking maybe I'll let it grow out again in a year or so, see what happens with it." He snorted. "Assuming it does."

"Shame if it doesn't," David said. "I like long hair on a guy."

Zach flashed him a quick smile, then turned his head away again. *Yeah,* he thought, thinking of the sketchbook upstairs. The pictures of Jerry showed he had a headful of curls, just like he himself had once had. "Okay," he said. "My turn for weird questions."

"Okay," David said.

"You said there's more to sex than just fucking, right? So how many guys have you actually fucked?"

David laughed. "Jeez. Three. Chris, Steve, and Jerry. The only serious relationships I've had, as in live-in relationships. I've had other relationships, but those three are the only serious ones."

"Who was the first?"

"Chris. My roommate in college."

"Were you scared?"

David came up on his elbow and looked down at Zach, who was watching him with solemn eyes and teeth worrying his lower lip. He looked so much like the child Zach that David had to chuckle. "Scared spitless," he admitted. "But Chris wanted it, so…." He shrugged. "I was fine with the other stuff, the frottage, the blow jobs, but…."

"The what? Frot… what?"

"Frottage." David grinned. "What we just did. What we did in the shower. Rubbing off on each other."

"It has a fucking *name*?"

The grin became a laugh. "Jesus, Zach, everything has a name."

"Not this," Zach said, pointing to the groove above his upper lip. "Try and find a name for that."

"Spaz. Dweeb. Microcephalic moron." David kissed him. "You are so mental."

"So this Chris guy *wanted* you to fuck him?"

"Yeah. He asked me to. I wasn't sure. I mean, shit, yeah, I wanted to, but all I could think was that it must hurt like a bitch, but Chris said not. He said it might hurt a little to start, but if I was careful, it wouldn't hurt. It would feel good." He shrugged. "I have to say it felt good from my perspective."

"Yeah," Zach said. "I can't imagine it feeling good from his perspective, but I've been with enough guys to know that there are some that really get off on it." He looked away, then asked shyly, "I'm sorry about last night. I just...." he trailed off.

"You just wanted sex and I was available," David said.

"No. No. I just," Zach swallowed, "I just wanted sex with *you* and that was the only kind I knew. I never knew about this other stuff. I mean, yeah, blowjobs. But I gave you one of those." He glanced back at David, ducking his head so he was looking up at him through his lashes. "Was it okay? I don't have a lot of experience with that."

"Good thing," David said, "because if you were more experienced with that you would have killed me."

"Did I hurt you last night?"

David knew he wasn't talking about the blowjob. "It hurt to start with, yeah. But by the time you were done, it felt good. I never thought I'd say it, but I wouldn't mind doing it again, if that's what you wanted."

"I can't give you what you want," Zach said. "I can't let you...."

"Did I ask?" David cut him off. He eased off the bed and pulled at the spread. "Get up a minute, will you?"

Zach obeyed and David pulled the spread off the bed and rolled it up. "That's two bedspreads I have to wash today," he complained, but folded down the top sheet and gestured for Zach to crawl under. "Later." He followed Zach into the bed, and put his arm around Zach's neck, shifting on the pillows until Zach's head was on his shoulder. "There. That's good. You comfortable?"

Zach put his arm across David's abdomen. "Yeah," he said with a contented sigh.

"Sleep. I'll wake you up in time for breakfast with your folks, okay?"

Zach didn't answer, and when David looked down, he saw that Zach's eyes were closed, the lashes long and dark against the curve of his cheek. His hand lay on David's belly like a limp starfish.

"Guess it's okay," David said, and closed his eyes.

Chapter Sixteen

ANNIE slid the strata out of the oven, breathing in the warm scents of cheese and egg and sausage. "God, that smells good," Jane said from her perch at the kitchen bar. "I love your strata. I'd eat it every morning if you fixed it."

"Yeah, and bitch at me when your scale made rude comments at you," Annie said, "which is why I only make it for special occasions. Though in my opinion, you could use a few pounds."

"When Richard gives up the business and I don't have to go to any more social events, I'm going to gain those few pounds and then some," Jane promised, "but I have to look sexy so those female vultures keep their hands off my hot man."

"Trophy wife," Annie accused with a grin.

"Right," Jane sighed. "Because every man wants a fifty-five-year-old woman by his side."

"This one does," Richard said from the doorway. "Especially a fifty-five-year-old woman who looks thirty-three. And besides, you're not fifty-five for another four months."

Jane waved her hand dismissively, but Richard caught it and kissed the palm. "It's totally not fair," she said, looking down at his dark head, "that a man gets better-looking as he gets older, and a woman just gets… older."

"Says the one who's the youngest of the three of us," Annie said, and tossed a potholder at Jane.

Jane laughed and turned to kiss her husband. Annie watched them a moment, a faint smile of amusement on her face; then her smile died and she turned back to her preparations. "The two of you take the coffee stuff into the breakfast room," she said over her shoulder, "along with that tray of rolls, and I'll be in with this once it has a chance to set up."

They obeyed, Richard snagging a cup of coffee and smacking a kiss on Annie's cheek on the way past. Annie laughed, but when they were gone, she rested her elbows on the counter and put her head down in her hands. *Damn it,* she thought. She should be happy for Davey. Yes, it would be a tough road for him if he wanted to drive it with Zach, but she knew that all along it had always been Zach that Davey loved. The months after Zach's disappearance had certainly brought home that fact; the endless nights of holding Davey while he grieved, listening to him weep late at night until she'd moved her bedroom downstairs to the guest room in self-defense, being patient with his abrupt mood swings, and the suppers gone cold and uneaten as he worked into the nights on the software he swore would have protected Zach.

She'd watched David get involved with other people, all the time knowing the relationships were doomed to failure, but she'd kept her mouth shut and let him struggle. She'd do the same this time. But God knew it wasn't going to make her happy.

"Mom, you okay?" David's voice came from behind her.

She whirled. "Oh, honey, you startled me! I didn't hear you come in."

"Sorry. You okay?"

"Oh, yes, of course. Just waiting for the strata to set. Where's Zach?"

"Stopped off at his place to change. Sleeping in your clothes makes for the dreaded grunginess, and not the Seattle-and-Nirvana kind, either."

"Good," Annie said absently.

"Seriously, Mom, are you alright? You seem sort of distracted."

"No, not really. Can you give me a hand with the burritos? They just need the cheese added and then they need to be wrapped. I've got to cut the strata."

"Sure," David said, and took the cheese out of the refrigerator and set to work. After a few minutes, he said, "Are you angry with me about Zach?"

"No," Annie said, "not angry. Worried. But you're an adult. I have to let you make your own choices."

"Are you worried that it's going to blow up and mess up your relationship with Dick and Jane?"

His mother shook her head. "No. I hope not. Maybe. No, I don't think so. Oh God, Davey!" She put down the knife and covered her face with her hands.

"Shit," David said, and put his arms around her. "It'll be okay, mamacita," he said softly.

"I'm just afraid, Davey," Annie said. "We've been a family so long, but I *know* that if it came down to choosing sides, it would be us against them, and I don't think I could stand it."

"If it came down to choosing sides," David said seriously, "you side with them because it will be me that's in the wrong. I made a promise to Richard when I was nine that I would always take care of Zach."

"You were *nine*, Davey!"

"A promise is a promise."

"But Zach's not a puppy or kitten that you can make a promise like that. Zach has to go his own way and find his own destiny. You won't always be there to protect him."

"No, I know. But I won't be the one to break his heart, either. If someday he wants to move on, that will be his choice. I won't."

"David, I don't want to hear that! You have to think about your own happiness too!"

"I know, I know." David sighed. "I don't want to sound like a stalker, Mom, but Zach's what I want. What I've always wanted. If he decides later on he doesn't want me, that's okay."

"But you'll be so hurt."

"Yeah," David said. "I'll be hurt. I'll survive. Just like we did when Dad died. We survive, we Evanses." He squeezed her tightly.

"I take it more than just sleeping went on last night, then?" Annie sighed and shook her head. "No, never mind, don't answer that, it's none of my business."

David grinned. "I'll tell Sandy and Alison that next time I see them. It certainly was your business back when they were dating. Bet they'll have something to say about it, gender inequality and all."

"Don't you dare, David Philip Evans. Don't you dare."

David grinned and went back to the burritos.

"YOU'RE sure you're okay?" David asked one last time as they went into the breakfast room.

"Drop it, Davey," Annie murmured back.

Mike Pritzger was already there, talking with Jane and Richard. David set the tray of breakfast burritos on the table, then turned and held out a hand to the young officer. "Morning, Lieutenant," he said cheerfully. "Sorry I didn't get a chance to talk to you yesterday."

Mike shook David's hand. "It's Mike, and no problem. Hope you had a good time on your date last night."

"Oh, it was… interesting," David said.

Zach burst into the room through the French doors. "Shit! I'm late," he gasped. "Sorry!"

"Don't be silly," Jane said with a smile. "It's just breakfast."

Sliding into the chair beside his mother, Zach whined, "But it's *Sunday*, and it's *strata*."

"Boy after my own heart," Richard said.

Zach grinned at them both, and squeezed his mother's hand gently.

The eyes Jane raised to Annie's were stunned. Annie gave her the faintest of nods; then Jane turned back to her son. "Do you want some juice, honey?"

"Sure," he said.

Annie pressed David's shoulder. "Sit down, boys," she said to David and Mike.

"Can I help with anything else?" David asked.

"It's all out and on the table," Annie replied, and took her own seat to start passing stuff around.

They were quiet a moment as they passed plates. When everyone was served, Zach squirmed around in his seat to dig in his pocket. "Here," he said to Mike, and reached across the table to hand him a twenty-dollar bill. "The money I owe you."

The others glanced up. "Just a private bet," Mike said, grinning widely.

"What about?" David asked curiously.

"Whether he could beat me in WD," Zach said. "Well, not *me*. My first score. Whether his first score could beat my first score. He did."

"Zach, a lesson," David said soberly. "When you're feeding someone a line of bullshit, less is more. Don't over-explain."

"It's not…!" Zach protested.

"Right." David glanced at Mike, who only rolled his eyes and grinned back at him.

THE coffee shop was fairly busy for a Sunday morning, but Brian was able to find a booth in a quiet corner. For some reason, his contact had insisted on meeting him at the ungodly hour of ten-thirty, and between Brian's late night and the drive from the Springs to Denver, he hadn't been to bed yet. It was his own damn fault, of course; he really hadn't intended on staying out so late, but there had been that hot blond he'd been working on all evening, and when the guy had invited him back to his hotel room… well, it had been all Brian could do to get out of there in enough time to get back to his apartment to shower and change out of his club clothes into something more respectable. He hoped this contact would be worth it. The last few weeks on this new assignment had been frustrating as hell; he *knew* there was more to be said on the story, but he'd run into continual roadblocks.

A young guy in jeans and a blue linen sports jacket came into the shop and paused in the doorway a moment before spotting Brian.

Pushing a pair of wire-rimmed glasses back up on his nose, he picked his way through the crowd to the table. "Brian McCarthy?"

"Right. You're Jeff?"

"Jeff Putnam," the guy said, and held out a hand. He was mildly attractive in a nerdy sort of way, but looked nervous.

"Have a seat," Brian said, shaking his hand and giving him his best non-threatening smile. He was an old hand at getting nervous sources to talk. "I was just going to get coffee and something to eat. I don't know about you, but I'm starved. What'll you have?"

"Just coffee. Um… Venti Americano, extra milk," Jeff said, and reached for his wallet. Brian held up a hand as he slid out of the booth.

"My treat," he said. "Least I could do, what with you coming out on a Sunday morning and all."

While he was in the line, Brian kept a discreet eye on his source. It would be just his luck, and in keeping with the way this assignment was going, for the guy to freak out and run away while he was waiting for the coffee and scones. But Jeff stayed put, only glancing up from the tabletop when Brian returned.

"They had cranberry scones," Brian said, "so I thought I'd give 'em a try. Want one?"

"Sure. Thanks." Jeff took the coffee and scone. "So what did you want to talk about? I have to tell you, I haven't seen Zach Tyler since high school—before the kidnapping and stuff."

"That's okay," Brian assured him. "This is really more of a human interest story, what with the two-year anniversary of his rescue coming up. The problem for me is that I can't seem to get a hold of him or the family to talk to; there's so much security with Tyler Technologies that I can't get to them directly. And the locals don't seem inclined to talk. I mean, I can understand them being defensive of the family; they're major employers in the area, and have contracts with the military, who are the other big employers around here. I don't blame them at all. But you're a writer; you know how things are when you can't get information." He nodded at Jeff encouragingly. Jeff nodded back. Brian smiled inwardly. *Bait taken and hook set*, he thought.

"No," he went on, "what I'm looking for is some background, some insight into what Zach was like as a kid, before all that shit happened to him. You know what I mean. You said that you'd been all through school with Zach?"

"Yeah. Yeah, we both went to Foothills Academy. It's a year-round private school, but it takes more than money to get in. Based on test results, the top thirty kids a year from the kindergartners in the area are invited to attend. Tuition's on a sliding scale based on the parents' income, so you have kids like Zach, who are not only smart, but richer than God, and you get kids like me, whose mom raised five kids on her own with a waitress job. Zach paid full price; I didn't pay anything. But we both got the same education, played on the same teams, took the same classes, and hung out together along with two other guys— Frankie Hernandez and Jesse Wilmot. We were pretty good buds. Were on the soccer team the year we won regionals. That was right before Zach disappeared. Put a damper on the awards banquet that year."

"So, you were like Zach's best friend?"

Honesty warred with ego in the guy's face a moment. Honesty won out. "No, it was the four of us, mostly, plus some of the other guys on the team. We were pretty tight. Zach's best friend was probably this older kid, Davey. He was the Tylers' housekeeper's kid. He went to Foothills, too, but he was probably two or three years ahead of us. He was kind of the kid's bodyguard and chauffeur, but he earned his way into the academy. As smart as Zach was, I think Davey was probably smarter. Zach was more of a smartass, though."

"Arrogant?" Brian suggested.

"Oh, no, not that way. He was just—funny. He was always coming up with jokes and stuff. Big on nicknames. For instance, our algebra teacher in third grade was a guy from Norway; had a really heavy accent. Zach called him 'Fortinbras' or just 'Fort' for short."

"'Fortinbras'?" Brian frowned.

"Yeah. From *Hamlet*. The one who comes in at the end after everyone is killed off."

"Oh, yeah, right. The guy who just conquered Poland or something. Not Hitler, the other one." Brian shot him a grin.

Jeff laughed. "Yeah, that's right. Anyway, Zach called him Fort and pretty soon everyone was. He called his parents 'Dick and Jane' from the old reading books; the principal's first name was Kirk, so of course Zach called him 'Captain'. It was just the way Zach was. But he wasn't mean about it. He was a nice kid. People liked him, and not just because of his money. " He sipped the coffee and went on. "That's probably part of the reason you're coming up against resistance in Wesley. The town might be just a suburb of Colorado Springs now, but it had its start as a silver-mining town back in the 1800s, when it was thirty miles from there, and it still thinks of itself as its own entity. And the Tylers have been a part of the town for generations. Rich Tyler's old man started Tyler Technologies back when 'computer' meant a guy with a slide rule. People remember that, and they're protective, you know? And when you got a kid like Zach, that everyone likes, and everyone feels sorry for, then they're even more so. It's an 'us against them' sorta mentality."

"Did you have a nickname too?"

"Yeah." Jeff grinned. "But I'm not sayin'."

"What was his friend Davey's?" Brian asked carefully.

Jeff thought a moment. "It was weird… Daffy? No. Taff. That was it. Something about him being Welsh. Most of us called him Davey, but Zach… Zach always called him Taff."

"DAD, you and Mom don't mind if I skip therapy today, do you? Since Mike's here, and all?"

"No, I don't mind," Richard said carefully. "Are you sure you want to do that? Both sessions? That's two days in a row, since you were out biking with David yesterday."

Zach thought a minute, then said, "Yeah… yeah. I think so. I'll go again tomorrow. I think by this point me taking a weekend break isn't a big deal. Do you?"

Richard regarded his son and smiled affectionately at him. "No, I think you're doing okay, Zach. I know your mother and I are pleased with the way you've opened up the last couple of weeks. You seem like you're feeling a lot better."

"I guess so," Zach said. He leaned back on the couch next to his father and picked at a thread on his jeans. "I'm getting there, I guess."

"Still having the nightmares?"

"Yeah," Zach admitted. "Not as bad as they were. I mean, I can usually get back to sleep after a while, and I usually only have one or two bad ones a night. And I didn't have one at all last night, that I remember. So I'm getting more sleep. I'm not needing to take a nap in the afternoons like a baby anymore."

"Well, your mother would say you're still her baby, but for my part, I'm glad." Richard tentatively put his arm around Zach's shoulder. To his surprise, Zach didn't pull away as he usually did, but settled in the crook of his arm.

"I know it's been hard on you guys," Zach said. "I know I haven't been the easiest person to live with. I know there's a lot of stuff I can't talk about yet and might never be able to. But I do love you guys, you know."

"I know." Richard squeezed gently.

"It's just that sometimes I don't know what you expect, and I don't know what *I* expect, and it's kind of scary." Zach was quiet a moment, then said, "I had a panic attack at Taff's this morning."

"Is that how you hurt your nose?"

Zach reached up and felt his nose with his fingers. "Is it that obvious?"

"It's a bit red and swollen." Richard grinned. "I'm thinking of calling you Rudolph."

"Funny," Zach nudged him with his elbow.

"So what happened? You bump into a wall or something?"

Zach hesitated, then said, "Um, no. Actually… Taff punched me."

Richard froze. "He did *what*?"

"It's not his fault, Dad. I was being a real dick to him. I… well, never mind how it all happened, just trust me. I deserved it and then some. I'm just lucky he wasn't really putting any power behind it."

"Do you want me to talk to him?"

"No! Jesus, no. It was totally my fault. And he felt bad

afterwards."

"David never hit you before," Richard said. "I mean, even when you were kids."

"No. But there were plenty of times I deserved it." Zach grinned at his father.

Richard grinned back. "God, it's good to have you back," he said, and kissed Zach's forehead.

"I'm not there yet," Zach said ruefully. "But I have my moments."

"Zach," Richard said soberly. "You know that whatever you want is okay with your mother and I, don't you?"

"Me."

"What?"

"You said 'with your mother and I'. It's 'with your mother and *me*'."

"I'm a programmer, not a grammarian," Richard said, "and that's not the point. My point is that we don't judge you—we won't, and we never have. You know that, don't you?"

"You mean about me being gay," Zach said. "I know that, Dad. Why bring it up now?"

"Because of David," Richard said.

"Oh." Zach tilted his head so it rested against Richard's shoulder.

"I don't know what's going on between you and David, if anything. I don't need to know. But whatever the two of you want is okay with me and your mom."

"What if what we want is to take over Tyler Technologies?" Zach grinned.

"Go ahead and try—you'll be able to wrest control of it from my cold dead hands," Richard shot back. "Besides, I know neither you nor David is the slightest bit interested in the company."

"Actually, you're wrong," Zach said. "I'm kind of interested. Not enough to actually *work* there, but you know, if you want to occasionally talk about it, or something." He yelped as Richard dug his fingers into his ribs.

"Are you abusing my son, Richard Tyler?" Jane looked over the back of the couch.

"Only in the most parentally necessary of ways," Richard said. He grabbed Zach in a headlock and proceeded to rub his knuckles over his son's head. Then he kissed the top of his head and released him.

"Assault," Zach grumbled, and scrambled to his feet. "Taff done eating yet?"

"Yes, he's in helping Annie clear, which would be a good idea for you too," Jane said sternly. "And Mike's up packing so he'll have that out of the way. What are your plans for the afternoon after therapy?"

"Dad says I can skip therapy today," Zach said. "Since Mike's here. I thought we'd take the Jeep up around Garden of the Gods. Even with his sister living in Gunnison, he's never been there and it's pretty cool."

"Davey going with you?" Jane asked delicately.

Zach snorted. "No, he's got stuff to do. He starts school on Tuesday, you know. And I guess teachers have to have their homework done ahead of time. But he's seen it. I told him we'd be back for supper and he could come by then if he wanted to." He cocked his head at Jane. "That's okay, right?"

"Duh," Jane said, and whacked him gently on the side of the head. He grinned at her.

"And you complain of my abusing him?" Richard said indignantly.

"Yeah, that's *my* job," Jane said, and bent to kiss Richard, then Zach. "Why don't you go help Annie until Mike comes downstairs, love?"

"Sure," Zach said, and went back into the breakfast room.

Richard reached up and hauled Jane over the back of the couch onto his lap. She submitted with a faint shriek. "You going to tell me what you and Annie were talking about in there?"

"I will, if you tell me what you and Zach were talking about in here," Jane said.

"Stuff. Guy stuff."

"Hmph," Jane said. "Well, we were talking girl stuff, so there.

Did he tell you what happened to his nose?"

"Yep. Nothing important. Walked into something. He had a panic attack last night at Annie's."

Jane sighed. "I'd hoped he was done with those."

"Apparently not. Give him time, Jenny. It's been less than two years, and you know what he said just a week or two ago about still having trouble believing it was all over. You remember what they told us at that hostage clinic: it might be years before he's put this completely behind him. But he's so cheerful today, it's like a miracle."

"I think he slept with David," Jane said.

Richard didn't say anything, just held her.

After a moment, she went on. "I'm scared, Richie. What if they do get involved…?"

"If they're sleeping together, I'd say they're involved."

"But what if they break up? What will that do to Zach? David's had several serious relationships already, and he's only twenty-five."

"Jenny, we can't play 'what if' with Zach's life. We have to let him manage it on his own."

"I don't want him hurt."

"Neither do I!" Richard dropped his head back on the couch cushion. "Damn it, Jenny, of course I don't want him hurt again. He's been through so much already. But you know what the shrink says— Zach's got to feel free to make his own choices and to learn to take responsibility for his own actions. We can't protect him any further than we have been." He sighed. "There have been more requests for interviews lately, what with the anniversary coming up. And practically any time I talk to the press about new product or anything, Zach's name comes up."

"We gave them all the information we were going to when he first came back," Jane said indignantly. "What more do they want?"

Richard shrugged. "They weren't happy with what we told them. They want more. They're like bloodhounds, Jenny; they know there's more to the story, and they want it. We didn't make a big deal of Zach's homecoming, but it's gotten out that he's living here now, and they want to talk to him directly. Get his 'perspective' on what happened. Hear it from the horse's mouth."

"We can't," Jane gasped. "Zach wouldn't be able to stand it. As it is, I worry about him leaving the compound at all. Does this mean we have to keep him home?"

"No. No, that wouldn't be good for him. Let's just keep working with the security team at Tyler. Zach's careful about not letting people know who he is and he looks different enough from what he did as a kid that he's been lucky so far."

"His luck's not going to hold forever," Jane said.

"No, but let's hope he's mentally in a better place by then." Richard touched his forehead to hers. "In a worst-case scenario, we give a controlled interview with somebody who'll let us authorize the story; that way we can manage what comes out. But I don't even want to do that to Zach. He needs to have some time to recover before he has to dredge it all up again."

"From your lips to God's ear," Jane whispered. Richard just folded his arms around her and held on tight.

Chapter Seventeen

"I DIDN'T get a chance to look around the one time I was here," David said. "Nice place. This stuff new, or did Alan leave it furnished?"

It was Sunday evening. Mike had headed over to his sister's in Gunnison, and David and Zach had left the house a little while ago, ostensibly to watch some movies at Zach's.

"No, most of his stuff was pretty old by the time he left," Zach said. "The kitchen table was his, but he had this grotty plaid couch I dumped immediately. Mom and Dad gave me the TV for Christmas."

David glanced around in puzzlement. The wine leather couch faced French doors leading out to the balcony overhanging the garage, and there was no sign of a television. "What TV?"

Zach picked up a remote from the end table and clicked a button. A screen descended from the ceiling in front of the French doors, completely blocking out the light and turning that wall into a movie screen. "You can set the size of the image," Zach said, and pressed another button. An ESPN sports show appeared on the screen, covering only a small portion of the center. "Twenty-six-inch," Zach said, and pressed another button. "Thirty-two. Thirty-eight. Forty-two… by six-inch increments, 'til you get to just about the whole screen. And the resolution doesn't change; it's still high-def." He grinned as the screen went black, then the words "Star Wars—Episode IV" crawled across the now-enormous screen.

"You are such a geek. I take it that's not a projection system, though." David went to the wall and fingered the edge of the heavy fabric curtain.

"No, it's new tech. Dad's thinking about buying the company. Not so much for this as for some of their nanotech projects. This is just a toy, though it might be a godsend to the movie theater industry: every showing is as crisp and high-definition as the first, no film to distribute, deteriorate, or jam projectors—no projectors. Just nanoflix."

"Nanoflix?"

"Yeah, that's what I called it. Dad liked the name, though."

The giant star destroyer cruised across the screen as David said thoughtfully, "You ever think about going back to school?"

"I think about it, yeah. You want something to drink?" Zach switched off the screen and it crawled silently back up into its holder on the ceiling.

"No, thanks. So... are you?"

"Drinking? Yeah." Zach turned from the fridge, a Corona in his hand.

"Going back to school."

"No."

"Why not? You're only twenty-two; it's not like you'd stand out or something. Didn't you get that scholarship to MIT?"

"MIT? Are you fucking nuts, Taff? I don't even have a fucking GED, and places like MIT won't even look at people with GEDs, anyway."

"That's bullshit. You could pass the GED in your sleep, and MIT would take you in a heartbeat."

"Because of my dad's money."

"Your dad's money didn't get you the early admission, Zach. You've got brains...."

"I *had* brains," Zach snapped. "Fuck, Taff, the first time I even heard of an iPhone was less than two years ago. I missed the digital revolution. I'm as clueless as a caveman. I listen to Dad talk about shit and he might as well be speaking Klingon. My folks got me the latest and greatest CAD software 'cause they know I used to love playing with it, and I don't fucking understand how to even open the program!" He threw himself on the couch. "I'm a fucking Neanderthal. I can't even work on newer cars 'cause I don't understand their computer systems." He drank, then set the bottle on the end table. "I'm down on points, Taff, and I don't know if I can catch up."

"You don't have to win the game, Zach," David said quietly, "you just have to play." He sat down beside Zach and threaded his fingers through Zach's. "Okay, maybe you're not ready for prime time. Maybe you need to just recover some lost ground. Get the GED, maybe take some classes at UCo...."

"No," Zach said. "Maybe some online classes. I'm not going to sit in a classroom and have people stare at me." He swallowed and his fingers tightened on David's. "Who I am and what I am and how I look—bad publicity for Tyler Tech, Taff. Especially if I'm taking remedial math classes and stuff."

"Fuck Tyler Tech. Hire a tutor, then. Hell, I can tutor you. I'm teaching a *class* on Computer-Aided Design. Sure, it's basic CAD, but you can use it as a refresher. Get you back up to speed. You can even audit some classes if you want. I'll bet the admin at Wesley will let you register under a fake name if your dad asks." He drew Zach's fingers up to kiss them. "It's not an insuperable obstacle, Zach. Just one small step after another."

"I feel like I'm stumbling around in the dark," Zach said wearily. "I don't know where to go or what to do. I gave up in Venezuela, Taff. Nothing was ever going to change except whatever bullshit Esteban was going to pull that day. But it was *familiar*, like it was all I'd ever known—all I ever would know. The only dream I had was to kill Esteban, and I knew that would never happen. I didn't dare think of what would happen after that. But here—now—I've got all kinds of choices, all kinds of options. And I don't feel capable of a single one."

"You are capable of *all* of them," David said fiercely.

Zach said nothing, just turned and slid from the couch to his knees, laying his head against David's thigh. David stroked the thick pelt of Zach's hair as Zach wrapped his arms around David's calves like a drowning man clinging to a piece of driftwood.

After a while David said, "What do you want to do, Zach?"

"I don't know."

"Well, what do you think you might *like* to do?"

Zach was quiet another long moment, then said, "Build things."

"What kind of things? Houses? Buildings?"

"High-speed rail. Fusion power plants. Spacecraft. Nanomedical equipment." Zach looked up at David, a spark in his eyes that hadn't been there before. "Stuff that integrates the green-tech that Dad's working on with stuff that'll make the future happen."

"See?" David smiled. "You do know what you want to do. And it's brilliant. Beautiful." He leaned forward and kissed Zach. "And do you know what I want?"

Zach released David's legs to cup his face. "What?" he breathed.

"I want to watch you do it." David kissed him again and stood. Drawing Zach to his feet, he pulled Zach's face down toward his. "I want to be there when you do it. I want to be right by your side when you show the world what you're made of." He traced Zach's cheek with one finger; his cheek, and his jaw, and his lips. "But you know what I want most of all?"

"What?" Zach whispered again.

"I want you to do what *you* want. Change the world—or not. Build a ladder to the stars—or not. Be what *you* want, 'cause whatever it is, it'll be great because it's you. And I love you."

Zach's eyes were blurry, but he could see well enough to kiss David. "Thank you," he said against those soft lips.

THUNDER rumbles. Esteban looks up from his computer where he's probably watching snuff porn, and says, "Puppy needs a bath." I whimper, knowing what comes next.

He gestures for Che to push the cage out into the middle of the camp, into the clearing that's open to the sky. Lightning flashes to brighten the black sky, but it's a camera-flash on a dark night, fast and fierce and gone instantly. I curl up in a ball as close as I can to the corner of the cage, knowing it won't do any good, that the wire of the cage gives no protection from the violence of the tropical storm. Unimpeded by leaves, the rain will pummel the ground—and me. Sometimes it hails, and while the cage does protect me against the bigger, bone-breaking hailstones, it does nothing to guard me from the stinging, pellet-sized hail. Rain or hail, it doesn't matter; it's going to *hurt.*

But it doesn't. The patter of raindrops is soft, and gentle, and warm. I remember a YouTube video of a choir of people imitating the sound of a storm by rubbing their hands and snapping their fingers. (Why do I remember YouTube? I'd never heard of it before the jungle swallowed me up.) This is like the finger-snapping—the soft pops of raindrops plopping.

I turn my face upward toward the soft rain, my eyes closed. A drop hits my lip and I lick, eager for the sweet taste of rainwater.

It tastes strange, metallic, like copper. Like blood.

I open my eyes.

Taff's dead face gazes down at me. It's scored and bloody, like the rest of his body, spread-eagled across the top of the cage. What I heard as the soft plop of rain are the drops of blood falling from dozens of knife wounds—little cuts, none of which individually would matter, but together have flayed Taff's skin from his bones. His dead eyes stare at me, unseeing.

I scream.

The dead eyes don't blink, but the dead lips form a word: "Zach..."

"ZACH! Zach, come on, wake up!!"

He blinked, and David's face swam into view, David's very alive, very frightened face. "Taff?" Zach's voice was hoarse and his throat hurt.

"Jesus, Zach, scare the fucking shit out of me, why doncha?" David's face was white, his eyes wild.

"Sorry. Nightmare."

"Nightmare, my ass," David said. "That *has* to be an understatement. I've never *heard* screaming like that."

Zach reached up and touched his throat. His skin was wet. "What, did you throw water on me or something?"

"No, dweeb. That's sweat. Fuck, I thought you were having

convulsions. Then I thought one of those panic attacks, but I didn't think you could have one of those in your sleep."

"No, just nightmares."

David sat back on his heels and rubbed his forehead. Zach sat up and grabbed his hand, pulling it away from his face. There was a big scarlet patch on one cheekbone. "I hit you," he said flatly.

"No big," David said. "You were just kind of flailing around and I walked into it. I've had worse." He reached out and brushed his thumb across Zach's lips. "Besides, now we're even for me socking you last night. You okay?"

"Yeah. Fine." Zach threw his legs over the side of the mattress and sat up.

"This happen a lot?" David asked quietly. "The nightmares, I mean?"

"Often enough," Zach said curtly. "That's why I moved up here. Used to wake my parents. Freaked 'em out." He stood and reached for his sweats.

"Where you going?"

"Need a drink. My throat hurts."

He went into the kitchen but bypassed the bottled water in the fridge for the bottle of Scotch on the counter, pouring himself three fingers' worth and tossing that down. He relished the burn on his raw throat before refilling the glass. Then he crossed the floor to the couch, dropped down onto the leather cushions and gazed out the French doors at the lightening sky.

A minute later David joined him on the couch, not saying anything, not touching him, just sitting there. Zach said roughly, "No point both of us being up. Go back to bed."

"Too much adrenaline in the system," David said. "Not sleepy."

"Sorry," Zach said, and took a swig of his drink. "And before you ask, no, I don't want to talk about it."

"Okay," David replied. He was quiet a moment, then said, "Wanna fuck?"

Zach froze in the act of raising his glass to his lips again. After a beat, he said, "Thanks for not asking that question when I had a mouthful of booze. This stuff's expensive."

"I thought about it," David said, "but you're right. Shouldn't waste the good stuff. So." He held up his hand. There was a condom between two fingers. "You—ahem—up for it?"

Zach set his glass on the end table, then reached out and took the condom. Then he said, "Beat you to the bedroom," and took off, David at his heels.

Inside, he stepped to the side as David came in and grabbed him around the waist, tossing him onto the bed. "For the love of pancakes," David gasped, "what the hell do you press?"

"Easily more than you weigh," Zach said, and pounced on him, pinning him to the mattress. "No wrestling shit," he murmured against David's mouth.

"No wrestling shit," David whispered. He wriggled his arms loose from Zach's hold and wound them around Zach's neck. "No shit at all. Make love to me, Zach Tyler. I'm yours."

Zach kissed him leisurely, thoroughly, then abandoned David's mouth for more interesting territory farther south. He loved David's body, the strong, lean muscles, the long bones and graceful conformation. A beautiful package. Then he made the mistake of looking up into that beautiful face as he licked into the divot of his navel and saw David watching him, his heart in his brown eyes.

Zach closed his own eyes. David loved him. David *loved* him. He didn't know what to do. Didn't know if he was even capable of reciprocating. He wanted David, true, but love—that was asking more than he felt ready to give. It was commitment. It was eternity. It was *prison....*

He flipped David over and started back up at David's neck, kissing the nape, safe from those eyes. He licked down the spine, pressing hot, wet kisses to each of the bumps of vertebrae. When he got to the small of David's back, he closed his hands on David's hips, hiking him up on his knees, then pushed his knees apart and licked down David's crease to his opening.

David arched his back, moaning as Zach's tongue stroked him, and his hand went down to curl around his own dick, his other arm supporting him. Zach nuzzled him until David was rocking back with every brush of Zach's tongue; then Zach fumbled for the condom he'd dropped on the bed and reached for the lube on the nightstand.

He eased into David slowly, carefully. They'd only actually fucked the one time last night, and he was worried about David still being sore, but it had been David who'd initiated this, so he figured he was okay. Still, he was careful, and took his time. He eased forward and kissed David again on the nape of the neck.

David turned his head so that he could kiss Zach. "That feels good," he said, a note of surprise in his voice. Zach smiled at him, then kissed him behind his ear. "Good," he said. "Cuz it feels great to me."

"You know," David said thoughtfully, "there *are* other ways of doing this."

"I know," Zach said, and slid his arm around David, across his chest, cupping the front of David's shoulder, pulling him close as he sat carefully back on his heels, David in his lap. "Like this."

"Oh," David said, and then as Zach rocked forward into him, "*oh*."

A shaft of early sunlight had broken through the bedroom window and Zach's movement had brought them into its illumination. Across the room, their bodies were reflected in the big mirror over Zach's dresser. Zach watched them move a moment, seeing David's skin bright in the light, his own dark sweats and dark hair a shadow behind him. "Look at you," he whispered in David's ear. "Look at you—so beautiful." And he was, his slim body a bright shaft against Zach's darkness, his lean thighs splayed wantonly on either side of Zach's, his elegant cock curved high. Zach slid his hand down to play with that lovely thing and looked up to see David's head thrown back against his shoulder, his sleek golden chest glittering with sweat and his breath coming hard. "Open your eyes," he said in David's ear. "Open your eyes and look at yourself. I want you to watch yourself."

"What?" David said in confusion, and opened his eyes. He stared at their reflections in the mirror. "Oh, my God, Zach."

"Watch yourself," Zach said. "Watch how beautiful you are," and he rocked forward again, his hand moving on David's cock. David reached his arms back to circle Zach's neck, freeing Zach from the need to hold him; he released David's shoulder and began to use both hands to caress his lover's body as he made love to him. When he felt David beginning to tense, he said urgently, "Don't close your eyes!" and met David's gaze in the mirror as those dark eyes glazed and his body surrendered to Zach's.

Then Zach was climaxing too, his hands pressing on David's hips and thighs as he plunged deep and came, then fell backward on the bed, David clutched to him. David rolled them both onto their sides and Zach straightened out his legs and spooned himself against David's back, oddly reluctant to disentangle himself.

After a while David said, "Well, *that* was interesting. It's not quite what I had in mind, but it was interesting."

"What did you have in mind?" Zach asked sleepily.

"I was thinking more in terms of face to face," David said. He turned his head to look at Zach. "I'd like to watch you come sometime. I know, I should have been able to see that this time, but quite frankly I was completely out of it. You do that to me, you know. Fuck me into oblivion."

"Is that a good thing?" Zach asked, not completely sure.

"Oh, yeah," David smiled, and kissed him. "Oh, yeah." He kissed him again then curled back into the shelter of Zach's body. Zach lay his head on his pillow.

IT HAD been easily five a.m. by the time they'd gotten back to sleep, so David was surprised when he woke at six-thirty to find himself alone. The apartment was silent, no sound of water running or footsteps, and when he rolled over and felt the sheets, they were cold. He got up and pulled his jeans on before padding barefoot out to the kitchen.

Zach wasn't there, either, but David's cell phone rested on the breakfast bar, so he picked it up and pulled up the Andrew application. "Good morning, David," Andrew said.

"Good morning, Andrew. Can you give me Zach's location, please?"

"I'm sorry, Dave. I'm afraid I can't do that," Andrew said in the voice of Hal from *2001: A Space Odyssey*.

David laughed. Zach had programmed Andrew to say that when he was about twelve. "Funny, Andrew. Where's Zach?"

"According to his cell phone, he's headed northwest on Route 24 at speed toward Cascade," Andrew said. "He had me open the concealed north gate twelve point six minutes ago."

"Thanks," David said, puzzled, and disconnected. Then he saw the piece of paper on the kitchen table.

It read, in Zach's oddly childish scrawl, "Had to go out. See you later." No salutation, no signature. David stared at it a long moment, feeling sick and confused. He let out his breath in an exasperated exhalation. Something told him he'd better get used to that feeling.

ZACH saw David about fifty yards ahead of him as he came over the last rise north of the house. He slowed the Ducati immediately, letting its engine drop rpms until it was a low, barely audible purr, the bike going just fast enough to stay vertical. David had to have heard it, but gave no sign, just kept running at his usual steady speed. Zack kept pace with him until he turned off on the track that would take him away from the main house and toward his own. Then Zach stopped and watched until he vanished before revving the engine again and driving into the garage.

He went upstairs. There was no sign David had ever been there: the bed was neatly made, the towels Zach had left on the floor hung back up, the bedroom garbage emptied and the sink devoid of the glass he'd had his Scotch in last night. The note he'd left for David wasn't on the table; he found it crumpled in the garbage and wondered if it meant anything other than David's tidying up before he left. Maybe David was pissed at him. Maybe he'd decided it wasn't worth the effort. That would make it easier on Zach; the decision taken out of his hands. If David wrote him off, he wouldn't have to worry about any of it. No fear of hurting David; no fear of David hurting him. No decisions to make. Done. Over. Just the rest of his life to go through alone, but that was okay. He could do alone.

He opened the refrigerator and took out juice and a couple of slices of Annie's homemade bread for toast. There was microwave bacon there, too, so he took that out as well and put the whole package on the paper plate he put in the microwave while the bread was toasting.

He ate the toast dry and the bacon crisp to the point of almost burnt, but tasted none of it.

The apartment was so quiet. Why would it seem so unusually so? It wasn't as if he was a noisy tenant at the worst of times. But today the silence was different—more hollow, more echoing.

More lonely.

"Shit," he said aloud, and tossed the paper plate into the garbage. No point in hanging around here; there was a fully equipped gym with his name on it at the house. And gyms didn't care.

Chapter Eighteen

WHEN Zach walked into the sunroom, his mother was telling the shrink, "Oh, we had a lovely day yesterday. Zach's friend the lieutenant came for the weekend, and David came for breakfast, and both Saturday and Sunday we grilled out. Zach took Mike up around the Garden of the Gods. Have you ever been there? The rock formations are just spectacular—oh, hello, honey." Jane smiled at Zach. "I was just telling Dr. Barrett...."

"I heard," Zach said shortly. He dropped into his chair, stretched out his legs and stared at the toes of his boots.

There was silence in the sunroom; then Richard said evenly, "That wasn't terribly polite, Zach."

"Sorry." Zach bit down on a smart-ass remark. His parents didn't deserve to catch the flak from his lousy mood. Even without looking up, though, he knew his parents were exchanging The Look, the one they always exchanged when he was being a dick. And he was. He didn't want to be, but he was. He sighed wearily and kept studying his toes.

"Often," the shrink said to Dick and Jane, "an exciting or enjoyable weekend leaves a sense of let-down behind it. One feels like one can't ever recapture quite the same enjoyment. Which is true, of course. We can't repeat our good days, but we'll have other days just as enjoyable in different ways. Did you have a good time yesterday, Zach?"

Zach shrugged. "I guess. Yeah. It was good. Okay, anyway."

"How are you feeling now?"

"Okay."

"Your body language doesn't seem to agree."

Zach shrugged again.

"Honey, did something happen last night to upset you?"

"No," Zach said, then more slowly, "No.... No, nothing *happened*. I mean, yeah, shit happened, but I'm not upset or anything from that. It was a good evening. Nothing bad happened. Well, I had a nightmare. And I...." he trailed off.

"What did you do?"

"I socked Taff," Zach said curtly. "Accidentally, so it wasn't quite payback for him punching me. But he wasn't mad." He looked up and met Dr. Barrett's eyes. "I'm sleeping with Taff," he said bluntly.

"Is this a new development?"

"Yeah. Since Saturday night." He glanced at his parents. "I figured you guys figured it out."

"Well, we suspected," Richard said. "Pretty confidently."

"How do you and Jane feel about this?" Dr. Barrett asked Richard. Zach looked up to watch their faces.

Richard hesitated, and then said, "Ambivalent."

"Join the club," Zach muttered, and went back to studying his feet.

"Why do you feel ambivalent, Richard?"

Zach's father sighed. "Well," he said, "it's a big step for Zach. We worry about him, but he has to take the opportunities he's presented with, and make the decisions only he can make, and starting a relationship is both a big opportunity and a big gamble. Jane and I both love David too—he's part of our family—but our main concern is and always will be Zach. We don't want him to get hurt, but we have to let him take the chance. It's not comfortable."

"I *want* Zach to have a good relationship with a good person," Jane said fiercely. "And David is a good person. As long as he won't hurt Zach. And David's been Zach's protector all his life, and I think Zach will be safe with David."

"What if I don't *want* to be safe?" Zach demanded. "What if I don't want David as a protector? I mean, Jesus! I'm not a little boy anymore. Okay, I'm not quite a normal grown-up, either, but I can take care of myself. You know," he said roughly, "*I* fuck David, not the other way around."

Jane went scarlet. Richard's hands clenched. "Just because we more or less approve of your relationship with David," he said tightly, "that doesn't mean that the details of that relationship are anyone's business but your own. I'm sure you think that this is an appropriate venue for sharing private information, but there is a limit, Zach."

"Why did you feel you needed to share that, Zach?" Dr. Barrett asked, unruffled.

Zach didn't answer right away. Finally he said, "They think I'm still a little boy. They think that if they're careful enough nothing will ever hurt me. But I'm not a little boy. I may be retarded, but I'm not *young*. I don't want David to protect me. I… I'm not sure yet what I *do* want from him, but I don't want that. But he does. He *does*. I feel safe with him, and that is *not good*."

"Why do you say that?"

"Because nobody's safe. Nobody has the right to feel safe, because it can all be taken away from you. David makes me feel safe and that makes me feel not safe." Zach shot out of his chair and started pacing. "I know, it's stupid. But I don't want to feel that way. I can't let myself feel that way. If I let myself, what will happen when I'm not safe anymore? I won't be ready. I won't be prepared."

"You'll be vulnerable," Dr. Barrett said.

"Yes! And I can't be. I *can't*."

"Zach, being vulnerable is part and parcel of being human."

"Then I don't want to be human," Zach said wildly. "I want to be, to be *Andrew*."

"Do you know what you're protecting yourself from?"

"No. Yes. Everything." He stopped pacing and stood before them, his hands fisted. "I'm scared. I'm really, really scared. And I don't know what the fuck I'm scared of. Everything, I guess. And David makes me feel not scared and that scares me worse than anything else."

"Fear is also a part of being human, Zach," Dr. Barrett said. "There's nothing wrong with being afraid."

"How do you *stop*?"

"Well," he said thoughtfully, "you can look at probabilities and rationalize them, but that doesn't always work. Or you can face whatever it is that you fear. There are different therapies for specific phobias."

"What about pantophobia?" Zach asked dryly.

Jane giggled, surprising everyone including herself. The shrink looked at her in puzzlement.

"It's from Peanuts," she explained. "Lucy's trying to analyze Charlie Brown and she asks him if he has pantophobia, and when she explains that it's fear of everything, he yells '*That's it!*' and she goes rolling over from the force of his yell. I guess you have to see it."

"I remember the cartoon," Dr. Barrett said. "That was in *A Charlie Brown Christmas*, right?"

"I think so."

Zach said, "We always used to watch that every year at Christmas. We haven't since I've been back."

"We will this year," Jane promised.

"Zach, back to your fears. Fear is normal, and most of the time more or less healthy. But not when it prevents us doing something that needs to be done or that we want to do. Maybe for your session this afternoon, you can make a list of things that you fear the most, and we can work on them."

"Okay," Zach said. He dropped back into his chair, stretched out his legs, and went back to studying his toes.

"WOODCHUCK CIDER," David said, and slid a five across the bar. "Keep the change."

"Thanks," Terry said. "How you been, Davey?"

"Decent, decent," David replied, and took the bottle Terry handed him. "I'm back for good, I guess. Got a job teaching at Wesley Community College."

"That so? Teaching what?" Terry opened a Woodchuck for himself.

"Art and design. It's a good gig. I start tomorrow. Thought I'd treat myself before I jump into the grind."

"Beth's sister taught there for a while. Math, I think. She said it was pretty nice there."

"Why'd she leave?"

"Married a Kansan."

"No shit?"

"No shit."

"Flatlanders," they chorused, and clinked bottles. Terry grinned.

"Haven't seen your little buddy around lately," he said. "Not that he's that little anymore. Holy shit, what did they feed the kid while he was away?"

"No much of anything, from what I hear," David said. "He's built up some since he got back, I guess."

"Yeah, musta. I didn't recognize him when he first started coming around here. Took me a few days, but then I heard that his folks had brought him back and figured out who he was. Wasn't what I expected, that's for sure."

"Thought he'd be this poor pitiful me type, didn't you?"

"I did. Nothin' pitiful about that kid."

"Nope," David said wryly. "He's got a mind of his own."

"Couple people come around askin' questions about him, but I ain't talkin'. I don't think anyone's figured out who he is yet, though. Like I said, he's sure a lot different. I remember when Beth worked for Tyler before the kids were born and we'd go to the company picnics and stuff. He was always such a friendly, happy kid. Not any more."

"Who's been asking questions?" David asked suspiciously.

"A couple people. Strangers, mostly. Reporters and that crap. But you know, this is a neighborhood place, not like some of those joints downtown. We know who our people are. And we don't talk about them to strangers." Terry glanced over David's shoulder. "Speak of the devil."

A body settled at the bar next to David, a warm and solid presence. "Taff. Terry."

"Hey, kid," Terry said. "Scotch?"

"What are you guys having?"

"Woodchuck Cider."

"I'll take one of those."

Terry served him the cider and then went off to attend to some other customers. They drank in silence a moment, then Zach asked in a low voice, "Are you pissed at me?"

David considered the question. "No," he said finally. "Not pissed."

"Then what?"

"I don't know, Zach. Not happy." David picked at the label on his bottle. "I'm not sure what I'm feeling right now, but it's not happy."

"I'm sorry. I just had to get out of the house. I didn't want... well, that's not quite true. I *did* want to stay with you. Too much. It scared me."

"You don't trust me not to push. I get it."

"It's not that simple."

"No, it never is." David sighed. "It's okay, Zach. It's a speed bump. Nature's way of telling us to slow down."

"I don't want to slow down," Zach said in a fierce undertone. "I want to be with you, Taff." He turned his head to look at David. "I'm scared as shit but I *want* you."

David closed his eyes as a shudder went through him at the hunger in Zach's voice, in his eyes. "I got it," he said.

"I wish I did," Zach said. "Come home with me, Taff."

David hesitated, then shook his head. "Not tonight. My first class is at ten and I gotta be there by nine to get stuff set up. And I want to go running in the morning. I need to get to bed at a reasonable hour."

"You will. I promise," Zach whispered.

David shuddered again. "Fuck," he muttered.

Zach leaned over so his shoulder brushed David's. "That's what I had in mind," he murmured.

"Hey," Terry said as he came by with a handful of empties, "I meant to ask you—you guys in a fight or something?"

"What?" Zach frowned.

"Well, your nose is all swollen"—Zach put his hand over his nose automatically—"and Davey's got a black eye."

Zach turned to David in surprise. "What?" He put his hand under David's chin and turned his head. "Fuck, Taff! You do!"

"It's not that bad," David said.

It wasn't, just a slight discoloration, but still noticeable. He'd been standing on David's other side, so hadn't seen it. "Jesus, I'm sorry."

"No big," David said dismissively. "It doesn't even hurt. It'll go away in a day or two."

"And in the meantime you start teaching with a honking big black eye," Zach said remorsefully. "I'm sorry, Taff."

"You sock him?" Terry asked interestedly.

"Accidentally," David assured him. "Shit happens, you know?"

"Don't I," Terry said, and carried the bottles over to the recycler.

"Well," Zach said thoughtfully, "if you have a black eye, maybe that will intimidate the students so they don't give you a hard time."

David laughed. "It's college, Zach, not high school. The kids are there because they want to be there."

"I wouldn't know." Zach finished his Woodchuck and pinned down a five on the counter with the bottle. "Well," he said reluctantly, "if you don't want to come home with me...."

"No," David said, "but you could come home with me."

Zach raised his head and gave him a hopeful puppy look. "Seriously?"

David sighed. "Yeah, seriously. And if you're trying to look like a bad-ass, puppy eyes don't help, dweeb. But you gotta let me get to sleep at a reasonable time and no nightmares, okay? *And* we go running in the morning."

"Okay."

A quick grin flashed on David's face and he added, "Besides, I moved the full bed from the guest room into my room this afternoon. It's still not as comfortable as your king, but a hell of a lot better than the twin."

Zach was grinning widely. "Excellent," he said enthusiastically.

David shook his head.

Chapter Nineteen

"YEAH, it went fine," David said, his cell phone tucked between his ear and his shoulder as he finished putting away the art supplies in the closet. "I'll tell you more if you bring a pizza by about nine. I'm starving."

Zach said, "Why didn't you stop and eat dinner? I thought you said you had a break at six."

"I had kids with questions after my class."

"You gotta make sure you eat," Zach said disapprovingly. "Don't let it happen again."

"Yes, Mother," David said. "I'm packing up now and should be home in a little bit. I'll provide the liquid refreshment and a salad; you provide the pizza. I think Mom has set-ups in your freezer; cook it before I get home, because I am not willing to wait."

"Nag, nag, nag," Zach retorted.

David grinned and disconnected. He was almost done, ready to go home, as tired as he'd ever been in his life, but with a real sense of accomplishment. It was going to be a good move. The kids in his Introduction to Watercolor and Basic Drawing classes were enthusiastic and interested; the ones in his CAD classes less so, since CAD was a required course for the tech program, but still most of them were determined to do well, if the number of questions they'd had after each class was any indication. And they were all subjects he was comfortable with, so that was cool. The kids had all been impressed with the fact that he'd done internships with both ILM and Weta, and that seemed to add to their enthusiasm.

But teaching five classes was going to be tough. The two

traditional art classes only met on Tuesdays and Thursdays, but the CAD classes were Monday through Thursday, with optional labs on Fridays. He had the suspicion that he'd be playing catch-up on his lesson plans during his off-periods on Fridays; these kids were chewing through his carefully ordered syllabi faster than he'd allowed for. He grinned to himself. Ah, better overworked than bored.

He turned off the lights in the art room and locked the door, hiking his backpack higher on his shoulder. Footsteps sounded down the hall, and he turned to see Bill Hernandez.

"How did it go?" Bill asked cheerfully.

"Great," David said enthusiastically. "These kids are awesome. I'm gonna really enjoy working with them. A couple of them brought in some of their own work for me to look at; I think there's some real talent there."

"I heard you yourself are working on a gallery show this fall?" Hernandez fell into step beside David.

"Yeah, I know someone in the Springs who's expressed interest in showing some of my stuff. I've got most of it in storage right now, but there are some pieces I've had good feedback on. That's for later this summer. Speaking of which, Frankie coming home on break?"

"No, he's got a summer associate position at a big firm in Chicago," Bill said. "He'll get home when he can, I guess, but these are the connections he's gotta make if he's going to get a position after graduation. Gone are the days when you're guaranteed a job anywhere."

"No fooling. Frankie'll be fine, though," David assured him. "He's a smart kid."

"Yeah, he's top of his class, so I guess I shouldn't worry, but I do."

"You're a parent," David said. "Well, when he does come home, let me know. I'd like to touch base with him again. Maybe we can talk Zach into going out for a beer or something."

"Frankie'd like that," Bill said.

"Well, I'll see you," David said as they reached the door. "I've got to get home and get some sleep before I have to deal with those cannibals again tomorrow."

Bill laughed. "See that you do," he admonished. "You need all your energy for this bunch."

THE gatehouse was quiet when David got home. He let himself in the front door and dropped his gear on the couch before dropping himself beside it. "God," he groaned, "and I get to do this all again tomorrow...." It had been a while since he'd had to jump to someone else's schedule, and it would take some getting used to. It wasn't as bad as when he'd worked for MoMA, though; fourteen-hour days were the norm there. This was only—he checked his watch—twelve hours. He groaned again.

His cell phone rang and he climbed to his feet to get the phone out of the pocket of the jacket he'd slung over the opposite end of the couch. Figuring it was Zach, he headed for the kitchen to start putting together the salad he'd promised as he answered without checking the number. "Hello?"

"Hey, Davey." The voice was sweet, with just a hint of a Jersey accent.

"Jerry?"

"Yeah, it's me. I just wanted to call and see how your first day of school went."

"I can't believe you remembered the date."

"Yep. I recall you were kind of excited about it even when you were trying not to be for my sake," Jerry's voice was wistful. "So how was it?"

"Good. No, great. I think I'm really going to like it. It's gonna be a shitload of work, but that's okay. It'll be easier once I get into the routine."

"That's great," Jerry said, and David could hear the smile in his voice. That was one of the things he'd always loved about Jerry. He couldn't hide his feelings to save his soul, even over the phone.

He opened the refrigerator to get out the baby spinach and radicchio. "Yeah, I think it is."

"I'm glad. How's Zach?"

David sighed faintly. "Fucked up. But he's improving."

"Yeah. PTSD is like that. When I was doing PT with the hospital, I worked with a lot of returning vets. It was grueling for me; I can't imagine what it must be like for them. That was part of the reason I went into sports medicine instead. I just couldn't handle the stress."

"Yeah, you always were too soft-hearted," David said affectionately.

"And you always wanted to take care of everybody," Jerry shot back, just as affectionately. "But I'm glad to hear he's getting better. Are you guys... you know, together yet?"

"Yeah." David opened the cabinet and took out the salad bowl. "Just this weekend. It's not going to be easy, though."

"No, I never thought it would be, Davey." Jerry's voice had gone serious. "I warned you about that, remember? But you've never really wanted anyone but him, so you better God-damned make it work."

"Yeah. I know. I am sorry, you know."

There was a knock at the back door, and David opened it. Zach came in with the pizza in a paper bag, started to speak, and stopped when he saw David was on the phone. Instead, he just waved with his free hand and moved around David to put the pizza on the table.

"Yeah, I know you're sorry. That's the hardest part," Jerry said wistfully. "We were good together and I know you loved me, and you know I love you. But sometimes love just isn't enough, is it?"

"No," David said. He put the bowl down and walked to the far side of the kitchen, leaning against the breakfast bar that separated the kitchen from the living room. "Sometimes it's not. God, Jer...."

"I know." Jerry took an audible deep breath. "That's the other part of why I'm calling, Davey. I just need to ask one more time: is there any chance in hell for us? Is there any way you're coming back to me?"

David swallowed and put his hand over his eyes. After a moment, he said raggedly, "No. Not... no."

"I didn't think so. That's okay. I knew that." Jerry let out a soft exhalation, then said, "I wanted to tell you before you heard it from any of our other friends. I've started seeing someone. He's not you, but he's a good guy. I think we have a future, or at least the possibility of a future."

"Do I know him?" David asked in a low voice.

"No. I met him at Kathryn's. He's an accountant—and despite that, a funny guy. You'd like him."

"Right." David laughed, a short, sharp, humorless bark.

"Seriously," Jerry said. "In a year or two, I'll introduce the two of you."

"Fuck, Jerry," David said miserably, "how the hell did we get here? It was so great in the beginning…. Was it really all my fault?"

"Yeah," Jerry said, "but I knew that going into it. So it's equally mine. And don't think of it as fault or not fault, failure or not failure. It's just the way the world works, David, my love. 'Merry meet and merry part, and merry meet again.' That's what life is about. We're just at the merry part stage."

"And merry meet again," David echoed. He swallowed. "Okay. In a year or two, introduce us. And I'll introduce you to Zach."

Zach looked up from where he was studiously cataloging the contents of the refrigerator. David tried to smile at him and managed a quirk of the lips.

"I'll look forward to that. In the meantime, Davey, keep in touch, please? I don't want to lose you completely."

"You won't."

"I love you, Davey."

"Love you too, Jer."

ZACH tried not to flinch at the words David whispered into the cell phone, or notice that David's dark eyes were glittering with unshed tears. He turned back to the refrigerator and took out a bottle of beer, not even paying attention to which one it was.

Behind him, David said in a voice thick with the tears he was refusing to shed, "I've got to change. I'll be back in a minute."

"Take your time," Zach mumbled.

He waited until David had left the room before sinking down on one of the kitchen chairs and putting his head on the table. "Fuck," he said aloud. This wasn't good. Jerry had apparently gotten a new boyfriend and David was not taking it well. *Shit,* he thought.

The back door opened and Annie came in, a cloth grocery bag in either hand. "Oh, hi, Zach," she said, puzzled.

Zach looked up. "Hi," he said.

"Is Davey home?"

"Yeah. He said he was going upstairs to change or something. I brought a pizza."

"I see that. Looks like someone started a salad."

"Yeah. Taff did. But he got a phone call. I think it was bad news." Zach heaved himself up out of the chair. "Maybe I better go home."

"What kind of bad news?" Annie put the bags down on the counter and started putting the groceries away.

"I don't know. It was his boyfriend—Jerry? I think he broke up with Taff."

Annie frowned. "David and Jerry broke up a long time ago, Zach. Well before he came back here."

"Maybe," Zach shrugged. "But I guess it's for good now. He's got a new boyfriend and Taff was pretty upset. I better go."

"No," Annie said decisively. "You better not. Go up and see if Davey's okay. I'll finish the salad and put it and the pizza in the fridge. You guys can heat it up again later if you want it."

"He won't want me hanging around," Zach said. "Not now."

Annie blinked. "Now why would you say something so incredibly stupid, Zach? You're a bright boy, and that was just plain dumb. Go see to David." She gave him a gentle push.

He hesitated a minute, then at her stern expression, turned and went up the stairs.

DAVID'S door was ajar; Zach pushed it open gently and stood watching a moment. David sat motionless on the floor by the bed, his arms around his knees, his head down and his cell phone held in both hands in front of his knees. The screen was blank. Zach sighed soundlessly, then sat down on the floor next to him, leaning back against the box spring. David didn't move. Then Zach lifted his arm and draped it over David's shoulders, and David started to cry, at first quietly, then louder and more fiercely, until he was shaking with the force of his wracking sobs. Zach didn't say anything, just sat holding him while he cried. He took the cell phone from David's nerveless fingers and reached up to set it on the nightstand, then put both arms around his lover and held him.

Finally David's sobs eased and he lay quietly back against Zach's shoulder. Zach smoothed the honey-blond hair back from his forehead. "You okay?" he asked softly.

"Sorry," David muttered.

"It's okay. Jerry's got a boyfriend, huh?"

"Yeah." David wiped his face with his hand. "Stupid of me to get upset. It's not like I didn't expect this to happen. I mean, he's sweet, and gorgeous and smart and anyone would be lucky to be with him. And I did leave him, not the other way around. But it still hurt. Isn't that stupid?"

"No," Zach said, and kissed him. David's lips were damp and salty and soft; he sighed faintly and leaned into Zach, putting an arm around his neck. Against his mouth, Zach said, "But he's not the only one who's sweet and gorgeous and smart, and I am so fucking lucky you chose me instead of him. God, Taff."

"Shut up and kiss me," David murmured, and Zach obliged. They necked a while, sitting on the floor, then Zach eased away and got to his feet, bending to lift David in his arms. "Fuck," David said in disbelief, "you *are* strong."

"Yeah," Zach shrugged, and set David down on the bed and pulled the linens away from the bottom sheet. "I see your comforter's a little small for this bed."

"Yeah, I probably need a new one, anyway. I think Mom made it for me when I was like six."

"It smells like you."

"Is that good or bad?"

"Good," Zach said, and unbuttoned David's oxford shirt before pushing him gently down on the pillows. He opened the shirt and ran his hands down David's chest and abdomen. "Pretty," he said. "I like that you're not all bumpy and muscular. Just lean and sleek. A 'wee sleekit beastie'."

"Great," David said in mock despair. "And I'm not so wee. I'm almost as tall as you are. I'm just not muscle-bound like you. And what's next? You'll say you like the fact that I don't have any hair on my chest?"

"You do." Zach used his fingernails to pluck one of the fine, almost invisible strands. David batted his hand away.

"Ouch, that hurts!"

"Whiner. Besides, I don't have that much either." Zach made a face. "Guess neither of us have a lot of testosterone or something."

"You have plenty for me," David said. "Besides, guys with hairy chests usually go bald. I like the fact that your dad still has lots of hair."

"Got a thing for Dick, Taff?" Zach grinned down at him as he unbuttoned David's khakis and slid them down his legs.

"Just yours," David murmured as Zach bent to kiss David's belly. He ran his hands over Zach's head. "Your hair's growing," he said, still in that sleepy murmur. "I can almost get my hands through it."

"Time for a haircut." Zach kissed David's hip, then nuzzled his groin, his cheek against the curve of David's cock. "God, you smell so good. Makes me want to eat you up."

"Come up here," David said, patting the comforter at his side. "I wanna kiss you."

"Not yet. I've got something I'm interested in here." He slid his arms under David's thighs, lifting his hips. "Push that pillow under your butt."

David obeyed and Zach let David's rear settle on the pillow, but kept his upper arms under David's legs, holding him so he could gently mouth David's balls. David groaned faintly. "Feels so good," he mumbled.

Zach smiled and rolled David's balls in his mouth, playing gently with them with his tongue. He tasted so good, spicy and musky, salty and sweet, all at the same time. David shifted, his hand coming down to curl around his cock and rub his thumb across the head; Zach reached up and put his hand over David's. "Let me take care of you for a change, Taff," he whispered. "Let me...." And he dragged his tongue over the silky skin of the tip of David's cock. David moaned again, and Zach slid his mouth down to bury his nose in the soft curls at the base, his free hand cupping David's testicles. David turned his wrist beneath the hand that held his and laced his fingers through Zach's, holding on tightly as Zach swallowed, taking David deep.

David lay under Zach's hands and mouth, exhausted from the crying jag and lost in wonder at the gentleness Zach was showing him. Sex with him before had been fierce and athletic, and David had loved Zach's hungry passion. But he didn't realize that he wanted this kind of loving, too, had missed it ever since he'd broken up with Jerry. When he finally came, it was still powerful, but slow, more a wave running through him than the electric shock of climax that rougher, wilder sex brought; a deep, easy, rippling sensation that had him arching his back and rocking up into Zach's warm, welcoming mouth.

Zach came up beside him then and lay on the pillow, smiling at him. "Was it good?" he asked.

David smiled lazily back at him. "Amazing. Where did you learn to do that?" As a kid, Zach had been sweet-natured, but he'd changed so much since his return that David hadn't realized that Zach could still show a tender side. How had he managed to keep the gentleness he'd always had as a kid through the long night of his captivity?

The smile faded from Zach's face and his eyes went shuttered again. "I just did what felt good," he said coolly.

"Shit," David said, "I'm sorry. I didn't mean anything...."

"I know." Zach swallowed hard, then said, "Esteban didn't make me do that much... only a couple of times. I think he was afraid of me in that way. I mean, he didn't make me do it until he knew for sure he'd broken me, but afterwards, once when I was, he sort of patted my head and I couldn't help myself. I growled at him." He shuddered. "He hit me then, but he didn't make me suck him off any more after that. I was glad. He smelled bad."

David rolled over and put his arms around Zach. "Never again," he said fiercely. "From now on you belong to *me*, Zach Tyler. And you make the choices, okay? I loved that. *Loved* it. But it's always gonna be your decision, got it?"

Zach gazed back at him with solemn eyes. "Why are you so good to me, Taff?" he asked in a small voice. "Why did you give up Jerry for me? Why did you come back here when for all you knew I could have been a ravening lunatic—more of a ravening lunatic than I already am?"

"I had to take the chance," David said. He smoothed his fingers over Zach's face, feeling the tiny scars along his jawbone, the rough sandpapery whiskers on his cheek. "I had to know if your captivity changed that one important thing about you."

"Which important thing?"

"Whatever it was that made you kiss me that afternoon. I'm hoping it was love."

"I've never kissed anyone but you," Zach said abruptly.

David blinked. "What?"

"I've never kissed anyone but you. That kiss—that was the only time I ever kissed anyone. Until Saturday. I didn't *want* to kiss anyone but you. I still don't."

"Good," David said, and kissed him. "Do you want to make love?" He slid his hand up Zach's jeans-clad leg.

"No," Zach said with a grin, "I want to eat pizza. Get under the blankets and I'll go get it."

Chapter
Twenty

"SO, I talked to Maggie today," Zach said as he dug his fork into the bowl of salad he and David were sharing.

David had been asleep when Zach came back with the bowl of salad, a platter of warmed-up pizza, and two bottles of water; Zach had set it all down on the dresser and pulled the comforter over David, sitting down at his drafting table to wait for his lover to wake up. A minute or two later, he had, blinking in confusion a moment before sitting up and giving Zach a sleepy smile. "Sorry," he'd said. Zach had told him no problem, and now they were sitting with their legs folded under, Zach on top of the comforter and David underneath with it tucked around his waist, the pizza platter and bowl of salad balanced on the comforter between them, just as they had when they were kids and Zach stayed over with David for one of Annie's absentee dinners.

David finished chewing his bite of pizza, then said, "Maggie? What about?"

"I asked if she could tutor me for my GED," Zach replied. "She asked me a whole bunch of questions, and when we were done, she said she thought that with intensive study I might be able to get it by the end of the summer. Then I talked to Dad this afternoon and he's going to talk to some of the professors he knows at UCo, and see if he can't get some of them to tutor me this fall and winter, and then maybe I can apply at MIT for next fall. Depending on how the tutoring goes. Might not really be for another year or two, but I've kind of decided to do that, so the timing is flexible."

David was staring at him, his pizza slice hanging limply from his fingers. "What? When did you decide all this, Zach?"

"I thought about what you said. And I thought, so what if I missed a couple years of high school? I'd already gotten the early admission thing from MIT. So it should mostly just be trying to remember what I knew, not so much learning things I didn't, right? And I thought about you offering to tutor me in CAD, and if you're still up for it, I'd like that. But I need stuff like biology and math, not to mention the usual core classes you gotta take, like literature and history and that. I thought Maggie's really smart with that stuff, and better than you at the history and literature, so if she can give me some real intense tutoring then maybe I can test out of some of the classes, and Dad has a lot of friends at UCo that he thinks would be willing to take some time tutoring me too. Talking with Maggie made me think that maybe you're right, I'm not so much stupid as I am undereducated, and that's fixable. And my therapy yesterday and today were about fear and dealing with fear, and I realized in my afternoon session today that most of what I'm afraid of is people making judgments about me and if I don't do anything to, to *improve* myself, then I deserve whatever judgments they make."

Taking a bite of pizza, David chewed a moment, then said thoughtfully, "Whoa. Info dump. Let me take a minute to process, okay? Cuz this is, like, completely a new direction for you."

"Yeah," Zach said anxiously. "You don't think it's stupid, do you?"

"Hell, no," David replied.

"Good. Because your opinion is important to me." Zach sighed faintly.

David brushed his fingers across Zach's hand. "I have a good opinion of you, Zach. I've always had a good opinion of you. Just the fact that you survived as well as you did all the horrible stuff that bastard did to you—that alone makes you a hero in my book. The rest is gravy." He grinned. "Really *good* gravy, like Mom makes for breakfast, the kind with the fabulous sausage in it." This time, he wriggled his eyebrows significantly. "Sausage *and* meatballs *and* gravy…"

"You're a moron," Zach said, laughing. "A sick, sick moron."

"Seriously," David said. "This is just awesome. Not only because I think you can do it, and do it well, but because it's moving forward.

You're taking control of your life instead of letting that bastard keep ruling it from beyond the grave." He took Zach's hand in his. "Sometimes I wish you *had* been the one to kill Esteban, instead of Pritzger and his dudes. Just because you deserve to have that revenge on him. But really, I think that it's better you didn't. Because that would have… I don't know, damaged you, you know? It would leave more scars on your soul than you have on your body. I can't imagine how it would feel to kill someone, but it must be fucking awful, even if you hate the guy. Even if he tried to destroy you like he did. But sometimes I think you feel like by not killing him you left something undone. This, though, this is so good, because it's you taking control again. You sort of killing Esteban, without actually killing him." David studied Zach's suddenly closed face. "I'm sorry. I don't mean to remind you of all that. But it's good, see? You're moving on."

"Yeah," Zach said expressionlessly. He put his half-eaten slice of pizza on the plate. "You want any more?"

"No, I'm good."

"Okay." He got up and picked up the platter and the bowl. "I'll take these down on my way out."

"Whoa—wait a minute," David said, confused. "You're leaving?"

"I probably should."

"Why?"

Zach stared down at the dishes in his hands. "It's late. You wanted to get up early to run."

"Not that late, and yeah, I'm tired, and yeah, I do plan to get up early to run. But you don't have to go. You could just stay over. We don't have to do anything if you don't want to. But we could if you do."

There was a long silence, then Zach said finally, "Okay. I'll just bring this stuff downstairs. But I'll come back."

"That's all I ask, dweeb," David said affectionately. "That you come back."

DAVID didn't know.

Mechanically, Zach moved around the kitchen, putting away the leftover pizza and salad, washing and drying the dishes and putting them into the cabinets, leaving the kitchen as tidy as David had left his yesterday morning. He understood now why David had done so: the mindlessness of his task kept him from focusing on what was really bothering him.

Too soon, though, he was done; the kitchen couldn't get any cleaner. Zach was left with nothing to do but as he promised, go back upstairs to David. Who *didn't know.*

He didn't know why it shocked him that David hadn't been aware of the facts. David himself had told him weeks ago that he knew little about Zach's experiences, and it wasn't like it was common knowledge anyway. His parents knew, of course, and Dr. Barrett; he'd assumed that Annie was in the loop, too, since she and his mother kept no secrets from each other. But there was no reason for David to know. Except that he'd fallen back into the habit of believing that David knew everything about him. All-seeing, all-knowing David, who never let Zach pull anything over on him, always one step ahead of him in the game. Even when he'd told Zach how little he knew of Zach's captivity, Zach hadn't realized on the gut level that he really *didn't* know anything about it. When Zach had told him about being Esteban's whore, David hadn't seemed as surprised as he was furious. Maybe that had fooled Zach subconsciously. Maybe that was why he was so shocked now at David's innocence.

He folded the dishtowel neatly and set it on the granite countertop beside the sink. The worst thing about the situation was that he'd been working under the assumption that David knew, and accepted it. Everything he'd been building in the last few days, every dream he had that this might actually work out, that David loved him enough to look past the scars, the panic attacks, the nightmares, the erratic behavior: everything had been predicated on the belief that David already knew the worst about him.

He swallowed against a heart that was beating too fast. It was too late. He couldn't let things change now. David was *his* and he was David's, and it would kill him if David rejected him at this point. He'd put himself out there, his scars and his neuroses and his nutjob behavior, and left himself vulnerable to David; and the idea of David walking away, leaving him hanging out there without him, was a cold fire in his chest, a pounding ache in his head, and chill numbness in his hands. He caught his breath. Losing David wasn't an option.

David can't ever find out. The voice in Zach's head was his own, but it was stark and cold, blasting through Zach's mind like a bitter winter wind, leaving behind a stunning clarity. The tension leached out of his body; feeling came back into his hands, his head stopped aching. It was a decision made all unconsciously, instantaneously. David couldn't ever know. No matter what, he could never let David know. He had to protect David from the truth. David, and this fragile new relationship they were building.

And it wouldn't be lying, not quite. He just wouldn't correct David's suppositions about Esteban's death. He'd have to make sure that his parents and Annie didn't tell him, but if they hadn't over the course of the last two years, they probably wouldn't. And Annie had kept in close contact with David over those years. No, he'd confirm it with his folks, but he was pretty sure they wouldn't tell David anyway. He took a long slow breath and let it out just as slowly. No. The subject would never come up, and he would never lie about it, and David would never know.

He went back upstairs quietly. David was asleep; Zach went and dug out a pair of relatively subdued plaid cotton pajama pants from the garish collection in David's dresser, and changed out of his jeans and into the pajamas, then eased into the bed beside David, trying not to wake him. David's eyes didn't open, but as soon as Zach had settled, he'd turned into Zach's arms, nuzzling unconsciously at Zach's T-shirt-covered chest. Zach slid his arm under David's neck and settled back into the pillows, letting David's head rest on his shoulder, the weight and the warmth so natural, so comfortable, so *comforting*, that he drifted almost immediately to sleep.

Chapter
Twenty-One

"BALANCE and symmetry are not the same thing," David said, pacing up and down in front of his Introduction to Drawing class. "Symmetry is balanced, true, but it's a static form. The eye settles on the symmetry and goes no further, doesn't invest in the piece. A good composition requires movement, to draw the observer in. The movement of the eye around the artwork makes the observer invest in the message that the artist is trying to convey. Balance creates the illusion of movement within the composition."

"How can you have balance and movement at the same time?" one of the students asked in puzzlement.

"Dancers do it," David said. "And martial artists...." He swung around into a side kick in demonstration, halting the movement halfway, with his foot in the air, his body in counterbalance. "Martial artists, and dancers, and athletes always have to be in balance, otherwise the power behind the movement is lost," he went on, holding the position effortlessly. "In art, you always want to make the observer feel that he is looking at a frozen moment in time; that any moment the action is going to continue. The way to do that is to compose the piece so as to draw the observer into the picture. Keep the eyes moving. Make them notice details. Make them see the art breathe. Make them believe that the next movement is only a second away." He finished the kick and swung back into his beginning position. "Balancing the elements of the composition so that the eye keeps moving is the challenge we're taking up next. You've had some experience with shapes and shading; now we're going to integrate those into a composition that contains both balance and movement. Between now and your next class, I want you to look at as many different paintings in as many different styles as you can and see if you can recognize how the artists use motion and balance. Good paintings, mind you, not your little brother's refrigerator art!" He grinned at them as they laughed. "Although, who knows? He might be a budding Picasso. Anyway, Thursday's class will be an audio-visual extravaganza, which I'm sure you're thrilled about. See you Thursday." He pointed to his eyes with two V'd fingers, then pointed the fingers back at them. "Look for balance. Look for movement. Look. Now get."

A few of them came up after class to ask him questions, a couple of them girls who he suspected just wanted to flirt with him. He was smilingly polite, but dismissed them as quickly and courteously as he could.

To his surprise, the last person waiting to talk to him at the back of the art room wasn't one of his students. It took a minute for him to connect the name and face. "Brian, right?" he said coolly. "What brings you to my humble classroom? Looking for art lessons?"

"No, thanks," Brian said, grinning. He held out his hand. "Formal introductions. Brian McCarthy. David Evans, right?"

David shook his hand reluctantly. "Right. So what can I do for you, Brian McCarthy? Aside from the obvious, and this is a completely inappropriate venue, so I'm hoping that this has nothing to do with why you hang out at places like Fat Charlie's. Because if it does, I'm kicking your ass from here to the front door."

Brian held up the hand David had just released. "No inappropriateness involved. Besides, I know you're involved right now, and as attractive as I find both of you, I'm cool with that. I wasn't for a while, you know. You strike me as a kind of laid back, low-key type of guy, and I couldn't see how you would be good for him. He's built up such a thick wall of ice around himself that I couldn't see how anyone like you could get through. After that scene at Terry's that one time, it surprised the hell out of me to find out that you were together. But I see now I was wrong about that."

"What changed your mind?" David asked, unwillingly curious.

"You did. Just now, really." Brian leaned back against the wall and folded his arms, regarding him thoughtfully. "The passion that you have for your work. Most people—and I'm guilty of it as well—think of passion as hot, fiery, impulsive. But listening to you made me realize that passion can be a deep, warm, steady flame too. The kind of fire that keeps a man warm at night—or melts an ice wall that would drown a flashier spark. You've got that kind of passion in you. I was a fool to misjudge you that way."

"I take it you think I've got something you want," David replied suspiciously.

"Oh, I'm not the patient kind, not really. You are. And he needs that. And he wants you—he called your name once, when he came screwing me. Made it pretty damn clear to me, anyway." Brian cocked his head. "Do you know the real meaning of the word 'passion'?"

"Suffering," David said.

Brian tilted his head in acknowledgement. "Suffering. And of course 'compassion'—fellow suffering. You suffer for him, don't you? I can't do that, and that's what he needs. Someone to share that, until he deals with what he needs to deal with himself."

"How do you know he's got things to deal with?"

Brian shrugged. "Man that closed off is that way for a reason."

"Seems like you've given him a lot of thought for someone who's not interested."

"I didn't say I wasn't interested. I just know how things are."

"So what did you want from me?"

"I just wanted to ask you some questions and maybe a favor."

David turned back to the big table he used as a desk and started putting his class's latest projects into a neat pile. "You can ask. No guarantees I'll answer."

"Well," Brian breathed. "At least you're honest. And I appreciate that. First off, Taff—you don't mind if I call you 'Taff' do you?"

David jerked around, a chill settling in his chest. "Yeah, I mind," he gritted out through clenched teeth. "Don't."

"Sorry." Brian raised his hands in apology. "I just heard that was your nickname—or is it only Zach that calls you that?"

"None of your fucking business," David snarled. "And if that's what you're here for, to snoop around about Zach, then you can just piss off. I don't talk about Zach."

"No," Brian said with a smile. "I know. I'm not asking you to talk about him, if you don't want to. I *am* asking if you could talk *to* him for me."

"No."

"David—just listen a minute."

"What are you, some kind of fucking reporter?" David swore.

"I'm not a reporter. I *am* a journalist...."

"Same damn thing. Get lost."

"No, it's not. A reporter files a report. A journalist writes a story. Zach has a fascinating, important story to tell. People don't understand what goes on when someone's taken hostage. It happens so often nowadays, all over the world, and people have become numb to it. They need a real person to associate with it, someone whose name they recognize. Someone who's *real* to them in a way that other people aren't. A face they can recognize, identify with...."

"Very noble," David said sarcastically. "And I suppose you get nothing out of this?"

"A story," Brian admitted with a grin. "A sale, a byline. Hell, maybe a fucking Pulitzer. Yeah, I get something out of it. Zach will get something out of it, too, something he needs more than all the support and love and *suffering* you can give him. Closure."

"Bullshit closure," David snapped. "He'll get David Letterman and Oprah and Jay Leno and Larry King and every two-bit *journalist* who wants to jump on the bandwagon digging into his life. He won't be able to walk down the street without some asshole trying to get his fucking picture or autograph. And why? Because he was *tortured*? No thank you. You stay the fuck away from Zach or so help me I will break your writing arm. Got it?"

Brian held up his hands again. "I take it that's 'no'," he said dryly. "I got it." He regarded David thoughtfully. "It's good you're with him," he said finally. "It doesn't make it easier for me, but it's good to know someone's got his back. See you around."

"Not if I see you first," David shot back, but Brian was gone.

HE DIDN'T even bother to stop at home, just drove straight to Zach's, seething all the way.

One of the garage doors was open, the interior brightly lit against the deepening twilight. He pulled the car around to the side by the exterior entrance to Zach's apartment, then walked back around to the front of the garage to look into the illuminated bay.

Zach straddled a bench, holding a piece of equipment up to the light, frowning at the object in his hands. His hair had grown out some; a lock fell over one eye and he blew upward absently to get it out of his way. David had seen him do that a thousand times before, but never since his return; for a brief moment, he saw the fifteen-year-old Zach, tousled hair hanging in his eyes, the bright light limning shadows along his high cheekbones, elegant nose, and sharp jaw. Then Zach shifted on the bench and the illusion was lost, and it was Zach the man he was watching—his features still fine, but stronger and more defined now, the jaw shadowed with a day's beard, the arch of the neck and curve of the shoulder strong with a man's muscle.

He must have made a sound or something, because Zach looked up at him, his crystalline blue eyes bright in the high-intensity lamps, and smiled, brighter than the lamplight. *Fuck Brian,* David thought, *what's not to be passionate about?* And his bad mood disintegrated under the force of that thousand-watt smile. "What are you doing?" he asked, stepping onto the brickwork of the garage floor.

"Trying to decide if I want to try and repair the alternator to the Mustang or try and find a replacement," Zach said. "Either way's a pain in the ass, but I think I'd rather try and fix it; it's original equipment, and finding a decent substitute for a forty-year-old car isn't going to be easy. With luck, it's just something minor."

"You'll fix it," David said confidently.

"How did your classes go?" Zach asked as he set down the alternator and turned his face up for David's kiss.

"Mmm…. Fine," David said, deciding right then and there not to tell him about the visit from Brian. "Better now. You eat yet?"

"No, I was waiting for you. DB brought over a slow cooker full of pot roast; I had to come down here to work because the smell was driving me nuts. And I had a late lunch at Maggie's, too, so I wasn't all that hungry. I am now." He got up from the bench and put the alternator on the work-stand at the back of the garage, then turned back to David. "Ready?"

David walked up to him, took his face in his hands, and kissed him fiercely. "Upstairs," he said, his voice low and husky.

"Whoa," Zach said, and grabbed his wrists. "Something tells me it ain't pot roast you're hungry for."

"Nope."

Zach grinned and released his wrists, then reached behind him and hit the switch to close the garage door. "Don't need to go upstairs for that," he murmured. "Ever get fucked on the hood of a '69 Mustang?"

David shuddered and rested his forehead against Zach's. "No, but I have the feeling that lack is shortly to be remedied."

"God, I love when you talk smart like that." Zach ran his hands through David's hair, pulling him in for another kiss.

David chuckled deep in his throat and reached for the button on Zach's jeans. Then he froze. "Shit," he sighed.

"What?" Zach drew back and studied him, frowning. "What's the matter?"

"No raincoats. No lube." David reached up and smoothed his fingers over Zach's furrowed brow. "Guess we'll have to do the Mustang dance some other time."

"Got lube," Zach said, and released him, heading back toward the workbench. Something flashed in the air and David reached up automatically to catch a small jar of Vaseline. "I use it for metal parts, but it'll do," Zach said, heading back to David.

"Yeah, but we still don't have condoms, and even if we did, you couldn't use that with it," David objected. "It eats the latex."

"Who said we're using condoms?" Zach's grin was blinding. "Got the results from my blood tests last week in this morning's mail."

David stared at him. "Zach...."

"I have been waiting so damn long for this," Zach said, reaching for the hem of David's shirt and pulling it over his head without unbuttoning it, then starting work on the waistband of his khakis. "This is it, Taff. This is us, forever and always, right?"

"Forever and always," David agreed, running his hands over Zach's chest as he toed off his shoes and socks and stepped out of his pants. He hiked himself up on the hood of the Mustang, his heels on the bumper, his knees splayed wantonly, and leaned back onto his elbows, eyeing Zach with a smoky gaze. Zach's color was high as he fumbled with the buttons of his own jeans. David leaned forward and grabbed Zach by the T-shirt, dragging him down on top of him. "Face to face," David murmured as he trailed kisses along Zach's jaw and up toward his ear. "Skin to skin and face to face...."

"I don't know how," Zach gritted out, his face flushed. He rested his hands on the hood of the car on either side of David's hips and dropped his head so he couldn't see the scorn in David's eyes.

"I do." David chuckled again, tilting Zach's face up to smile away his lover's embarrassment. He slid down a little and wrapped his legs around Zach's hips, using his heels to push Zach's jeans down to the floor, and slid his hands over Zach's rump and up under his T-shirt to run his hands over the ragged skin of Zach's back.

ZACH closed his eyes, loving the gentle touch of David's hands, the heat where their bodies rubbed together, the scent of David's neck, David's soft, rough breathing. David's body shifted beneath his and then his hands were on Zach, the heaviness of the petrolatum warming and softening as David caressed him, and then he guided him gently in. Zach sank into his welcoming heat, and David pulled him closer, his mouth finding Zach's, his warm, slippery hands sliding back up over the scars on Zach's back, holding him, safe in the grasp of arms and legs and body. Zach buried his face in David's neck as they moved together, came together, and lay together after, sated, nerveless, boneless.

Finally David murmured into Zach's ear, "I think I'm permanently stuck to the hood of this car."

"You'll make a hell of a hood ornament," Zach drawled, pulling back a little to look at him. "Ugh, I think I'm permanently stuck to you."

"Would that be so bad?"

"No," Zach said with a grin, "but I don't think I can sell the Mustang with *both* of us as hood ornaments. The weight would throw off the engine's torque." He pulled away and went over to the side of the garage by the Mustang. He'd parked it in the bay nearest the interior car wash station, because when it had arrived, it had been covered with dust from its trip on the flatbed, and he'd wanted to wash it before starting to work on the engine. Now he ran warm water through the faucet into the floor drain, dampening a shop rag and wiping himself off. But an imp of the perverse made him turn up the pressure on the hose and whip around, shooting warm water all over the Mustang and David.

David lunged for him, shouting, and Zach got him full in the face for a brief moment before David wrestled the hose from his hand and turned it on him. They chased each other around in the warm spray, fighting over control of the hose; then David upped the ante by grabbing the car shampoo Zach had used on the Mustang a couple of days before and squirting it at him. In moments they were both not only wet, but slippery and sudsy. "That's one way to get you to take a bath," David gasped just before Zach let him have it in the face again with the spray. He slipped and went down on the wet brickwork, laughing like a hyena.

Zach slid down the side of the Mustang to sit beside him, laughing just as wildly. He peeled off his soaked T-shirt and wiped his face with it. "Not much point in leaving this on, is there?" he laughed, and handed it to David, who put it to the same use.

"You realize all the rest of our clothes are soaked now too?" David asked, and tossed Zach's shirt onto the sodden pile of clothes in front of the Mustang.

"I've got a washer and dryer in the apartment," Zach said. He reached over and slung an arm around David's neck, hauling him across to sit in his lap. His other arm went around David's waist. "That was fun," he said peacefully.

"Yeah." David grinned and tilted his head back against Zach's shoulder. "And we got the come washed off the car too."

"Yeah, like I was really worried about that," Zach said dryly. "Taff, can I ask you a question?"

"Sure." David twisted around to look at him. "What?"

"How come you never pushed the face-to-face thing? I mean, it was good. Really, really good. I mean, you mentioned it maybe twice, but always kind of in passing, like 'we gotta try that someday' sort of thing. But you didn't push it. Doesn't it feel good to you that way? Cuz I gotta tell you—it felt real good to me."

"It felt great." David rested his head back against Zach. "But it's more... I don't know. Intimate. You see everything that's going on in your partner's face then. And I thought—I thought maybe you weren't ready for that. That you weren't ready for that kind of intimacy. You know. Crap like that."

"What changed your mind this time?"

David reached up and pulled Zach's face down to kiss. Against his lips, he said, "'Forever and always.' Forever and always, Zach."

Zach's heart gave a great thump and his arms tightened around David. "I think I've got it figured out," he said softly. "About the love thing? Cuz I think I do love you, Taff. There isn't gonna be anyone else, ever. Just you."

"I hope so," David said softly, and kissed him, then got to his feet. "Come on, let's get these clothes washed and some food in us."

They picked up their wet clothes and went up the inside staircase to Zach's apartment, stopping by the little laundry unit to toss them in the washer, "Since they're all full of detergent now, anyway," said Zach. Then Zach found them both sweats and T-shirts. "If we stay naked we're never going to get any food in us," he told David, who just grinned in his sweet, sleepy way.

"CAN I ask you a question?" Zach said over the pot roast.

David took a swig of beer before answering, "*Another* one? You just asked me one a little while ago. Sheesh. Give a guy an inch and he takes a foot."

Zach flicked a carrot at him; David bobbed and caught it in his mouth. "Asshole."

"Dweeb. Go ahead."

"Who was the first guy you were ever with? The one in high school you never told anyone about?"

David sighed. "Well, I promised I wouldn't ever tell, but shit, high school was seven years ago... Matt Brewer."

"*Matt Brewer*? The quarterback from Wesley Community High School? Holy *crap*! He was *gay*??"

"Obviously." David snickered. "His mother hired me to tutor him so he'd pass math, or he'd blow his scholarship to UCo. He occasionally made jokes about gay boys in public, but I don't think we'd had three study sessions before he was on his knees with my dick in his mouth. I mean, I knew I liked it from when Maggie and I fooled around, but God, what a rush when it was a guy doing it. If I hadn't known about it already, I'd have known I was gay then."

"Matt Brewer. Matt Fucking Brewer. Damn." Zach was shaking his head in wonderment. "I always wondered who it was you tossed Maggie over for. I mean, when I was a kid, I figured you guys would get married right out of high school and it fucking broke my heart. Cuz I *knew* you were gay, even while you were going out with her; I just figured you were going to stay in the damn closet forever."

"Well, I wasn't going to come out in high school," David pointed out reasonably. "Talk about a disaster waiting to happen. Even if Foothills was a pretty liberal school, we did a lot with the kids from Wesley Community, and there was a whole big anti-gay bunch there."

"Apparently not Matt Brewer," Zach said.

"Nah. He was okay. And I didn't toss Maggie over for him. I'd busted up with him long before I came out to her. I did tell her I cheated on her, though not with who."

"Whom," Zach corrected absently.

"Speaking of which, how's the tutoring going?" David grinned. "Speaking of tutoring."

"Good. Maggie thinks I can probably take the GED in a week or two and pass it. Dad talked to the school, and the next time the school district's running the test is the second week of July, so I'll probably take it then. The results take two weeks so I should know by August first. So that gives me a couple of weeks yet to study. With time off for the Fourth of July party at Tyler."

"So you're going?"

Zach took a deep breath. "Yeah. Yeah, I'm gonna try. I figure if I get there early before too many people are there, I won't be like making an entrance or anything where people are going to be noticing me. I'll just... hang out, or something. You're coming, right?"

"Yeah." David regarded him thoughtfully. "How much of us do you want on display there, baby?"

Zach looked up at the endearment. "You mean, *us* us?"

"I don't know any other us's around."

"Oh. Well. I don't know."

David shrugged. "It's up to you. Best buds or madly in love—your call."

"Can I let you know?"

"Of course." David reached across and took his hand. "We do everything at your speed, love. I told you that in the beginning. You set the pace."

"It's a lot of responsibility."

"You can handle it." David grinned. "Pass the pot roast, I'm still hungry."

Chapter
Twenty-Two

"I CAN handle this," Zach said, staring at the pale, hollow-eyed reflection staring back at him. "I can handle this, no problem. It's just a barbeque, right? Hot dogs, brats, chicken, steaks, corn on the cob, apple pie, all-American tradition, fireworks, music, people, crowds of people, hundreds of people, *thousands* of people... oh, shit. I can't do this." He leaned forward, resting his head on the bathroom mirror, trying to decide if he should puke first or panic first. Puking had a distinct lead, but the tingling in his fingers and the shortness of breath told him that panic was gaining.

"Zach?" his father's voice called from the living room.

Zach hauled in a breath and tried to answer but nothing came out. A moment later Richard appeared in the bathroom door and said, "I thought I'd find you hiding in here."

A squeak emerged from Zach's throat. He gave Richard a desperate look, then lunged for the toilet, where he brought up his breakfast. That, oddly, staved off the panic attack, so when he raised his pale, sweaty face to his father's concerned one, he was breathing normally and more or less calm. "I think I have the flu," he said hopefully.

"I think you have acute butterflied stomach," Richard corrected. "Done?"

"I guess." Zach straightened and reached for a paper cup to rinse out his mouth. "Now I have to brush my teeth again," he complained.

"Poor baby," his father jeered gently. "Seriously, Zach. Flu or nerves?"

"Nerves," Zach said. "I think."

"Brush your teeth."

Zach obeyed, making as big a production out of it as he could manage to waste time. His father stood in the doorway the whole time, his arms folded and a wry expression on his face. Finally, Zach said, "Okay, I guess I'm ready."

"You don't have to come if you don't want to," Richard pointed out. "You were the one who said you thought you were ready. If you really don't think you are, you don't have to do this."

"Yeah, I do," Zach said with a sigh. "I need to be able to handle people around me."

"You've been going out for several months now to clubs and stuff," Richard said. "There are people there."

"Yeah, but not people who *know* me," Zach said. "Not people who work with my dad and knew me when I was a little kid, and stuff like that." He rubbed his stomach with his fist. "They're not quite strangers and not quite friends. I can handle either of those. It's the in-between kind that I have trouble with."

"It's not just you," Richard assured him. "Right now your mother's in the bathroom redoing her makeup for the fourteenth time. She's already had on eight different outfits and is back to the one she put on originally." He shook his head. "We've done this Fourth of July barbeque for the last fifteen years with only a couple years' exception, but to your mother, it's still always the first time." In a softer voice, he said, "You always used to love the Fourth. It'll be fine; you'll have a good time."

"You know this is gonna play hell with your security team's program for me," Zach said. "There'll be people here with cameras. My picture's gonna get out, and security's gonna get tougher, you know."

"You're the one who's going to be most affected," Richard said. "Does it bother you that you're going to have to be more careful when you leave the compound? Are you worried about people wanting to talk to you about what happened? I'm pretty sure no one will have the discourtesy to bring it up today, but after today, you'll be fair game."

"I have to do this," Zach said doggedly. "I have to know if I can deal with this, if I have any thought of going to college. I have to be able to deal with people. It's like the last stage of the process, Dad.

Right now, the idea of all those people... Jesus, I'm ready to puke again! But I *have* to do this. I have to." He started to shake.

Richard threw his arm around his son's shoulders. "Zach," he said urgently, "it's going to be *fine*. They won't turn into monsters, I promise."

Zach shot him a look. "Am I that obvious?"

"Well, it *was* what you were worried about, wasn't it?"

"Not in so many words," Zach said, "but I guess so. It's that same feeling, anyway. You'd think I'd be beyond that now. You'd think the old brain would have figured out that there aren't real monsters."

"There are," Richard said soberly. "You lived among them for five years. But there aren't any here, I promise. And even if there were, you can deal with them. You're strong—so strong I can't believe it. I don't mean to put pressure on you if you think you really can't deal with it. I just believe in you and want you to believe in yourself too."

Zach turned and rested his forehead on his father's shoulder. Even after two years, he still hadn't adjusted to the fact that he was a good two inches taller. David and Dad were the same height, and he was taller than both of them. It blew his mind. "I know," he said, his voice muffled. "I *know* I can handle it; I just don't *feel* like I can."

"Two years of therapy rears its ugly head," Richard said cheerfully. "You can distinguish between what you know and what you feel. That's more than most people can do."

"Most people don't have two hours of therapy daily," Zach said dryly.

"Come on, then, if you're coming. We have to go winkle your mother out of her shell, and I thought you wanted to get there early so you don't make an entrance."

"Yeah." Zach gave Richard a brief squeeze before letting him go and taking one last look at the mirror. "Do I look okay?"

"Ghastly," Richard teased, then shoved his shoulder gently. "Come on."

"ZACH! Hey, Zach!"

Zach turned at the sound of his name called over the rattle and rumble of the crowd around the beer tent. There had to be a thousand people here at least, and he pretty much only recognized a few of them. The two guys pushing through the crowd weren't in that select group, but they looked to be about his age, and they *were* faintly familiar, though he couldn't say who they were. They both stopped and grinned at him, and suddenly he *did* know who they were. "Jesse? Jeff?"

The shorter of the two turned to the one in glasses and poked him. "I *told* you he'd recognize us!" and he turned back to Zach and shoved out his hand. "How ya doin', Zach?"

"Good, Jess," Zach said, and shook his hand, then Jeff's. "What are you guys doing with yourselves these days?"

"Jeff's in grad school; I'm working at an accounting firm in Colorado Springs. My dad still works here, though, and when Jeff found out I was coming today he tagged along. Honest to Jebus, Zach, you done grewed!! How tall are you now?"

"Six-two," Zach said.

"You pump iron?" Jeff asked interestedly. He didn't, that was for sure; he was as lanky as he'd always been, just a bit taller. "I tried that once. Tore a ligament."

Zach laughed. "I had a physical therapist teach me how to do it right."

"I knew there was a reason," Jeff said cheerfully. His grin faded. "Look, Zach, you got a minute?"

"Sure," Zach said, the hair on the back of his neck prickling. "What's up?"

Jeff led him and Jesse around the side of the beer tent out of the direct line of the entrance. "A few weeks ago, maybe three or so? Some guy was asking questions about you. Said he was writing a story on you. I didn't tell him anything he couldn't have found out anyplace else, but he was mostly asking about when you were in school, what you were like and stuff, not anything about now—not that I know anything about now, anyway. Anyway, I didn't tell him much, and he didn't stick around and push. But I wanted to tell you about it but couldn't get home until this weekend and didn't have your email address or anything."

Zach's throat was thick, but he took a breath and after a moment was able to say, "That's okay—it happens. I don't know how he found out you went to school with me, but things like that happen. I haven't talked to the media and they don't like that. They want you out there, hitting the talk shows and being on reality TV and crap like that, not minding your own business. What did he ask about?"

"Oh, just what you were like as a kid and stuff. I did tell him about the nicknames." Jeff flushed. "I hope you aren't pissed about that."

Nicknames? Zach stared at him a moment, then guffawed. "You didn't tell him *yours*, did you?"

"Hell, no!" Jeff said indignantly. "I have a *little* pride!"

THEY hung out together for a while, then went off to acquire some food. It being a Tyler barbeque, it wasn't just hot dogs and hamburgers, but steak and pulled pork and ribs and corn dogs, all eaten to the competing sounds of country, blues, jazz and rock bands. Kids rode on carnival rides, couples played midway games trying to win each other stuffed animals, and as soon as it got dark, fireworks exploded overhead.

It was all way, way too much, and when David appeared at Zach's elbow and discreetly disengaged him from his friends, he was way past ready to go find a quiet spot to sit and watch the fireworks and decompress. David, in his usual efficient manner, had found such a spot, on a rise of ground closer to the house than to the area set off for the barbeque, close enough to still hear the music, but far enough that they might have been alone in the world. "How are you doing?" David asked as they settled down on the plaid blanket he'd left there earlier.

"Okay. Despite throwing up in front of my dad this morning, it hasn't been a horrible day. Once I got here and people started coming, it was okay. It was good to see the Jays," Zach admitted, "and it was kind of fun to see some of the old guys that have been working at Tyler forever. Some girls flirted with me. It was weird."

David lay down and gazed up at the fireworks. "What did you do?"

"I *think* I just flirted back," Zach said. "Either that or I'm engaged. Can I ask you a question?"

"Since when has permission given or not stopped you? Go ahead."

"Have you ever kissed a girl?"

"You *are* kidding, aren't you?"

"No. Have you?"

"Duh! I dated Maggie for five years, dweeb. There was considerably more than kissing that went on."

"Did you have *sex* with her?" Zach stared at him, wide-eyed.

David laughed. "No. Just a lot of screwing around, you know. She was kind of into the whole 'good girl' prom queen thing, and frankly, I wasn't all that interested. Why?"

"Well, I've been spending a lot of time with Maggie lately…."

"Not thinking of switching sides?"

Zach frowned at him, then shook his head. "No. I love Maggie, she's great, but she's definitely not my type. Besides which, Alex can kick my ass. No, I was just wondering if you got, like, turned on by her. I mean, I don't, but you must have, if you dated her so long and screwed around, and stuff. I'm just curious. I mean, I can't even *imagine*, you know, being with one of the girls I was talking to today. It just… it just felt so weird to even think about it. The flirting, and all."

"Zach, I was a teenage boy. *Everything* turns us on. I read someplace that the average teenage boy gets a dozen erections a day. Besides, I told you before that I already knew I liked blowjobs by the time Matt Brewer blew me—I just liked it a whole lot better when it was a guy on the other end. *Obviously* I'd had some experience before that."

"Oh, okay. It's just weird, you know. And I was just wondering about you and Maggie."

David cocked his head. "Feeling threatened?"

"No. It's just… weird, you know. Knowing you and she dated,

and when I'm hanging around with her, I'm always wondering if she ever, you know, wanted you back or something. If Alex wasn't just a second-best...."

"You *are* joking, right? Maggie is *nuts* about Alex. Haven't you ever seen the two of them together?"

"Yeah, they're friends with my folks and I've seen them at least once a week since I came back here. But that doesn't mean anything. I mean, it could be she's just good at hiding it." Zach rested his chin on his knees, carefully not looking at David.

"Oh," David said slowly. "I get it. You're not really asking about Maggie, are you?"

"Of course I am. Hello? Asking about Maggie by name?"

"But that's not really what you're asking. What you're asking is whether or not *you're* second choice.... To who, I wonder?"

"Whom," Zach said.

David ignored him. "Not Maggie—you know I love her but not in that way... Oh. Jerry. You think I screwed up with Jerry or he dumped me or something and I'm making it up by choosing *you*? You're an idiot, Zach, you know that? And while you come by your rotten self-image honestly, it's really annoying."

"Fine," Zach said, and started to get up. David grabbed his arm and yanked him back down.

"Shut up and listen to me," he said savagely. "If anything, Jerry—and Chris and Steve and fucking Matt Brewer for that matter, *and* Maggie—have all been my second choices. All of them. Because every relationship I've ever had has had this big ugly lummox of a Zach Tyler hanging over it. So shut the fuck up about Maggie and Jerry and every other person I've ever even looked at twice, and I'll ignore all the strangers you fucked in the ten months, okay?"

"That bothers you, doesn't it?" Zach asked slowly.

"You bet your ass it does. Shit, Mike Pritzger bugs me, and I don't think I've ever met anyone more het than he is. I'm jealous of everyone who takes your attention away from me. Okay, that sounds like a stalker, and I'm not that, but you know what I mean."

"I think it means you love me."

"Well, duh."

"Okay," Zach said. "I get it. I'm just being stupid again. And paranoid. It's just... I guess I'm so nuts about you I can't understand why everyone else *isn't*."

"Well, we'll just blame it on taste. De gustibus non est disputandum."

"'There is no accounting for taste,'" Zach said.

"Glad you haven't forgotten all the Latin tag lines I taught you."

"Most of them. I think the only other one I remember is something else about 'brevior saltare something something viris est vita'."

David chuckled. "'Brevior saltare cum deformibus viris est vita.' 'Life is too short to dance with ugly men.' Good thing neither of us hot young dudes fall under that category."

"Ego much?" Zach flopped back beside him, lacing his fingers through David's. "When I was talking with the Jays, Muffin told me that some reporter talked to him about me a few weeks ago. Was asking about when I was a kid. He said he told him about the nicknames, but not anything else. What?" David's hand had suddenly gone tense.

"Nothing," David said.

"Something," Zach corrected. "What is it?"

"Oh, I just think I ran into the same guy. He called me 'Taff'. I shut him down, and told him to stay away from you, but he knows who you are."

"He does." Zach's voice was flat.

"Yeah." David took a breath and let it out in a long exhalation. "It was that Brian guy."

"Brian? The surfer dude? He's a fucking *reporter*?"

"Apparently."

Zach was quiet a moment, then said, his voice bitter, "Well, talk about your past coming up and biting you in the ass. I know where he got the 'Taff' part, anyway."

"He told me."

The sound of the party seemed distant in the silence. Finally,

Zach said, "It was before we got together. I haven't cheated on you, Taff."

"I never thought that," David said in surprise.

"Oh. Good." His fingers tightened around David's. "He didn't act like a reporter. He didn't ask questions or anything. The only thing he was interested in was getting fucked."

"I don't know," David mused. "He sounded like he was interested in more than that."

"Well, I'm not. Not with him, anyway." Zach released David's hand and sat up, wrapping his arms around his knees.

David put his arm behind his head and his other hand on his stomach, just relaxing and staring up at the stars. "I know you're not," he said easily.

"Taff?"

"Haven't gone anywhere."

"Do you think, that maybe, if all that happened didn't happen—that if we'd started, I dunno, seeing each other back then, that we'd be here, now, like this?"

"Probably not," David said. "Maybe hanging out, friends or something. But not together."

"Why not?"

"Well, even if we were together that whole next year, with you putting off going to MIT and me working at Tyler before college, sooner or later you'd end up in Boston and me at UCLA. We'd write and talk and email and videochat for a while, but separation's hard on a relationship. Sooner or later you'd meet some hot young science geek or I'd meet some hot young actor wannabe, and we'd end up just doing the whole 'we'll still be friends' crap."

"I wouldn't have done that."

"Sure you would have." David smiled at Zach when he turned to look down at him. "We were a lot younger then, and that's how that sort of thing goes."

"That's why you didn't want me in the beginning? Because you thought it was just a crush or something? That we'd end up splitting up anyway, so why waste the time?"

"Gee, zero to asshole in sixty seconds," David complained. He sat up and imitated Zach's posture. "For the record—and for the hundredth time—you *know* why you threw me for a loop when you kissed me."

"I know what you said." Zach looked over at him out of the corner of his eye. "So what's gonna happen when I get accepted to MIT? You gonna figure I'll take up with some hot science geek and forget about you?"

"No," David said, "because I'm coming with you."

"To Boston?"

"No, to Shanghai. Of course to Boston, dweeb. Someone's gotta look out for you."

"I can take care of myself."

"Of course you can," David said. He slung his arm around Zach's neck and hauled his head down to rub his knuckles across the top. "Dweeb. But there's another reason."

"My hot bod? Cuz while I'm damaged, I'm not *deformibus?*" Zach squirmed around and leaned until David collapsed back on the ground, then started tickling him. David smacked his hands away playfully.

"Cut it out, ya maroon."

"Because you love me?" Zach teased, dodging David's grasping hands and going for his ribs again.

"Forever and always," David said.

Zach froze, then rested his hands on either side of David's chest. The grass was warm and crisp beneath his fingers. "Forever and always," he agreed, and kissed him, so gently David wanted to weep, then rolled over to lie beside him, gazing up at the fireworks, his fingers laced in David's.

"HAVE you seen Zach?" Jane asked Richard worriedly as they left the picnic site. Annie was staying behind to organize the staff they'd hired for the event and make sure everything got cleaned up and off the grounds by daybreak so that Tyler employees could get back in the parking lot in the morning. It was nearly that now, somewhere past three a.m., and everyone was tired, but it had been Jane and Richard who'd run the event, not Annie, so she'd shooed them on their way home, claiming not to be the slightest bit worn out.

"David told me he'd found a spot for them to watch the fireworks and that he was going to rescue Zach, but that was hours ago. I did check with Andrew and he said they had gone through the footgate up toward the house about ten o'clock. I'm sure they're together."

"Mm," Jane said, taking Richard's arm and leaning against him as they walked up the path toward the house. The moon was still up and between that and the stars and the faint glow from the lights still on at the picnic site, it was easy enough to see their way. "I'm glad about that. Do you think we'll have repercussions from Zach coming to the party today, Richie?"

Richard shrugged. "Maybe, maybe not. If we do, we'll deal with it when it happens. What...?" He looked up the slope of lawn to the west of where they walked.

"What is that?" Jane asked curiously, also noticing the long line of shadow at the top of the rise. It was barely visible, just a patch of darkness against the star-strewn sky.

Richard took her hand and they left the path, climbing the slope up to where the shadow lay. "Oh," Jane said softly.

It was Zach, asleep on his back on the plaid blanket David had brought to the barbeque. David lay beside him with his head on Zach's chest and Zach's arm around his shoulders, also deep asleep. They stood a moment looking down at the two young men. "They look like little boys," Jane whispered. "Look at Zach's face—he looks like he's six again."

Richard slid his arm around his wife. "Wouldn't it be so much easier if he were? If we knew what was coming and how to stop it?"

"Oh, yeah," Jane sighed. "But he isn't, and we can't. And I think we'd better wake them up; they'll get all crunchy from sleeping on the ground."

"No doubt," Richard agreed, "though not as badly as you or I would. Zach!" he called softly. Jane bent to touch his shoulder.

ZACH started awake, flinching back at the sight of a tall shadow looming over him and another crouched beside him, but there was something pinning him down. Terror rushed over him and took his breath. He gasped, trying to get enough air to scream, but then his eyes adjusted to the dark and he realized with a start that it was his mother beside him and his father standing at his feet. He breathed out a sigh of relief. "Oh! Mom. Dad." He glanced down at the object pinning him to the ground and saw David, sound asleep on his chest. "I guess we fell asleep."

"I guess you did," Jane agreed. "It's past three—you guys are going to be stiff in the morning if you stay there all night. Besides, it's getting kind of cold out here."

"Yeah." He didn't say anything for a moment, just concentrated on getting his racing heart to slow down. Then he shook David's shoulder gently. "Taff."

David murmured, then opened his eyes to meet Zach's. "Hey," he said softly.

"Audience," Zach said.

David blinked and looked around. "Oh. Hi, guys." He sat up, wincing, and stretched. "Guess we fell asleep."

"That's what I said," Zach said. "What time is it, anyway?"

"Goblin hour," Richard said. "Roughly around three. Party's over and we're going home. You boys have a good time today?"

"I did," David said.

"Me too," Zach admitted. "After I stopped freaking out. People weren't as bad as I expected; most of them were pretty cool. The ones that talked to me, anyway. The ones that just stared at me like I was a wild animal escaped from a zoo—them I ignored." He gave them a twisted grin and folded his arms behind his head.

"Lot of them?" Richard asked carefully.

"A few. Relatives of employees, mostly, I think. Most of your people just came up to me and told me how well I was looking." Zach made a face. "I know they meant well, but it got old fast. Fortunately, you only have so many employees, so once I'd shaken everyone's hand, they left me alone. You remember the Jays?"

Richard frowned. "Pete Wilmot's boy Jesse and that other one?"

"Yeah. They were there. I talked to them for a while. I think we might be getting together sometime in the next few weeks for beer and pizza or something. Maybe a Broncos preseason game if I knew anyone who could get tickets." Zach batted his eyes at Richard, who snorted in amusement.

"The crowds didn't bother you, honey?" Jane asked in concern.

Zach sat up and leaned against David's shoulder. "A little," he admitted. "I got a little claustrophobic at times, but just was careful not to let myself get anyplace I couldn't get out of, so I was okay."

"And he didn't need his hand held all day long, either," David said. Zach stuck his tongue out at him. "I left him for hours at a time and he was fine." He grinned back at Zach. "I don't say I wasn't *watching* him the whole time, but he didn't know I was."

"You're like an old fusspot," Zach said. "I was fine."

"I know," David said. "Didn't I just get done saying that?" He poked him. "Come on, I'm tired and I have to teach tomorrow."

Zach scrambled to his feet and David followed.

"Still," Jane said, smiling, "I'd say that was a pretty successful experiment, don't you, honey?"

"Yes, Mom," the two younger men chorused.

Jane laughed.

Chapter
Twenty-Three

"AND then, Frankie says 'But Sister, I thought you were a *guy!*'"

The table exploded with laughter. Zach pounded Jesse's shoulder with his open palm. "You jackasses! You set Frankie up, didn't you?" he demanded, grinning widely.

"You bet your ass we did," Billy Krepwith, one of their old school friends, said from across the table. "Frankie needed to get taken down a peg or two, especially with that John Marshall crap."

"So what did the nun say?" David asked as he poured himself another glass of beer from the rapidly diminishing pitcher.

"She laughed her butt off," Jesse said. "Good thing she had a sense of humor about it, or Frankie'd be on his way to hell right now. Anybody hear from him lately, anyway?"

"Yeah, I got an email from him a couple of days ago," Zach said. "Taff got Frankie's from his dad at the college, so I emailed him and he sent back." He pulled out his phone and queued up his email. "'Wish I could be there'—I told him we were going out for pizza tonight—'and had the chance to kick Muffin's ass for getting me drunk last time I was in town. Didn't get rid of the hangover for three days.'"

They laughed again. Zach glanced around the table in satisfaction. There were six of them: himself, David, Jesse, Jeff, Billy, and Taiwan Burgess, who'd played forward on their soccer team the last season before Zach's 'adventure'. That was what he'd taken to calling it to himself, in his attempt to get beyond the nightmare of it. Dr. Barrett wasn't so sure that it was a good thing to lighten it up that way, but it gave him a non-threatening frame of reference. Dr. Barrett *was* pleased about this evening out, as well as the reason for it: Zach had not only passed his GED with flying colors, but an interview with a pair of professors from UCo who had connections at MIT had resulted in Zach not only getting set up for tutoring by the pair, but a letter of interest from Admissions at MIT. If he got through the program the UCo professors had set up for him, he'd be starting at MIT in September of next year, just a little over a year from now. The thought had his heart beating a little faster, and he wasn't sure if it was excitement or fear.

David glanced over at him and gave him a quick grin. "Thinkin' about MIT again?"

"How could you tell?"

"I dunno," Tai said, "maybe the way you get even whiter than you are normally, white boy?"

The guys laughed, and Billy shoved the pizza over his way. "Come on, eat up. Gotta get your strength back—you're wastin' away from the stress."

Laughing, Zach said, "Fuck you!" and took some more pizza.

Jeff drained the pitcher and said, "More beer?"

"Yes!" they chorused.

Zach laughed happily.

IT WAS well past midnight when they finally finished up, and Zach was ready to go home. It had been a good time; it was great reconnecting with his old friends and none of them seemed too judgmental or curious. Billy and Tai had both commented on the scars around his neck; Billy had declared them "heinous" and Tai "wicked," but both were more interested in finding out his workout schedule and how the hell he'd gotten so big. Tai was working at an advertising firm in the Springs; Billy at NORAD in their data analysis department, so they'd kept in touch with each other over the last couple of years. They'd greeted Zach exactly as if he'd just been away at school for a while, with friendly punches and smart remarks. He grinned to himself as he said goodbye to them and wondered why the heck he'd been so hesitant about seeing any of his old friends again.

"Yeah, guess I better get going too," Jesse said. "Lynda'll be pissed if I'm home too late, and that is not a pretty sight, Lynda pissed.

You're lucky you don't have those issues, Zach. Sometimes I wish I was gay too. It'd be a lot easier."

Zach froze. "What?"

Billy hooted. "You think we didn't know you were gay, girly-man? Since, like, fifth grade!"

He glanced at each of his friends, wide-eyed. "You.... What?" He looked at David, who just covered his smile discreetly with his hand. "Did you know about this?"

"That you were gay?" David asked cheerfully. "Oh, I'd suspected."

"No! That *they* all knew!"

Jeff laughed. "Yeah, well, like Billy said, we've known since about fifth grade. About the time we all started getting interested in girls and you didn't. We didn't say anything, cuz frankly, it wasn't anybody's business at the time, and I don't think anyone else knew, but shit, Zach, we all hung around together for years! You think we're stupid or something?"

Zach shook his head slowly. "No.... No, of course not. I just didn't think.... Well, I didn't think I *acted* gay or anything...."

"You didn't," Jesse assured him. "Like Muffin said, nobody else knew. Well, maybe Coach Faber, but he didn't say anything either. Broke a lot of little girls' hearts, though, you know, never paying attention to any of them. Everyone said you had a major crush on Maggie Richards, Taff's girlfriend, and that's why you never went out with any other girl."

"You guys are wacked," Zach said, shaking his head in amazement. "You knew, but nobody else at school did?"

"Hell," Jeff said, "we were your best buds. I don't think anyone else even suspected, though."

"And it didn't bother you?"

Jeff's face went all thoughtful. "Maybe at the beginning we thought it was a little weird. And once we actually *knew* what 'being gay' meant—I mean, eww. But to each his own, I guess, and if you think about it, sex in general is kind of weird and gross anyway." He grinned and slung an arm around Zach's neck. "So when I say 'I love you, man'—you take it the right way, okay? Cuz I'm not into butt-munchin'."

Tai made gagging noises.

"You guys," Zach said, "are all assholes. And I love ya. Not in the butt-munching way, of course."

His four friends were laughing when they left the restaurant.

David looked around. The pizza joint they were in was Bella's, one they'd all hung out at in school; but he hadn't been here in years. It had been like practically every other pizza joint he'd ever been in, from New Zealand to New York: dark, a bit grungy, noisy, and comforting in its sameness. It still was. He felt a beer-infused sentimental affection for the place, even though neither the beer nor the pizza was impressive in its quality. "Good place, huh, Zach?"

"What? Taff, I think you're drunk."

"I think you're right. Are you?"

"I don't think so. I only had two beers."

"How come? I mean, used to be two beers was your warm-up to the evening of pounding Scotch. You haven't drunk any Scotch lately, either, from what I remember." He stood, and clutched the back of his chair as the room swayed gently. "How come you haven't drunk any Scotch lately? That I remember?"

"I don't know." Zach regarded him with an amused look on his face. "Don't need to. I sleep okay these days."

"It's cuz you're sleeping with me," David said confidentially, in an undertone.

"I think you're right. Look, I gotta take a piss. You gonna be okay while I'm gone?"

"I'm not that drunk," David said dryly. "You go ahead. I'll wait for the bill."

"Don't try and pay it," Zach chuckled. "God only knows what you'll come up with."

"Fuck you," David retorted with a grin, and sat back down.

ZACH was coming out of the bathroom when someone stepped in front of him. He stopped, frowning, then recognized the sun-streaked blond hair and handsome face.

"Hi," Brian said. "How you doing, Zach?"

"Fine," Zach said curtly, and went to step around him.

Brian put out a hand. "No, wait. I've been hoping I'd run into you. Do you have a minute?"

"No."

Brian touched his arm gently. "Not even a minute. A second. I just want to talk to you."

"I know what you want to talk about, and I'm not interested." Zach took another step to the side.

"I've seen the reports," Brian said.

Zach froze. His eyes flicked to Brian's face. The man's expression was sympathetic. "What reports?"

"The reports about what happened to you. What happened to Esteban. What *really* happened in Venezuela." He reached into the breast pocket of his jacket and put a card in Zach's hand. "I want to hear about it, Zach. Please. Now—later—whenever you're ready."

DAVID took the bill from the middle-aged waitress and thanked her for putting up with the rowdy crowd. "Aw, you guys weren't bad," she said with a smile. "Loud, is about all. Celebrating something?"

"Yeah, you could say that."

"Well, whenever you're ready, you pay me. Need any change?"

"No. In fact," David dug into his hip pocket for his wallet and gave her his Visa card. "Put it on this."

She took the card and the leatherette folder with the check. A few minutes later, she was back, and he signed the credit slip, adding a twenty-five percent tip for her good-natured and patient service. "Thanks," she said, giving him a glowing smile as she took the folder.

He watched her head back to the server's station; then his eyes went past to where Zach stood, talking to a tall blond man in a tan blazer. A bit dressy for a pizza joint, he was just thinking, and then he recognized him. No. Oh, no. Not tonight, not when Zach was still glowing from a great evening out with friends like normal people took for granted, not when he was feeling so happy and positive and *normal*.... He lunged to his feet and stormed over to where they stood, shouldering Zach gently aside so that he faced the journalist.

"I THOUGHT I told you to stay away from him," David said savagely, reaching over and taking the business card from Zach. Fury radiated off him; even stunned and numb as Zach was, he recognized the barely suppressed rage. It just added to the air of unreality about him, feeling David so furious; David, who was always so calm, so easy-going, except when he was fighting with Zach. Distantly, Zach wondered why David was so angry. He was never angry with anyone except Zach.

"I'm not talking to you," Brian said calmly. "I'm talking to Zach."

"You're *not* talking to Zach," David retorted. "I'm not letting you."

"I sort of think that should be Zach's decision." The journalist's voice was reasonable. He glanced beyond David to Zach. "What about it?"

"What do you want?" Zach asked unwillingly.

"I want a story. I want the *whole* story. I want the truth." He met Zach's eyes. "I want to know what really happened."

"Learn to live with disappointment," David snarled. "It's none of your fucking business."

"Look, *Taff*," Brian shot back, "Zach doesn't need you running interference for him. He's perfectly capable of defending himself. He's capable of a lot more than you give him credit for. Aren't you, Zach? You can take care of yourself."

"Yes," Zach said.

David turned to look at him. "It's a con," he said urgently. "Saying 'yes' puts you in the frame of mind subconsciously to agree with him. It's the oldest trick in the book. Don't say 'yes'. Say 'fuck off" the way you did me."

Zach looked at him, weary, but saying nothing.

"Tell me no, Zach," Brian said, "if that's really what you want to say. But you don't need David to protect you, do you?"

"No," Zach said, but he was agreeing with Brian.

David said painfully, "Zach...."

"I don't need you to protect me, Taff," Zach said. "I love you, but I don't need you to protect me."

"Yes, you do! This guy is gonna run roughshod over you. He'll drag all kinds of shit into the open. Do you want everyone knowing your business?"

"Maybe it's time."

"Zach! This is what I mean!"

"Davey," Brian said, "he really doesn't need you to protect him, any more than he needed those soldiers to free him."

"What are you talking about?"

"Those soldiers didn't get Zach away from Esteban, did they, Zach? You freed yourself."

"Yes," Zach said. He could hear his voice quavering and shut up before anyone else noticed.

"What are you *talking* about?" David repeated angrily.

"Zach knows what I'm talking about."

"Zach...."

"Yeah. I do. I did." He took a deep breath, then let it out slowly, a long exhalation redolent with pain and grief. "What do you want to know? What it *felt* like?"

"Yes," Brian said softly. "What it felt like. What you felt."

"I felt his windpipe crunch when I crushed it," Zach said, speaking to Brian but watching David's face. *I still hear it sometimes. I remember that. I remember the way it felt, standing on his back with him on the floor beneath me, feeling the muscles convulse under my bare feet and trying to stay standing by digging my toes into his ribs, and the feel of his come trickling down my legs as I rode him like a circus bareback rider.* "I remember the leather of the leash cutting into my hands." He opened his hands and looked down at them. "There was blood on my hands," he said, "but no place else. He didn't bleed. He choked to death. *I* choked him to death."

He looked back up at David. "They said what I did was impossible. He was twice my weight and solid muscle. His neck was thick and hard and I was eighty-six pounds and all bones. But I did it. I killed him. I yanked him off his feet and garroted him with my own leash until he was dead."

David's face was white, his eyes black holes. He said nothing, just stared at Zach as if he were a stranger. Zach turned to Brian. "You'll get your interview. I want to talk to my lawyers and we'll get back to you." He plucked the card from David's resistless fingers. "One way or another, you'll get your story." Then he turned and walked out of the bar. A moment later they heard the roar of his engine as he gunned it, and the rattle of gravel as he sped away.

David turned to look at Brian, stunned and speechless. Brian said, "It was all in Captain Rogers' report. I got a copy of it—heavily redacted, of course, but I could read between the blacked-out lines. Thank you, FOIA."

"I didn't know," David said numbly.

"No. Not many people do. I wouldn't, either, but I have contacts in the State Department." Brian regarded him compassionately. "You don't give him enough credit. You still think of him as this unworldly, sheltered little fifteen-year-old, but he's so much more than that now. He's been through things that you and I—God willing—will never have to go through."

"And you're still going to write your fucking story," David said bitterly.

"Yeah. Because he needs to tell it and the world needs to hear it. But I can tell you this—if you care at all about that kid, you will move your ass and catch up to him, because if you don't, I will, and it will have *nothing* to do with the story."

David looked at Brian, really looked at him, then turned and ran for his car.

Chapter
Twenty-Four

IN A haze of misery, Zach parked the Ducati under the overhang and climbed the stairs to his apartment, opening the door and stepping inside, then closing it and leaning back against it in exhaustion. Surprisingly, he was calm; no sign of a panic attack threatening. But he felt dazed and numb, the only thing clear in his memory of the last hour David's shocked, horrified face and his own voice, coldly recounting the murder. He reached behind him and threw the rarely used deadbolt, then slid down to the floor and leaned back against the door, too drained to even stand.

It was only a few minutes later that he heard feet pounding up the stairs, then the doorknob rattling. "Zach? Zach! Lemme in, Zach. Come on, I know you're in there, Jesus, let me in!" Then the jingling clatter of keys and the scrape of one being hastily shoved in the lock, and the click of tumblers and the pressure of the door as David tried to open it against Zach's weight. Zach set his sneakers on the tile floor of the entry and braced himself against the door. "Zach! Cut it out. Let me in."

"Go away, David," Zach said dully.

"No! Come on, let me in. I need to talk to you."

"I don't want to talk."

"Fine, then I'll talk, you'll listen."

"I don't want to listen, either."

"What do you want, then?"

"For you to go away."

There was a thump of frustration against the door and when the voice spoke again, it came from lower down, as if David had mimicked

Zach's position on the porch. "I'm not going away. I need to see you, Zach. We need to talk."

"No, we don't."

"Open the fucking door, Zach."

Zach ignored him, just pushed back until he heard the door latch again, then reached up to throw the deadbolt again. He dragged himself to his feet and grabbed a kitchen chair, wedging it under the doorknob so even if David got the door unlocked again, he wouldn't be able to open the door.

"Zach? What are you doing?"

"None of your fucking business."

"Jesus, Zach, what is the matter with you? Why won't you let me in? I need to be with you, Zach. I need to talk to you."

"There's nothing to say."

"Nothing to say? Christ, are you *crazy*? There's a *lot* to say. A lot I need to say. Please, Zach. Let me in. Please. God, don't be doing anything stupid!" He pounded on the door. "Open this God-damned fucking door right now, God damn it, or I'm going to get your parents and your mother is going to be so fucking upset she'll probably fall apart, and your dad will have a heart attack, and...."

"All right!" Zach shouted. "Just *shut the fuck up!*" He jerked the chair from under the knob and unlocked the door, yanking it open so David practically fell into the room. "What the *fuck* do you want???" He dropped onto the chair and folded his arms.

David stood in the doorway, his hair looking like he'd been dragged backwards through a bush and his eyes wild. "Don't ever do that to me again," he gasped. "Don't ever scare me like that again."

Zach shrugged.

"What is the matter with you?" David demanded. He went to his knees beside the chair, putting his arm across Zach's lap. "Why are you acting like this?"

"Why are *you* acting like nothing's wrong?" Zach retorted. "You're pretending like I just all of a sudden started acting weird for no reason. I *saw* your face, David. I saw what you were thinking. And just because you somehow decided that you needed to pretend you didn't hear what you heard doesn't mean I'm ready to just forget what I said. Or how you looked when I said it." He shoved David's arm away and stood, slamming the chair back against the wall. "I'm not going to kill myself or anything stupid like that, so you can go home with a clear conscience, okay? We're done. I'd be stupid if I didn't realize that. So you don't have to say anything. Just… go away."

"What do you mean, 'we're done'?" David asked in confusion. "What did I do?"

"What did *you* do?" Zach laughed humorlessly. "You didn't do anything. You're just David. Perfect David. God's gift."

"What are you talking about? What are you saying? I don't understand, Zach. Why are you saying this?" He reached out to touch Zach's arm, but Zach jerked away. David stared at him in disbelief, his eyes filling. "Zach?"

"Go away, David. Just… just go away."

White, David stumbled back. Zach put his hand on David's chest and pushed him gently outside. "Zach?" he tried again, but Zach shook his head, not meeting his eyes. God, this was killing him…. He closed the door again behind David, locked it, and put the chair back under the knob. Then he went and sat on the sofa in the dark, staring unseeingly out the French doors. His thoughts tumbled like stones in a polisher, never still enough to focus on, just noisy and flickering sparks against dark.

When the sky was starting to lighten and his head was aching and his eyes were like sandpaper from lack of sleep, he dragged himself up from the couch and went to pull the drapes closed against the morning sun. As he reached for the cord, he glanced down to see David's car still parked on the concrete in front of the garage. Frowning, he removed the chair from under the doorknob, and unlocked and opened the door.

David looked up from where he sat against the porch railing, his arms around his knees and his face pale and drawn, his eyes reddened from crying. "You been there all night?" Zach asked expressionlessly.

David nodded.

There was a long moment of silence, then Zach held the door open. "You might as well come in, then."

David got awkwardly to his feet and followed Zach into the apartment.

"You want some breakfast?"

"If you're having some."

Zach nodded, then went into the kitchen and took some rolls out of the freezer. David went to the coffeemaker and started coffee. They worked in silence, going through the same motions they did most mornings, but without the usual joking and teasing and affectionate touches. *This must be what it was like to be married to someone who didn't love you anymore,* Zach thought. This must be what it was like to live in a failed marriage. Only he and David weren't married and weren't likely to be. The thought caught in his throat and he made a choking sound. David whirled and said, "Are you okay?" in a voice that trembled.

"I'm fine," Zach said. Even to his own ears he sounded like he was strangling. He put the rolls in the oven and closed the door, then turned around.

David was watching him. He met David's eyes, then looked away. "Zach," David said.

"No."

"No what?"

"No, I don't want to talk about it. No, I don't have anything to say. No whatever fits the bill."

"I wasn't going to ask anything."

"Then why are you here?"

David let out a long exhalation. "I'm here," he said carefully, "because I love you and because you're upset and I want to be here. That's all."

"How can you say that?" Zach demanded, his voice rising sharply. "How can you say anything like that after what I said last night?"

"Which part? The 'we're done' part or the 'not going to kill yourself' part?"

"Neither! Jesus, are you being deliberately obtuse? I *fucking killed a man,* David! I'm a murderer! And you stand there like it's no big deal when I *saw* how you looked when you heard that."

"Yeah, okay!" David shouted. "I was shocked! It's not an easy thing to hear, you know—what it fucking *felt like* to strangle someone? And knowing it was you and that you were driven so far over the edge that it was the only way out for you? Jesus, it just about killed *me*." He sucked in a ragged breath. "And it fucking hurt that I didn't know, that you didn't trust me enough to tell me about it. That I had to hear about it from a stranger—a fucking reporter, God damn it. That you weren't sure enough about me to even tell me the truth. That you've been lying to me all along."

"I thought you knew," Zach said miserably. "Up until a few weeks ago I thought you'd known all along and that you were okay with it. Not that I killed someone, but the circumstances. And then you made that speech about how if I *had* killed him it would have damaged me and all that crap. And I realized that you didn't know—and that I didn't want you to know. I didn't want you to know how fucked up I really am. I didn't want you to *ever* know because then you'd know the truth about me."

"I already know the truth about you, Zach," David said. "The important things. Like the fact that you try harder than anyone I know at anything you do. That you take life way too seriously. That you don't have a great self-image despite being the most fucking wonderful person I've ever met." He paused and scraped with one finger at an invisible smudge on the countertop. "That no matter how hard I try, I can't be enough for you. I can't protect you. I can't take care of you. I'm just not enough."

"What are you talking about?" Zach demanded. "You're everything I want."

"But I'm not what you need."

"Bullshit. I need you. When I left Bella's last night I thought I was going to die. I felt like I'd had part of me cut off. And there wasn't a damned thing I could do about it because it was my own fault. And here you are thinking it was *your* fault I fucked up?"

"Not my fault," David said tiredly. "But my responsibility. At least, that's how I felt at Bella's. And that bastard Brian was right, damn him to hell. I can't protect you." He laughed humorlessly. "God, you'd think I'd have figured that out seven years ago? But no, here you are back, and I fall right back into that mindset. Protect Zach."

"What are you talking about?"

David sat down at the table, his coffee mug forgotten on the counter. Zach took it, added cream the way David liked it, and set it on the table in front of him, then got his own and sat down across from him. David sighed. "Do you remember when my dad died?"

"I remember the funeral," Zach said. "I don't really remember your dad, though."

"You were only about six at the time, so that doesn't surprise me. During the luncheon afterwards, you got restless, and I took you out of the restaurant and let you run around for a while to wear you out. Then we sat on the porch of the restaurant and you fell asleep on my knee. While we were sitting there, your dad came out and sat down on the step next to me. He started talking about my dad, and how when he met him at MIT he—your dad—was only seventeen and it was his first time away from home and how my dad was already a sophomore and how he took your dad under his wing and taught him how to go on, and watched out for him and everything. And how my mom watched out for yours at Radcliffe, so it was kind of like the Evanses always looking out for the Tylers. And that he didn't know what he was going to do without Phil keeping an eye on him the way he always did, helping him with the business side of the company, and helping him bounce ideas, and stuff. He was crying and that freaked me out some, but I said I would help him if he wanted me to. And he said, no, he'd have to learn to manage on his own, but he'd appreciate it if I would watch out for you. Of course I said I would. I tried to keep that promise, Zach. I failed once, epic fail on a galactic scale, but when you came back, I jumped right back into trying to protect you again. But you don't need me to protect you. Brian was right. You can take care of yourself."

"No," Zach said. "He was wrong. I need you, Taff."

"No, you don't." He reached over and put his hand on Zach's. "You really don't. But I think it's gonna be hard for me to deal with that. That's why"—he took a breath—"that's why I'm not going to go with you to Boston next year."

Zach jerked his hand back. "Then it *is* over," he said dully.

David said carefully, his face pale and his voice shaking, "If that's your choice."

"*My choice?*" Zach lunged to his feet. "My choice? You just sat outside all night long to tell me we're over and you think it's *my choice?* That's rich, Taff. You couldn't just take my word for it last night. Couldn't just go away and let it be done. No, you had to hang around to tell me this? What do you call this, 'closure' or something? You asked what you did wrong last night. You made me think you wanted to make this work, to get past it, to move on, but here you are dumping me and trying to make me think it was my decision? That's bullshit. You're fucking with my head."

"What are you talking about?" David was on his feet now, hands fisted. "What the hell, Zach? I didn't say *anything* about breaking up with you! I *love* you!"

Zach backed away until the breakfast bar stopped him. "What are you talking about, Taff? You said you weren't going to come with me next fall!"

"I'm not. But that doesn't mean I don't want to be with you until you leave...."

"Oh, 'forever and always or twelve months, whichever comes first'?" Zach's voice was bitter. "Well, what if I say 'fuck MIT' and don't go? You gonna stay around forever then?"

"You are going to MIT," David said fiercely. "You are not going to let whatever you feel for me stop you, ever, do you hear me? And I *am* going to stay around forever. I *meant* forever and always, damn you!"

"You confuse the hell out of me, David! I don't know what the hell you want from me!"

Zach's headache was pounding now, threatening to push his eyeballs out from the inside. "I don't understand you," he said. "I don't understand any of this. Christ, I think my head's gonna fall off." He closed his eyes and turned around, leaning on the breakfast bar, his face in his hands.

He heard the scrape of the chair legs on the flagstone floor, then warm hands settled at his temples. "I'm sorry," David whispered. "I'm so sorry. I didn't mean I was leaving you. I didn't mean anything even remotely like that. I meant forever and always, Zach. I still do." He rubbed Zach's temples gently with his fingertips, working his thumbs over the base of his skull.

Zach stood braced against the breakfast bar, his hands clutching the edge, his eyes closed, feeling David's warmth all along his back, his steady, strong artist's hands easing the tension in Zach's neck and head. "About Esteban," he began, but David cut him off.

"Don't talk about him if you don't want to," he said firmly.

"I don't want to," Zach admitted. "But I want you to understand."

David's hands slid down to Zach's shoulders and turned him around to face David. "I understand, Zach. I don't need to know anything. Tell me whatever you want, whenever you want. But I know enough. I know *you*. Nothing you can tell me will change any bit of that." He cupped Zach's face with his warm, steady hands. "I love you. Sometimes love isn't enough. And sometimes it *is*."

Zach closed his eyes again. "I don't know, Taff. There's so much you don't know, so much I haven't told you. How do I know that when you've heard it all that you'll feel the same way about me? And if—when—I talk to that journalist guy, you'll hear it. All of it."

"Have your parents heard all of it?"

Zach shook his head. "Most of it they know. But not all."

"Will they still love you after they hear what you have to say?"

Blinking, Zach said, "Well, yeah… I guess. They know the worst, anyway. About what I did to Esteban."

David snorted. "You think *that's* the worst? You are such a dweeb, dweeb."

"What can be worse than knowing your kid is a murderer?"

"A., you're not a murderer. I'll bet that Esteban dude killed a shitload of people before you took him out. Your doing that was justifiable homicide in my book, for that reason alone, not only because of what he did to you. And B., knowing about practically *anything* he did to you is a lot worse than hearing that you killed him." David dragged Zach's head down onto his shoulder and kissed his ear. "I try not to think about it, but just the little you've told me breaks my fucking heart, love. It just makes me *insane*, knowing you went through shit I can't even imagine. And still came out in one piece."

"Well, not quite. I'm sort of back in one piece, more or less," Zach mumbled into his neck. "After years of therapy."

"No. He didn't break you."

Zach pulled back. "Sure he did. I broke, Taff. I buckled under, did what he said, was what he wanted me to be. I never expected to get out of there; I just expected to eventually die. How is that not broken?"

"Because, dweeb, when you had your chance, you took it. I can't tell you how many times I've seen people back down when they had their chance, afraid of the risk, afraid to be brave. And they weren't in a situation as... as *fraught* as yours. Hell, there have been times when I didn't take a chance, because I was scared. And it wasn't life or death—it was just... just life." He drew back and cupped Zach's face again, his brown eyes searching Zach's earnestly. "A broken man wouldn't have even tried to kill Esteban," he said urgently. "A broken man wouldn't have even *thought* about it. You *did* it. You took the chance. And you got out. You won. He lost. And you aren't letting what happened to you stop you anymore. Like last night. You went out with old friends. You laughed and made jokes and ate pizza and there wasn't anything about Esteban there to haunt you, was there? Not until that asshole made his move."

"No. It was... it was normal," Zach admitted. "I mean, it was what I think of as normal, and the guys seemed to think it was normal. No weirdness at all involved." His fingers closed around David's wrists. "Kind of a far cry from what I was doing when you first came home—the pickups, the drinking...."

"Hey," David said, "that was just another way for you to fight back. You weren't going to be what he tried to make you. You *aren't* what he tried to make you."

Zach closed his eyes. "I'm still not where I want to be," he said. "I'm still, I don't know, still afraid."

"News for you, dweeb. Everybody's afraid. You just gotta suck it up and move on." He kissed Zach gently. "Deal with what you can and back-burner the things you can't. Just like you're doing."

"I don't know how I'll get along without you in Boston," Zach said.

David snorted. "You'll do fine. We've got a whole year to work on your confidence. Hell, kids way younger than you go off to college on their own; kids who have their own hang-ups and issues. You'll be in good company. You think I was okay when I went off to UCLA? *Hell*, no."

"No?"

"No. Because it was only a year after I lost my best friend and the love of my life." He bumped foreheads with Zach. "You won't have that problem, because you will *never* lose me. I will be here."

"Forever and always."

"Forever and always," David echoed. He pulled Zach close and rested his head on Zach's shoulder. "I'm tired, dweeb. What say we crawl into bed and catch a few hours of sleep before you have your therapy session?"

"Is that what you want to do?" Zach asked.

"Why? What do you want to do?" David raised his head and grinned at him.

"Well, drag you into the bedroom and make love to you until you can't see anything but me, of course."

David grinned. "News for you, dweeb," he said again. "I already can't see anything but you."

Chapter Twenty-Five

"OKAY, it's set," Brian said, and sat down in the chair across from the couch. "I'm going to use this recording solely for reference, to support my notes. Once the article is completed to both our satisfactions, the tape will be destroyed to protect your privacy, as per the agreement we just signed. Is that acceptable?"

"Yes," Zach said. His voice shook.

On his left, Richard squeezed his arm gently. Jane took his right hand and laced her fingers through it. But it was at David that Zach looked, turning his head to where his lover sat behind the couch, his arms folded on the back. David met his eyes, his own warm, and reached out one hand to touch Zach's cheek. *I love you*, he mouthed, and Zach's lip quirked upward in an attempt at a smile. Then Zach turned back and took a deep breath.

"The last thing I remember is walking out of the airport in Costa Rica. It was humid, but cooler than I'd expected…"

Epilogue

Four years later

"IT'S A particular honor for me to be here today," Richard said to the crowd in Killian Court. And crowd it was; at last count, more than twelve thousand tickets had been accounted for. His own family had two; Jane and David sat together somewhere in that vast sea of faces. "Not only as a graduate of this school, though that is something that I have always been proud of. But today my pride goes beyond just that of a graduate of—in my humble opinion—the best science and engineering school on the planet." That won a roar of approval from the students and spectators. "No, today my pride, and my gratitude, is all wrapped up in the *people* of MIT: students, professors, staff, administrators. I am proud of my son and what he has accomplished in the past three years here. But I am equally proud of the school that took him in and helped him accomplish those things. Your support and protection and education and encouragement means the world to me and to my family.

"Unless you live under a rock—and I think history has shown that MIT students live very much in the world—" another laugh of approval, "you know about my son Zach. It was technology that helped us find him five, nearly six, years ago when the world believed—when I believed—him dead. Technology that drew on inventions and developments pioneered here and at other schools. Technology that shows the truth of what we do: that whatever the plan or process or product, what we do affects what we become and defines what we are. The world tends to see us as 'ivory tower' academics, or wild-haired geniuses, or evil scientists; we may see ourselves as dedicated scholars and researchers; but one thing we cannot forget is that we are also people. We bear the same few chromosomes; we are made up of the same chemicals. We are fragile. We break."

He looked at the students until he found Zach's face. "But we are also strong, strong enough to survive horrific situations; and strong enough to reach out to each other, to offer a hand or a shoulder to another human being...."

"HE'S SUCH a good speaker," Jane whispered, her hand in David's. The brim of her straw picture hat shadowed her blue eyes, but they were still as crystal-clear as Zach's as she looked up at him. "He totally hates public speaking, but he does so well at it. I'd be a nervous wreck, shaking in my shoes."

He smiled down at her, then shifted on his hip so that he could pull out the ball cap he had stuffed in his back pants pocket, shook it out, and put it on his head, pushing his Wayfarers up on his nose. That was better. It wasn't a particularly hot day, but the sun was fierce and he needed the extra shade the cap bill gave him. Jane looked at him and giggled. Okay, he thought, grinning back at her, maybe the virulent purple cap with the fluorescent orange "MIT" on the front didn't exactly go with the neat cream linen suit he wore, but Zach had given it to him last night for this very purpose. "It's gonna be hot as hell out there in the sun," he'd told David, "and everyone's supposed to tell their guests to wear hats. So since I knew you wouldn't have one, I got you one."

"Could you have found one a little more, I don't know, gaudy? This is awful conservative," David had replied dryly. Zach had laughed, and kissed him, and one thing led to another, and all in all it was a pretty nice reunion. Zach had come pretty far in the last couple of years. There had been times after the article had been published that Zach had backslid into reclusiveness and fear and belligerence, and he still had plenty of hang-ups that he was still working out, but being on his own and among his peers here had given him a lot more confidence, just as David had promised him when he'd left on his own that first year. He'd been terrified even to get on the plane, and it had taken all of

David's resolve to let him go alone. David had cried, and so had Jane, and Richard had held onto both of them as they watched Zach walk down the terminal on his own. It had had horrible echoes of that plane trip to Costa Rica. And Hell, and points south.

But this time it was okay. This time he'd gotten to where he was going, and after a few hysterical phone calls, had settled into life as an undergraduate. He'd even gotten to the point of being able to tease David about running off with some hot young science geek. But he hadn't. When he'd come home for holidays and on break, it was always to David.

And last night, David had given a graduation gift to Zach, in a sense—a new job for David at Foothill College in Palo Alto, and a lease on a townhouse in Mountain View, for the both of them. An easy commute for David to school, and Zach to Stanford, where he'd be pursuing a graduate degree with a concentration in nanoscience. School for Zach, and mountains for David. The Santa Cruz range wasn't exactly the Rockies, but then, the Rockies didn't have surf spots within an hour's drive. David grinned to himself. He was *so* looking forward to teaching Zach to surf. Had to keep ahead of the kid somehow….

Richard finished his speech to roaring applause and went to sit with the rest of the speakers. Jane let out a long sigh. "Well, that was good," she said in relief. "He did a nice job."

"Yep," David said. He put his arm around Jane and squeezed gently. "Both of them. And you. You did a nice job too."

"Sometimes I wonder," Jane said, smiling up at him. "But today… no. Not today."

THE Massachusetts sun is warm on my face and hands, and a cool breeze stirs the tassels on the caps of the students in front of me. I listen to the speeches and try not to react when my father mentions me. It's a good speech, despite that. The memories it brings back are ones I've come to terms with. And the listeners seem to enjoy it.

Then the speeches are suddenly done and names are being called. The time passes in a blur until suddenly I'm standing at the edge of the stage, and the university president is calling, "Zachary John Tyler." It takes a second, but then I realize it's me.

I'm not sure for a moment as I walk across the stage to shake his hand that it's actually real. That these past few years weren't a dream. That I won't still wake in the cage that still occasionally haunts my nightmares. But it's real, all of it. The stage floor squeaks quietly as I walk across it, the president's hand is slightly damp from all the warm palms that have pressed it before, the leather of the diploma case he hands me is padded and soft in my fingers. The roar of the students chanting, "Zach! Zach! Zach!' is a shocker; I turn in surprise and see them on their feet, grinning in approval.

I guess I've made friends here. That's good.

I step down from the stage and return to my seat, to let the rest have their moment. It's good I'm at the end of the alphabet; it's not much later that the final benediction closes the ceremony. My heart is too full, and I'm afraid I'll start to cry. Already some of my female classmates are in tears.

I will miss them. Miss here. But I've got a graduate spot at Stanford waiting for me, and I'm excited about that too. I want to try California. I want to learn to surf.

The final congratulations and then the air is filled with flying mortarboards. I'd always thought that tradition was kind of stupid, but here I am, caught up in the moment, hurling my own cap into the air and laughing and screaming just like any other kid.

I might be older than a lot of them, but today I am just like any other kid. The thought takes my breath away.

Hugging and kissing and shaking hands, my classmates and I are gradually separated by the influx of family members hungry for their own hugs and kisses and photo ops. I've already arranged to skip that part of the festivities and just buy the professional photos; Dad is going to meet me at the entrance to the Court and walk with me to the reception at the Kresge Oval.

He's there, grinning and damp with the nervous sweat he gets whenever he has to speak in public. I ignore that and hug him tightly. There's the flash of cameras; not from paparazzi this time, but from my friends and their families. That's okay.

Then we walk out of the court and down Massachusetts Avenue

with the rest of my classmates to the reception.

I see them right away. Mom, looking beautiful and so much younger than she is; Annie, grinning like a girl; Maggie and Alex and Annabel, with Annabel's little sister Jessamyn in Alex's arms; Sandy and Alison, both of them waving like idiots; Mike Pritzger and Captain Rogers; Jesse and Jeff and Tai and Billy and Frankie; Brian, in this company looking uncomfortable for the first time since I've met him. When he sees me, though, a smile lights his handsome face. I grin back.

And then I'm walking over the sun-warmed grass toward them— no. Not toward them.

For five years, I dared not dream of him; these days my dreams are rarely without him. We've survived kidnappings and death and anger and sorrow and loss; months of separation and the pitiless light of publicity. David has been my anchor, my ballast, my north star. As he once promised, he has been with me the whole way, even while I was here at school and he thousands of miles away in his beloved mountains. He will be at my side when I leave for Stanford. He has been at my side through it all.

I walk across the grass in the sunlight, into his arms.

I am home.

An unrepentant biblioholic, ROWAN SPEEDWELL spends half her time pretending to be a law librarian, half her time pretending to be a database manager, half her time pretending to be a fifteenth-century Aragonese noblewoman, half her time... wait a minute... hmm. Well, one thing she doesn't pretend to be is good at math. She is good at pretending, though.

In her copious spare time (hah) she does needlework, calligraphy and illumination, and makes jewelry. She has a master's degree in history from the University of Chicago, is a member of the Society for Creative Anachronism, and lives in a Chicago suburb with the obligatory Writer's Cat and way too many books.

Song lyric included in text is from "Little Boxes"—Words and music by Malvina Reynolds; copyright 1962 Schroder Music Company, renewed 1990.

Dramatic Romance from DREAMSPINNER PRESS

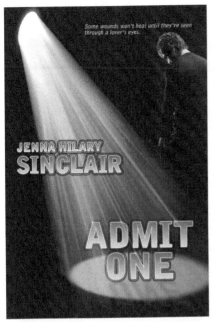

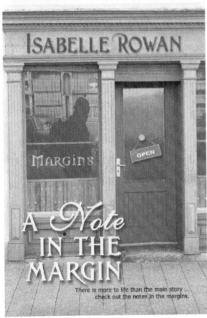

http://www.dreamspinnerpress.com

CPSIA information can be obtained at www.ICGtesting.com
Printed in the USA
LVOW01s1724070414

380671LV00015B/1130/P